THE RUBY LOCKET

MELISSA WRAY

ODYSSEY
BOOKS

Published by Odyssey Books in 2020
www.odysseybooks.com.au

ISBN: 978-1922311245 (paperback)
ISBN: 978-1922311252 (ebook)

A catalogue record for this book is available from the National Library of Australia

For Toby and Molly.
May you follow your dreams.
Always. Xo

'You do not think of what is lost,
only yourself and this life.
Retribution comes at a cost,
can you afford to pay the price?'

~ Mother Nature ~

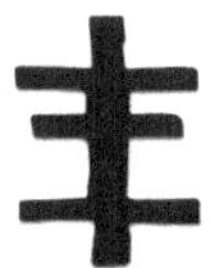

Chapter 1

Saxon

A coloured stain spreads across the sky in all directions. Tints of pink and purple blend together, sending a sign of the warm weather to come. I look around, but there's nothing else to see, except the body slumped on the ground. Her legs are bent one way, while her body twists the other. The wasteland stretches out behind her. It gives no clues of where she has been. There are no footprints to show from which direction she's travelled.

The landscape around our town is barren, making it impossible for anyone to survive in. Yet, somehow this girl has made it all the way here to Nevertyre. Alone.

'Do you think she's alive, Manny?' I say.

'Nope.'

The 'p' pops from his lips, so confident in his response.

'Well, she's not from around here,' I say. 'She must be a rambler.'

'Shut yer mouth, Saxon,' Manny says, looking around. 'It don't matter where she's from 'cause either way she's dead. Now let's go!'

I grab hold of Manny's arm. 'We can't just leave her out here to rot.'

The mangy animals around these parts haven't got to her yet, but that doesn't mean they won't if given the chance. It will soon be night and they'll come sniffing around looking for their dinner.

Manny checks his watch. 'We're already late and Constance will be gettin' worried.'

The days are longer at this time of year, but it will soon be night. We don't want to be out here when darkness falls.

'Manny! We gotta burn her. It ain't right not to and you know it.'

We stare at one another, each brother waiting for the other to give in. It won't be me. It never is.

'All right, fine,' says Manny. 'We'll come back and get her early tomorrow morn, before work. But you can help me take her to the crematorium.' Manny's footsteps crunch on the gravel as he walks off, ending the discussion.

I pinch the bridge of my nose. A habit of frustration picked up from my late father. It doesn't sit well with me to leave the body out in the open all night, but Manny won't change his mind now it's made up. That's something we both have in common. I squat and look at the girl, careful to keep some distance. Her long, black hair is matted and spills out around her head. Her skin is blistered and peeling. Dirt streaks her face with dark lashes crusted closed. She might have been pretty before death found her.

I shake my head at a life wasted so close to sanctuary. I look at her face, willing her eyes to open, unable to move away just yet. I've seen dead bodies at Manny's work before, but something about this one holds my interest.

'Saxon, come on!'

I ignore the call of my older brother and move toward the girl. It's difficult to judge her age. People that live outside the communities can appear older than they are. I'm in my seventeenth year so if I had to guess, I'd say this girl was a similar age. It's hard to tell through the grit and grime though. I shuffle closer again, careful not to touch her. Sunlight glints off her neck where a silver locket is nestled on her collarbone. A single red stone sits in the middle, like an eye watching me. I cup the necklace and lean forward for a closer look.

'Help me,' whispers the girl.

I scramble backward. 'Manny! Get over here, she's alive.'

I wait to see what she does next, but there's no more movement. No other sound. Is my mind playing tricks? Did I imagine her voice?

'Hello?' I crawl toward the girl. My fingers shake as I reach out to push some clumped hair from her face. 'Can you hear me?'

Her eyelids flutter open and light blue eyes pierce through me, the same colour as the day sky on a sunny morn.

'Please … help me.'

I lean closer, but her eyes are closed once again. Footsteps grow loud behind me.

'What game are you playin' at, Saxon?' Manny leans over me. 'She's dead, yer fool.'

'I'm playing no game brother. She spoke to me. I swear, on our parents' graves, this girl is still alive.'

Manny's face distorts at the oath I've given. He knows it is not offered lightly.

'You swear it?'

I nod. 'She asked me to help her.'

I stand eye to eye with Manny. We are identical in height, but nothing else.

'Damn it! What are we gonna do now?' says Manny.

'Suppose we better take her home.'

'Take a *rambler* home? Has the sun scorched yer brain?'

'Calm down, it'll be one night.'

'No way, Saxon. No bloody way. We don't need Agents knockin' down our door for housin' a rambler and breakin' the law.'

'Nobody will know.'

'Don't be stupid, of course they will! Nothin' ever stays quiet round these parts for long.'

'So what? I'll deal with the Agents if it comes to that.' I shrug. 'Won't be anything new for me.'

'No, Saxon. Absolutely not.'

'Come on, Manny! Let's just take her home and see what Constance thinks.'

The defeat rolls over my brother as his shoulders droop. Manny always relents when Constance is involved. She's his weakness, his Achilles heel. That's why my sister-in-law is a good ally to have and no match for Manny's stubborn ways.

'Yer damn tinker, one night.' Manny points a finger in my face. 'One night and then she's gone.'

I retrieve the wheelbarrow. 'Good thing we sold all the veggies. We can move her in this.'

'I ain't pickin' her up.' Manny crosses his arms. 'This is your daft idea.'

'What are you afraid of? Look at her! She's nothing but skin and bones.' I scoop up the lifeless body. 'She's hardly gonna cause us any trouble.'

'She probably won't last through the night,' says Manny, kicking the ground.

'Then what are you worried about? If she dies … well, we haven't broken any laws, have we? We can just report her after that.'

I lay the girl in the wheelbarrow, taking extra care with her head. The girl's crumpled clothes are like a pile of torn rags in the barrow. Her collarbones jut out from below her neck, ready to snap. One shoe is lost while the other is barely whole. Where did this girl come from to end up like this? Wherever it was, she must be some distance from home.

'Ain't nobody travels alone out there and survives,' I say. 'She's a fighter, Manny, you'll see.'

I push the barrow along the path, trying to avoid the bumps. There's a story to go with this girl. I just hope she lives long enough to tell it.

Chapter 2

Kerina

Consciousness comes to me slowly. The warmth of my body, the buzzing in my ears, the lingering scent of soap tickling my nose. I groan as I force my eyes open. My vision blurs from the brightness. For a moment I think I have woken beneath the outdoor sky, but the stillness around me suggests I am indoors.

I look up and find myself lying beneath a sea of painted colour. Swirling patterns of vibrant red, purple, and yellow frame the ceiling above. Splatters of blue, orange, and green cover the rest of the surface. Someone has taken great care with the design. I adjust my body and the bed frame beneath me squeaks, loud and grating. The noise startles me.

'Easy there.' A woman appears beside me.

'Don't touch me.' I try to push myself from the bed, but my limbs buckle.

'I won't harm you.' The woman holds up her hands in surrender. She is dressed in civilian clothes, not a uniform. The difference calms me for some reason.

'Do you have a name?' asks the woman.

My eyes flit around the room. It is sparse with only a wardrobe, small table, and chair. A sheer curtain covers the window. There's nothing else to suggest danger to myself. I assess the stranger before me, but my mind is foggy. Instinct tells me this woman is not a threat, but my brain warns me to be wary.

'A name would help,' the woman encourages. 'You can tell me.'

'Kerina. My name is Kerina.'

'Such a lovely name for a beautiful young lady.' The woman pours some liquid into a glass. 'Drink some water, please. We tried dripping fluid into your mouth while you slept, but it was not such an easy thing to do.'

I ignore the offered glass of water. 'Who are you?'

'I'm Constance, and this is my home. And it's okay, you are safe.' Constance takes a sip of water and re-offers the glass. 'It's not poisoned, so drink up.'

I accept the glass this time. As soon as the cool liquid hits the back of my throat, my gullet opens and I finish the water in loud, slurping gulps. Constance nods her approval and refills it.

'Where am I?'

'You're in a community called Nevertyre.'

'Never … tyre? I've not heard of it before.'

'We are one of the biggest communities around these parts.'

I lift the bedcover. A green nightshirt covers my body. 'You … dressed me?'

'Of course! Your clothes were rags and they stunk. They weren't coming inside this house. Besides, you have nothing I haven't seen on me or my sisters.'

Embarrassment sweeps over me and I pull the blanket higher.

'Don't fret. You were filthy, Kerina. I tried to clean you as best I could, but again, it was not such an easy thing to do.' Constance caresses her swollen, pregnant stomach.

I watch this strange woman I know nothing of, but who's seen me naked as the day I was born.

Knock, knock. The door opens and a tall man appears. He steps forward before stopping abruptly. A grim look settles on his face. 'You're awake then.'

I force myself to sit up. My body protests against the movement and pain rips through my stiff joints. The man makes no attempt to come closer.

'You can come in,' Constance says as she reaches for his hand and pulls him into the room.

'Why is he here?'

'This is Manny, my husband. Don't be afraid, Kerina. He'll not harm you. It was he and his brother, Saxon, who found you and brought you to our home.'

There is no recognition when I look at this curly haired stranger. He could be anybody coming in here to harm me. Or he could be a person who has some answers for me.

'Where did you find me?'

'We were comin' home along the outskirts of town. We'd been at the market selling our plants.' He clears his throat. 'You were in a bad way, just collapsed on the ground. I thought you were *dead.*'

'Manny, don't frighten her.'

'I'm not afraid,' I say.

'Good, 'cause I ain't tryin' to scare yer. I'm just speakin' the truth. Saxon was the one who thought different. Yer can thank him for your life.'

My life? Was I really so close to death?

'How long have I been here?'

'You've been in and out of consciousness for three days,' says Constance.

'Three days?' I raise my fingers to my cracked lips.

Constance leans toward the bedside. I flinch from the sudden movement.

'Don't be scared. I'll not harm you, Kerina.' Constance offers me a tin of salve. 'It will help.' She applies the lotion to her own lips. 'Just rub it on.'

I inhale the citrus scent before applying the ointment. It soothes the chaffing instantly.

Constance sits the tin on the bedside table. 'So, where did you come from?'

I stare out the window, but can see little from this position. 'What is Nevertyre near?'

'The next closest community is Middtown. Why? Is that where yer from?' says Manny.

'I ... no ... I don't think so.' I realise the answer escapes me. A flitter of panic stirs in my body as I try to remember. 'I'm not sure.'

'Not to worry, you'll recall it soon enough,' says Constance. 'Manny, can you tell Saxon to come and meet our guest? Perhaps send some soup with him. Kerina will be hungry now she's awake.' She looks at me. 'Are you hungry?'

My stomach grumbles in response.

'Well, if that's not a clear sign of hunger, and right on cue.' Constance laughs. A tinkling sound that almost makes me smile.

'I'll tell Saxon to bring some soup,' says Manny, fleeing the room.

The door closes behind him. The thud jolts me back to my situation. For three days I've been unconscious, lying here lifeless. For three days these people have been caring for me, tending my wounds, and trying to hydrate me. I have no recollection of any of it, and what about all the days before? Manny said they found me on the ground, nearly dead. How did I get there?

I trawl through the passages in my mind and try to recall my home, my friends, my family. Anything that might help to piece things together. Instead, my memories elude me. I know my name but nothing of where I came from. My chest tightens and I try to ignore the fear creeping in.

Chapter 3

Saxon

It's only been a couple of weeks since I tended to this job, but already the earth is overgrown. I tug out the weeds surrounding the base and scoop up the fallen leaves. The pink blossoms remain bright on the tree. They look pretty against them, as though they have been glued in place. The colour creates a striking contrast to the branches.

I adjust my knees to alleviate the dull ache. Two glass jars are buried beneath me in the earth. A boulder etched with two names marks the spot. *Shayne and Marlane Vespa.* The ashen remains of my parents are compact inside their glass tombs. Each one is deep below the surface. I know because I helped Manny bury them almost ten years ago. It's hard to believe two big personalities fit into such a small space. My father was usually serious, but when he laughed, he meant it. Deep, rumbling, contagious laughter. My mother was more carefree and often enjoyed playing a joke on her husband as well as her two sons.

I make sure not to disturb the dirt covering their final resting place. The Burn scorched the communities and destroyed both natural and man-made resources many years ago. As timber diminished because of the Burn, wooden coffins were considered a waste of resources. A new law passed that everyone must be cremated. Nobody is buried whole anymore, at least not by choice. The thought makes me shiver. What if the dead weren't really dead? Were people ever buried alive?

I tug on my necklace. A metal ball dangles on a string of black leather. Ash from both my parents fills the centre. The cool, smooth surface helps to ease the ache of knowing I can never touch either one again. Manny wears the same necklace as me. He had them made especially for both of us.

'I still miss 'em every day,' says Manny, placing a hand on my shoulder.

'Bloody tinker, Manny! Some warning next time.'

Manny bows his head, ignoring my emotional outburst. His hand remains clasped on my shoulder as we stay locked together in silence, both with our own memories.

I was only eight when our parents died. Manny says we were boys, forced to become men the day the Agent came to our house with the news. I remember the loud, demanding knock at the door. I knew straight away something was wrong.

'*Your parents are dead. The Primo Dictor is sympathetic and thanks you for their service.*' The Agent shoved a wad of tokens at Manny and left. Their bodies were delivered, already cremated, in jars a week later.

The Primo Dictor lives in Middtown and rules the nearby communities to ensure order. Our parents were killed while working for the former Primo Dictor of Middtown. My mother was a nanny on special occasions for visiting guests. My father was the head chef for important events. He was famous for his desserts.

After a while, Manny squeezes my shoulder. 'You okay, little brother?'

I stand up. 'I just miss them more some days than others. Stupid, huh? It's been almost a decade.'

'It ain't stupid at all. Don't matter if it's been one year or ten years, grief is grief.'

'Saxon!' Constance calls from the back door, oblivious to her interruption. 'Can you bring some soup please?'

'Be there in a minute.'

The back door slams shut.

'Why is *your* wife asking me to bring her soup?'

'Damn, she's impatient! She just asked me to send you in to meet the girl.'

'How is the rambler?'

'Don't call her that.' Manny looks around. 'Seems *Kerina* has no memory.'

I snort. 'What do you mean, no memory?'

'She gave her name, but that's all she could tell us,' says Manny.

'Could or would?' I cross my arms. 'Seems hard to believe she'd forget her whole past.'

Manny laughs. 'You always were a suspicious tinker. Not everyone has a hidden agenda. You can trust people sometimes, Saxon.'

'That's your problem, Manny, you're too trusting. You always have been. Just like when we were kids, and I'd talk you into anything, no matter how mad we knew Dad would get.'

'That weren't trusting. That was just a big brother lookin' out for his little brother. As it should be.'

'Story of your life hey, Manny?' The truth of the words is hard for either of us to ignore.

'Damn it, Saxon. Ain't no need for yer feelin' guilty talk,' says Manny. 'I don't regret havin' to look after you one bit.'

'But you shouldn't have had to, that's the point.' I pinch the bridge of my nose. 'I better get that soup.'

I turn to leave. Manny will never understand the guilt I have bottled inside for him having to raise me alone. I certainly didn't make it easy at times. Still don't.

'Hey Saxon, did you notice Kerina's wrists when you carried her home?' Manny says.

'No, what about 'em?'

'Scarred purple all the way round, they are.'

'Like a birthmark?'

'More like somethin's rubbed against her skin.'

My eyes narrow. 'Do you think she's got no memory, or that maybe she doesn't want to remember?'

'Has Rudolph been fillin' your head with ideas again?'

'Shut up! I'm old enough to think for myself. Besides, I read it in one of them old magazines. It's something called am-nee-sia.'

'Well, whatever that girl's past, I just hope it don't turn up here. Now you better get in there or Constance'll be after yer.'

'That's all I need. Her bossing me around as well as you.'

'Watch yer mouth about my wife.'

'It's true, ain't it?'

Manny shoves me playfully. 'Yep, but don't you *ever* tell her I said that.'

I walk toward the house. Manny knows me well. I am suspicious of most things. After our parents died, we had to grow up quicker than most. I learnt some lessons the hard way and soon realised that my gut instinct was a good weapon to have. I've been listening to it ever since. That instinct is calling out loud and clear about the rambler inside our house. There's more to her than we know. Good or bad, I'm not sure.

But suspicions and instinct aside, something about Kerina intrigues my curious mind. She's proven her ability to survive by making it to Nevertyre on her own. That alone tells me she is tough in mind and body. But the memory loss will need further investigation. There are things about Kerina that don't make any sense. What was she doing out in the wasteland alone? Where is she from? What is she hiding? She's got some big secrets and I plan to find out what they are.

Chapter 4

Kerina

Thump, thump, thump. The noise vibrates from the wooden bedroom door, but this time nobody enters. My body tenses, waiting to see who stands on the other side of the divide.

'Come in,' says Constance.

The door opens and a different person waits in the doorway. He stares at me, his dark eyes appraising me. This must be the brother they spoke about before. He's tall like Manny, but built differently. He fills most of the space, broad and strong. I lift my chin and keep his gaze. He looks curious, cautious, but not as hostile as Manny was.

'Saxon, bring the soup closer. And get another pillow so our guest can sit up more comfortable.'

Saxon says nothing. He sits the soup beside the bed then leaves. I force myself upright, gritting my teeth as my body complains with aches and pains. My skin is tender and my joints stiff. I adjust myself until the pressure is more comfortable, puffed from the effort.

Saxon returns, plumping a pillow. Something in my scowl must halt his approach. He hesitates before stepping toward me.

'Back off. I can do it.' I reach out for the pillow.

He releases his grip, a smirk pulling on his lips. I have the urge to slap it right off his face. I position the pillow as graciously as I can, trying not to grimace. I am not completely helpless as I have been for the past three days, yet my limited ability leaves me frustrated.

'This is Manny's brother Saxon,' says Constance. 'And this is our *rambler*, Kerina.'

'Rambler? Why would you call me that?'

Constance lowers her voice. 'A rambler is a stranger to the community. All visitors must be reported for clearance to stay in Nevertyre. We shouldn't call you a rambler though, in case somebody overhears us talking.'

'Why does it matter if they hear?'

'We'd be arrested.' Saxon's gravelly voice booms through the room.

I turn to him. 'Arrested? Yet you still brought me here.'

Saxon nods.

'Why?'

'Didn't want the wild animals to eat you.'

'Saxon!' says Constance. 'I already told Manny not to frighten her.'

I suspect he is trying to rile me up, or test me. Either way, I know he is playing with me for some reason.

'But you haven't reported me … have you?' Their silence answers my question. 'So, you could still be arrested?'

'I ain't afraid of being arrested.' His stance shifts and he seems taller somehow.

I suspect his bravado comes from previous run-ins with the law. Or something worse, stupidity.

'Why did you bring me here, really?'

He pauses before speaking, his stoic façade slips momentarily. 'Nobody should die alone.'

The words fill the space between us. I was alone and very close to death. Does he know somebody who died in such a manner?

'And now that I'm not dead?' I smooth out the bed cover. 'Will you hand me in?'

'Why?' He steps toward me. 'Have you got something to hide?'

'Saxon!' says Constance. 'She's barely woken up. Don't be rude.'

But Saxon ignores his sister-in-law. 'Where are you from, *Kerina*?'

'Not Nevertyre.' I glare at him.

'It seems Kerina has no recollection of her home at the moment.'

Saxon and Constance exchange a look before Constance shrugs. 'Perhaps it will return after some nice warm soup. You must be hungry, Kerina. Eat up.'

The steam rises from the bowl. I reach for it and the tangy scent makes my mouth water. How long has it been since I last ate a cooked meal?

'It shouldn't be too hot,' says Saxon.

I blow on the soup anyway and scoop it up. The rich pumpkin flavour assaults my taste buds. My stomach clenches and rumbles in response.

'Take it slow. There is more where that came from. Saxon grew the ingredients for it.'

It's my turn to evaluate him. He doesn't flinch from my gaze. Someone who tends to vegetables in the garden suggests a caring nature, yet a lack of fear of authority suggests careless. Which is his real temperament?

'Don't be too impressed. It wasn't so hard.' Saxon crosses his arms.

'Saxon works hard in the fields to grow our crops,' says Constance.

'Did you cook it as well?' I say.

'No, that was my brother's doing.'

I slurp the liquid. 'Tell Manny thank you. It's very tasty.'

'Manny can't grow a weed to save himself, but he sure can cook,' says Constance, laughing. 'That's why those two have always made a great team.'

Saxon opens his mouth to speak, then closes it. A silent conversation seems to take place between the two before Saxon looks away.

'Eat up, Kerina,' says Constance.

I swallow another mouthful. The warm, orange liquid slips down my throat. I try to eat slowly, but my body has other ideas. A mouthful goes down the wrong way and I suddenly choke on the liquid. I cough and splutter as Saxon takes the bowl from me. I lean forward, gasping as he bangs against my back, firm but not hard. Slowly my body regains control and my desperate gulps for air slow down. My long, dark hair falls forward. I push it off my face and scoop it down one side, leaving the back of my neck exposed. Saxon gasps and pushes me away from him.

I look up, startled by such rough movement. 'What's wrong?'

A mixture of fear and shock contort his features. His hands are poised mid-air, as though bracing himself to catch something.

'What's the matter with you?' I say.

He composes himself. 'It's nothing. I have to go.'

He passes the soup back, but averts his eyes and leaves without looking at me again. 'Strange boy,' I say, embarrassed by his actions. I flatten my hair down, settling it back into place. Something about me made him react that way, but what?

Constance shrugs. 'Sometimes the known is worse than the unknown.'

She leaves me alone in the room. I try to understand what just happened. But no matter how hard I try, I can't make sense of her words, or Saxon's actions.

Chapter 5

Saxon

I walk briskly along the dirt-covered path. Remnants of the old road are still visible in places along the way. The black substance that vehicles used to drive from place to place on is now cracked and broken. The wheeled machines sit discarded by their owners long ago. Most have been rolled to the outskirts of the community, abandoned and useless. The fuel to power them ran dry years before. Over time, the vehicles have formed a ring around the community. A fence line, so that we are secure inside, or perhaps it is to keep strangers out. Now the cars are only used as hiding places for children to play in, or for young lovers to meet, so long as their parents don't find out.

'Manny and Saxon, if I catch you knocking around inside those abandoned heaps …'

Our mother would warn us, but I always managed to talk Manny into exploring. Young as I was, adventure and bending the rules came naturally to me even then. We would disappear for hours and never get caught. Sometimes during our fossicking, we would find relics from the past jammed down the back pockets of seats. Manny once found a golden coin. It had an image engraved on it, along with a year and number. It became his prized possession and he hid it, even from me.

A breeze scuttles past, blowing me forward on my mission. It cools the perspiration on my neck. I wonder about Kerina's family. Where are her parents? Are they worried? Does she have any siblings? A shiver runs through me as I ponder over the symbol on her neck. Until now, I'd only heard whispers of such a birthmark. This girl, with no knowledge of her past, carries a mark that could make her a most wanted person, not only in Nevertyre, but any community. But for some reason she seemed oblivious to it. Could she really not know?

I want to confide in Manny, but my brother doesn't believe in such stories. He only understands facts, not fairy tales. My suspicion is that Constance has seen the mark, but I dare not ask her. Not yet anyway. Besides, she might not have heard the stories about the birthmark. If so, she would not know its significance. There is only one person I trust to find out more. One man I can ask the questions nobody else will answer for fear of reprisal.

'Saxon!'

I tut at the voice and ignore the call of my name. I can't be waylaid today.

'Saxon, wait!' she persists.

I walk quicker, pretending not to hear Anastasia.

'*Saxon!*'

Several people stop and turn. I sigh and wait for her to catch up, unable to ignore her calls any longer. Anastasia walks toward me. Her dress clings agreeably to her shape. It's tailored from Witon, a material designed to adjust to the heat of the day. It can be worn in summer or winter with little additional clothing necessary. Fewer resources and regular use make it perfect for our sustainable way of life. The cost of the material is beyond the reach of most people who live in the community though.

Anastasia's blond hair is styled around her face, framing it perfectly. The short-clipped cut is also a sign of wealth. Nobody else bothers with such trivial maintenance. It is an extravagance few can afford, or worry about. My own hair hangs below my shoulders, chopped intermittently by Constance, or pulled back by a band.

'I'm in a rush, Anastasia, what is it?'

'A rush? What could you need to do that is so urgent?' she teases.

'My brother sent me on an errand and he's got no patience if I'm late,' I lie.

She walks her fingers along my arm. 'Surely you have time for me? I've not seen you in so long.'

'We were speaking just a week ago.'

Anastasia frowns. 'So what? Can't you speak with me now?'

She is not used to being dismissed so easily, but I don't have time for her flirtations today. We've been on dates together and she was happy to oblige with a few stolen kisses. But it was harmless fun and I made no promises to her.

'Perhaps we can meet up later in the week?' I suggest to placate her. 'Will you be at the screenshow?'

She maintains a pout but I can tell she is pleased with my question. 'I suppose I might go. But only if you'll sit with me?'

I laugh at her persistence. Anastasia is a young lady used to getting what she wants.

'I'll sit with you the entire time.'

'Do you promise?'

'Yes, I promise! But I must go.'

I take the opportunity to disengage myself from her and hurry along the path. Crumbling structures lean toward each other. Some maintenance is done on the buildings to ensure there are no collapses, but mostly they are left to ward off the elements alone. The drab exteriors are a contrast to the plants scattered about in pots. Splashes of coloured flowers planted in warbles line the streets. Everyone uses the water-soluble balls to help grow things. Warbles eliminate the need for ongoing watering.

I near the market. As well as a meeting place for bartered sales and community events, it is a place to acquire knowledge without the sharply tuned hearing of Agents to listen in. I take note of the faces moving about the area. Nobody seems out of place, but I can't be too careful. There are always new Agents being moved around the communities to police the people. Agents that keep a very watchful eye on things and report back to the Dictor of each community.

It's busy today as I walk between the crowds. I pass the spot where Manny and I sold all our vegetables only a few days ago. A new person has taken up the space to sell their home-grown goods. That's the way the market works. Anyone can sell things, so long as they have a valid permit.

On the bench seat in the distance, I locate the person I seek, old man Rudolph. His fuzzy white hair is caked with dirt and grime. People take little notice of him as he watches the activity around him. His hair might be dull, but his eyes are sharp. Rudolph makes it his mission to blend in and be overlooked, but to hear every-thing. Over the years he has managed to do it well. He has a talent for picking up secrets nobody should share so openly. Rudolph is a loner, yet the strange-looking man is someone I trust whole-heartedly. He comes and goes to Nevertyre, neither a resident nor a rambler. But he's been a consistent father figure to Manny and me all our lives and can give me the answers I seek.

First, I detour into the bakery to make a purchase. It will be a mouth-watering offering Rudolph won't be able to refuse. The man might sleep rough, but he has his pride. It pays to remember such things. That was something my own father taught me.

Chapter 6

Kerina

I shove the heavy covers away from my body. The night dress is too big for my petite frame. If my mind won't give me any answers, then perhaps my body will. I kick the covers off completely and they drop to the ground. The first marks I see are the purple bruises around my wrists. Each one is marked like a scar trying to fade. Did Saxon and Manny tie me up when they brought me back here? I glide my fingertips over them like a feathered caress. They don't hurt, but my body shivers, uncomfortable from the touch. I might not know how I got them, but my body seems to remember.

I bend my knees. My legs fold, stiff but not painful. I lift one leg upward for closer inspection. The same purple mark from my wrists surrounds the ankle. I sit forward to see both ankles carry the circular stain. I reach down and feel an indentation. The skin is not as dark as my wrists, but it's still noticeable. They look to have been restrained in some way, but how? And by who? My gaze travels back up my legs. They show patches of yellow and brown marks, the bruising almost gone. Some grazes are still evident on my knees, but they cause no discomfort. It seems I have healed well from the rest and care provided by these strangers. It can't be them who caused the purple marks.

I remove the nightshirt and run my hands over my body. My stomach is flat and my hips protrude slightly. My ribs ripple against my skin, but they're not tender to touch. My breasts are full. Not the size of Constance's ample bosom, but a handful all the same.

There are no more unexplained scars or bumps. I run my fingertips along the collarbone and they meet in the middle. I cross my hands and let them settle around my throat. I squeeze my eyes shut to allow the other senses to take over. My skin is warm to touch and my breath echoes in my ears. Darkness settles in my mind as I wait for a memory, or even just a fleeting moment to return. Neither obliges.

There is a sharp knock at the door. It startles me and I scramble to pull the nightshirt up. The effort leaves me breathless. I wait, but nobody forces their way in. Instead, they knock again.

'Kerina?'

'Just a minute.' I quickly dress myself. 'Come in.'

Constance enters. 'Manny and I have to go out and Saxon has gone to the market. You will be alone for a while.

'Okay.' I try to settle my breath, but Constance misses nothing.

'Are you all right? Do you need anything before we go?'

I shake my head. 'I think I have slept too much but ...' A yawn interrupts me.

Constance steps closer. 'Your body has been through so much, it must rest. Listen to its needs.'

Her words make sense, but my mind is too active with questions.

'Did I have anything with me when I was found?'

'You mean like a bag or something?'

I shrug. 'Maybe. It seems strange I would be carrying nothing at all.'

'What is the last thing you can remember?'

I hesitate to share. I have not settled my thoughts on these people, or if they can be trusted.

As though reading my mind, Constance speaks. 'We are in danger by keeping you here, Kerina. We have nothing to gain and much to lose.'

I want to believe her, but everything is still so confusing. Constance moves toward the end of the bed and perches on the edge. She rubs her stomach. 'You can trust us to help you.'

'I remember … feeling alone.' I work my way back through my memories. I push my mind to recall something, anything specific. 'There is a figure in my mind, but it is blurred and far off in the distance.'

'What can you tell me about the figure?' asks Constance.

I reach forward. 'Each time I try to reach out to touch them, the image blows away, like a windstorm.'

'What are they wearing? Are you in danger?'

'If I try to focus on the face, I only see the blurred outline. I feel like they are my friend, not a threat, but I can't be sure.' I clench my fist and thump the bed.

'Give it time, Kerina. Your memories will return, I'm sure of it. In the meantime, perhaps there are some things we can do to hurry them along.'

'Like what?'

'I have a friend who is good with remedies.'

'I will try anything if it might help.'

'She believes you might be suffering from something called "dissociative amnesia".'

'What is that?'

'It's when your brain has blocked out important memories, usually to protect yourself. There is often a trauma of some type involved. Your trek through the wasteland would certainly have been traumatic enough. The good news is that there are some triggers that could help restore the memories. That's where my friend, Janoah, could help.'

'I'd like to meet with her. Do you trust her enough to arrange a meeting here?'

'Of course. Janoah can be depended on without question. Oh, I just remembered! Speaking of triggers …' Constance rushes toward the wardrobe. 'You did have something with you. You were wearing this when you arrived.'

I open the material carefully. Inside is a silver necklace, polished and sparkly. A ruby stone sits in the middle, staring at me.

'I took it off when I was trying to clean you up. I didn't want it to break.'

'It's beautiful,' I say, holding it closer.

'Is it familiar?'

'No, but it might help.'

I hold it up to my neck, imagining myself wearing it. The light weight settles on my skin and calms me straight away. As though it is meant to be there.

'I will arrange for Janoah to see you. Perhaps the two of you together will find a way to release your memories.'

'Thank you.'

I scrunch up the necklace, afraid the past is not worth remembering.

Chapter 7

Saxon

The scent of fresh bread fills my nostrils as I stumble out of the bakery. The crowd is thick and I jostle past each person going about their business. The old man still sits alone on the bench seat. Nobody is willing to stop and speak with him, except me.

'Rudolph? You with us?'

'Of course. What about you, young Saxon? Are you with us?'

'Of course.'

Rudolph laughs. 'Good lad. Come sit with a miserable old tinker for a moment.'

Talking with Rudolph never takes only a moment. His yarns always take much longer, often embellished for entertainment purposes—so I learnt as I grew up. But when I was younger, I believed every word he said.

I settle next to the old man. 'I got a free rock cake.' I hold it beneath Rudolph's nose so the fresh, sweet smell wafts past and he cannot refuse. 'Do you want it?'

Rudolph reaches for it. 'That's very kind of you.'

I could never just give it to Rudolph. It would embarrass him to accept something for no reason. So, each time I create a new one.

'Lots of shoppers around today,' I say.

'A lot more Agents walking round as well, new ones. Sneaky bloody tinkers,' grumbles Rudolph.

People move along the strip of shopfronts. Temporary stalls are set up on the street to trade items for the right price. Tokens or bartering is the accepted currency for the outside traders. But only tokens are allowed in the indoor stores. They sell nutrient packs and other essential items and will not barter from the fixed prices. Nutrient packs are the main sustenance in communities ever since they were developed to feed the masses.

My eyes flit from one person to another. The grey and red-trimmed uniform of the Agents does little to help them blend in. The stunner lasers hanging from their hips look like batons, but are much more powerful and crippling. They are capable of expanding up to three metres to debilitate an offender. The Agents are the only people assigned such a weapon.

'Why do you reckon there're more Agents?'

Rudolph shrugs. 'It's not them you have to worry about.' He points to the crowd in front. 'An Agent has to know where to look for trouble first.'

'Filthy lagers.'

'Everyone has a price, Saxon. Don't ever forget that.'

I would never dob someone in just to receive a few extra tokens, but many people do. Desperate or liars, the Agents don't care why such information is supplied. They just respond to the tip-offs.

Rudolph takes a mouthful of the dessert. 'This is almost as good as the ones your father would make.'

I bite into the rock cake, a treat we can't really afford. Rudolph's comment is another reason I enjoy the older man's company. He never shies away from speaking about my parents, always eager to pass on a story about them. Rudolph has lots of memories from when he and my father Shayne grew up together. The two of them were best friends.

I lick the crumbs from my fingers and clear my throat. 'Do you remember the story you once told us ... about the Okodee people?'

Rudolph moves closer and lowers his voice. 'Why do you ask?'

'It's just ... I haven't heard any mention of it from you in years.'

Rudolph relaxes and creates some space between us again. 'What do you want to know?'

'Do you believe the stories are real? That such people with extraordinary abilities exist?'

'I believe it sure as you're sitting next to me. I believe it sure as the wrinkles on my face are many.' Rudolph grips my arm. 'It's no bedtime story, my boy, no dreamland tale. It's fact. Okodee people live out there among us, and they are the most powerful of us all.'

'But *how* do you know it to be true?'

'Is this man bothering you?' An Agent towers over Rudolph. 'Move along, old man. No loitering.'

'No trouble here,' I say. 'He's just making conversation while I rest.'

I would like to drop my gaze from the penetrating stare of the Agent but instead, in a small act of defiance, I hold it higher.

The Agent steps closer to me. 'What's your name?'

'I'm goin', I'm goin',' says Rudolph. He stands and stumbles toward the Agent. 'Leave,' he hisses at me.

'Get off me.' The Agent tries to push Rudolph away, but the old man is stronger than he looks and slumps further against the Agent. 'Get off me before I take you to chambers and lock you up for the night.'

I disappear into the crowd, thankful for the distraction. You should never give an Agent your name. The less they know about your life, the better. With a rambler recuperating back at our house, it would not be wise to have an Agent poking around my life. If the Agent found out we hadn't reported a rambler, we would all be thrown into chambers, Constance included. We'd have to stay there until a judicial hearing to determine the threat of the rambler. It wouldn't matter that Kerina was near dead when we found her. The rules state, *Any newcomer must be invited to stay after reporting their arrival.* If not, they risk being sent back into the wasteland. Kerina might have survived it once, but it could be a different outcome for her if there were a second time.

Chapter 8

Kerina

Darkness surrounds me as I thump my hand against the cold, concrete floor. The echo is dull and flat. I am alone in the confined space, my ragged breath the only comfort. There was somebody here with me before, but they are gone now.

Wails of terror float through the air toward me. I don't know who they belong to, or what is causing them. I pull on the restraints and cover my ears to block out the noise, but the effort does little to stop the yelling. Thud, yell, scream, thud, yell, scream, over and over with no reprieve. Suddenly the door to my confinement opens. An Agent steps in. 'Your turn.'

I wake screaming and disorientated. A figure stands over me, shaking me awake. I lash out at their touch and punch with all my strength. *Smack.* I connect with something hard and lunge away from my attacker. Something restrains me and I roar in protest. I realise the bed sheets are tucked in tightly around me, making me thrash and kick.

'Kerina, you're safe. It's Saxon and Constance.'

I tear the sheets off and roll out of the bed. 'Get away from me.'

My legs are weak and I collapse to the ground. I drag my body across the floor until my back hits the wall and I can't go any further.

'Don't be afraid,' a voice says softly.

It confuses me. I remember that friendly voice. It calms me as I try to focus on it.

'It's okay, Kerina. I promise nobody here will hurt you.'

'I'm safe?'

'That's right. It's me, Constance. Saxon's here as well. Remember, he brought you some soup?'

I swallow my fear, remembering the warm pumpkin soup that was brought to me earlier. It tasted so good. There was a woman who offered to help get my memory back. I press against the thumping rhythm of my heart and look around. A face comes into focus.

'Constance?'

'It was just a bad dream, Kerina. I promise nobody here will hurt you.'

Saxon appears, holding his nose. Blood smears his fingers and the red stain makes me gasp.

'Did I do that?'

'Lucky shot,' he mutters.

I stare at my hands, imagining the strength that must have been exerted to smash his nose like that.

'What happened, Kerina?' asks Constance. 'What frightened you?'

I cover my ears. The faceless screams still ring inside my head.

'It was a stupid dream. I'm sorry I woke you both.'

Constance kneels in front of me. 'You can trust us.'

I know Constance speaks the truth, but I still can't bring myself to reveal the nature of the dream. How can I explain it when I don't know what it means? They are sure to think I've lost my mind.

'I'm fine. It really was just a bad dream.'

'She says she's fine,' says Saxon. 'Let's get her back to bed.'

Constance pauses, waiting for me to share more.

'Don't fuss, Constance. I feel silly waking you.'

Constance sighs. 'Very well. So long as you're sure, Kerina?'

'I am.'

To prove it, I try to stand. I haven't the strength, though, and my legs buckle. Saxon grabs me around the waist and catches me. He scoops me up as though I am made of feathers and carries me toward the bed.

'I can walk by myself,' I say, struggling against him.

He releases me to a standing position. 'You're trembling.'

'I'm cold.'

I glare at him. We both know I'm lying on this warm night.

He steps back but keeps one arm around my waist. 'At least use me as a support.'

I stand straighter, pushing him away, and take a wobbly step.

'Do it your way then.' He crosses his arms and watches.

I concentrate on the bed. My brow furrows and I grit my teeth. I know how to walk. I just need to remind my body. I slide one foot forward while the other drags behind. I grip my limb and lift the leg. It follows my direction and I repeat the gesture, moving closer to the bed.

'Nearly there, Kerina,' says Constance.

The effort has made me breathless, but Saxon's smug words spur me on. I swing my arms and step forward. With one final effort, I collapse to my stomach on the bed. Saxon moves toward me.

'Step back. I don't need your help.'

I flip over and sit on the bed. My heart beats so fast that I wonder if it will explode. I might be weak within my body, but my mind is strong. I smile and the strength spreads through my body as I catch my breath. I can do this. I can get my memories back and make sense of my past.

Chapter 9

Saxon

'**I** don't need you to chaperone me.'

Manny grabs me in a headlock and rubs his knuckles against my scalp. 'I sure don't plan on being yer babysitter tonight li'l brother.'

I push him away. 'Better not let your wife find out what you're up to.'

'What's that supposed to mean?'

I shake my head. 'I ain't stupid. I know what you're doing.'

Manny grins. 'It's all a bit of harmless fun.'

'Until you bet more than we can afford and Constance finds out.'

'It's tonight only, with *lots* of players. Zeb's got a game going.'

'Zeb! Are you crazy?'

'There's lotsa tokens to win, Saxon. It could support us through the winter.'

'Or leave us to starve.'

Manny gets in my face. 'Just keep yer mouth shut to Constance and I'll meet you back here later.'

I pinch the bridge of my nose as he walks off. My brother might be older by several years, but he doesn't always act it. Zeb is not known for his generosity. Manny's a tinker if he thinks he can compete with Zeb.

The line curls out the door for the screenshow. *The Great Adventure.* It's one I've not seen before.

'Saxon! I already got your ticket,' yells Anastasia, hurrying toward me.

'You didn't need to do that.'

She swats my hand away as I try to pay her. 'Don't be silly. My father got free tickets.'

Her father is a Dictor, the community representative of Nevertyre. Rumour has it he is the most malleable of the Dictors from all the surrounding communities. Whispers suggest he provides the least resistance to the Primo Dictor in Middtown.

I accept the ticket. 'Well, at least let me get a drink for you.'

She nods. 'Strawberry bubbles.'

I leave Anastasia with her friends, each born into families of wealth that allow carefree lifestyles. None know what it is like to wake cold and hungry.

As I wait in the line, I can't help feeling disappointed that Kerina couldn't come. Constance thought the experience would be too much for her and wouldn't allow it. It would have been good to see if being around other sounds and smells jogged any of her memories. Hopefully, the session with Janoah tonight will help. Janoah has a certain way with people. Constance says she can help mend souls, whatever that means.

'Next,' calls the attendant.

'One strawberry bubble and a fruit cider.'

These drinks are an indulgence, unnecessary but enjoyable. I walk back to Anastasia and her friends. They giggle as I get closer.

'I do hope you're not talkin' about me, ladies.'

This only increases their laughter, each caught out whispering about me behind my back. Anastasia's friends find our friendship amusing. They tolerate me as though I am a plaything, still new and interesting. But I'm under no illusions. I know they are not my friends.

'Ask him,' says Lia, Anastasia's best friend.

'Ask me what?' I say, sending her my most charming smile.

Anastasia reaches for her drink and takes a sip. 'They want to know if it's true.'

'Yes, it's true. I'm just as funny as I am handsome.'

Anastasia runs her hand along my arm. 'Both true rumours, but not the answer we seek.'

'Did you really meet a rambler?' asks Lia.

I try to keep the teasing grin on my face, but it slips. All girls wait for my answer. I feel protective of Kerina and don't want to reveal anything about her. Especially after what I know about her mark, but most importantly not with these girls whose parents all work in positions of power. I remind myself they can't know about Kerina, it's not possible. It must be a mistake.

'How did you hear such a story?' I say, trying not to panic.

Anastasia bounces on her feet. 'I have my sources of information as well, you know.'

'Yes,' says Lia. 'She doesn't just rely on listening at the base of her father's office door.'

The girls erupt in laughter. Anastasia joins in, not fazed by their teasing.

'You might need to check your sources, Anastasia,' I say, dismissing the gossip.

If these girls have heard of a rambler at our home, it won't be long until an Agent comes knocking.

'It wasn't gossip,' says Anastasia. 'My uncle said your brother told him about a rambler that once stayed at your house. Way back when you were boys.'

'Ohh, yes! That's true.' I laugh, relieved. 'It was a long time ago, so long in fact I'd forgotten about it till now.'

'That must have been weird,' says Lia. 'A stranger in your home, sleeping in your bed.'

'I can barely remember them,' I lie.

Anastasia watches me, making no comment. Drum sounds rumble through the area, indicating the screenshow will soon begin.

'Quick, let's get our seats,' says Lia.

I follow the noise, ignoring the sidelong glance from Anastasia. I'm happy for the distraction, but knowing her, it won't last long. I lied about my recollections of when I was a boy. The rambler from my youth is someone I have thought about often, and not because they were scary or strange. The man's face is still fresh in my memory, as though I only saw him yesterday. I will never forget how he was taken from our home, dragged kicking and screaming and discarded into the wasteland, never to be seen again.

Chapter 10

Kerina

'Kerina, I want you to meet a special friend of mine. This is Janoah. She is someone I would trust with my life.'

Janoah reaches for my hand to shake. It's a formal greeting normally used by strangers and authority figures. Members of the community who are friendly with one another adopt a more relaxed squeeze of the shoulder in greeting. I hesitate to shake the outstretched hand.

Janoah bows her head. 'Do not be afraid of me, child. I mean you no harm and wish only to help.'

I'm struck by the beauty of this woman before me. Her straight white hair hangs so long, she must be able to sit on it.

'You are very pretty,' I blurt out.

'That is kind of you to say.' Her lime green eyes twinkle. 'But I am sure you have seen others prettier than I.'

I try to conjure up faces of other women I've met, or been introduced to, but my mind is blank. Janoah must sense my fear because she quickly places her hands on either side of my face.

'We will work on your memories. They *will* come back. In the meantime, be not afraid of what you don't know, no matter how scary it might seem.'

'I'm not afraid.' I pull back from her grasp. 'I just want answers.'

'I shall leave you two alone,' says Constance, closing the door behind her.

Janoah smiles. 'Kerina, I want to try to relax you completely, so that your subconscious might have the chance to come through.

Many times, when trauma has been experienced, our mind buries what we cannot process. Whatever it thinks we cannot handle.'

'Will my memories return?'

'You were found nearly dead. You have suffered a massive trauma to have arrived here. I believe I can help loosen some memories. But I must be honest when I tell you that some may never return.'

Janoah removes the pillows and sets them on the floor. She sets up a candle on either side of the bed.

'These are ylang-ylang scented and will calm your nerves.'

The flames flicker against the cream-coloured walls. Janoah pulls out two sprigs of purple flower and sits them beside the candles.

'The lavender will relax you. Please come and lie down.'

The scent is strong, but not unpleasant. I do as she asks, ignoring the tremor rippling through my body. Janoah ensures my arms rest beside my body. Then she uncrosses my ankles and wipes oil on the soles of my feet. I flinch from the cool, wet touch.

'This is peppermint and will help with your concentration. Now, close your eyes.'

'You're not doing magic, are you?'

'Not the kind that uses spells. I am a healer, yes, but I use only natural remedies. Now please, do as I say.'

I take a deep breath, close my eyes, and focus on the past. My memories are hidden and I need to find them. A strong, smoky scent fills my nostrils.

'This incense is called Lotus. It is to help open your mind's eye.'

The smell is strong for a minute before becoming weaker. Waves of the scent waft beneath my nose. Stronger, then weaker. Stronger, then weaker.

'Kerina, you must keep your eyes closed until I say. You might fall into a deep state of unconsciousness, but I will be here waiting for you. I will keep you safe from your memories. Do you trust me to do that?'

I nod, determined to open my mind and unlock the secrets of my past. Constance mentioned that amnesia can be acquired through a trauma to protect oneself. That is what she thinks I have. But surely if I can just pluck out one thread of memory, the rest will unravel.

'Let's begin, Kerina. I want you to think about this room. Think of the people you've met here. Think of the things they have done to help get you better and strong again. You are safe here and they will protect you, so feel that security.

'Now visualise outside the house. Picture some flowers set in warbles. Inhale their scents. Feel the grass against your feet and the sun on your skin. Relax your body so your mind can open.'

Listening to Janoah's voice, my mind begins to wander. I visualise the flowers, the grass, the sun. The strong lavender and sweet peppermint scents make it easy to picture a garden.

'Kerina, I want you to think back to how you got here. Don't fight the memories and allow your mind to follow them wherever they take you.'

I inhale deeply. A pressure moves up my body, from my toes to my shoulders.

'Manny and Saxon found you. Can you see Saxon looking over you? You asked him to help you.'

I conjure up Saxon's face, trying to imagine what it must have looked like when he found me. More pressure is applied to my collarbone.

'You were alone when they found you. Did you have companions before that? Try to picture the road you took to get here.'

Snippets of memories begin to form, hazy but real. My body becomes heavy and I can feel it sinking into a relaxed state. I don't fight the images swirling inside my head, trying to break free; instead I embrace them, feeling hopeful.

Chapter 11

Saxon

We each take a seat in the middle of the theatre and settle in for the screenshow. I remember the first time Manny ever took me to one. The huge people on the screen scared me. The volume was so loud that the booming voices frightened me and I covered my ears, refusing to remove them until the end. A long time ago, everyone had smaller screenshow screens in their homes. They're still around if you search, mostly discarded and broken. After the Burn, energy sources were destroyed, along with so many other things. Power was eventually restored after a long time, but as solar power only.

Anastasia elbows me in the ribs. 'So tell me, my sweet Saxon, are you hiding something?'

I pretend not to hear her question, but she leans closer.

'You paled like a full moon when Lia mentioned the rambler. If I didn't know better, I would think you thought she referred to a different rambler than the one from your childhood.'

'Your imagination is ripe.'

She leans closer and whispers, 'You can always trust me, Saxon. I don't plan on following in my father's footsteps.' There is a determination in her expression I have not noticed before.

'Why would you say that about your father? What footsteps do you mean?'

'You might think I don't know about the way things work, Saxon. But I know plenty!'

She checks for anyone listening, but nobody is taking any

notice. They are too absorbed in the opening scenes of the show.

'I'm not a fool. I know what a puppet my father is. He must have his reasons for doing things in such a way, and I don't pretend to know what they are. But I do know that when I make choices, they are with good intentions, without the possibility of accusations of unjust actions. The choices when I rule Nevertyre will be made because it is the right thing to do.'

I sit back, stunned by her revelation. I've never heard Anastasia speak in such a way, especially about her own father. He is the Dictor of Nevertyre, after all.

'What are you trying to say, Anastasia?'

She leans in as though kissing my neck, but instead whispers, 'I'm saying that you can trust me not to run to my father and tell him things you might choose to confide in me. Understand this, Saxon. My actions will always be honest and true.'

I am confused by her outburst but certain she speaks the truth.

'Now tell me, Saxon, what are you hiding? Or should I say … whom?'

'You're right, I do have a secret.' My lips almost touch her ear. 'But you must promise not to tell anyone.'

She caresses my cheek. 'I swear it. Nobody will hear a thing from me.'

'There is a rambler at our house, right now.'

Her thumb freezes mid-stroke.

'They have no recollection of where they came from, so we don't know much about them.'

'They can talk the same as us?'

'Of course, but she doesn't say much. She's still weak from the journey.'

'A girl? I want to meet this rambler.' Anastasia moves my face to look directly at her. 'And you're going to make it happen.'

When Anastasia wants something, she usually gets it.

'Before I can agree to this request, tell me, what other things do you know?'

Anastasia takes my hand in hers. She peers up at me through her lashes. 'Don't you trust me?'

I laugh at her flirtations. There is no denying her beauty, and she does have persistence.

'Trust is hard to earn, but easy to lose,' I say.

She pouts. 'I'm hurt that you think I might deceive you.'

'I've never heard you speak this way, is all.' I move back to put some distance between us. 'I'm not sure what to think.'

'Ahh, you want proof, is that it?'

'An example would be a good offering of mutual trust.'

That determined look returns to her face. 'I know your friend Rudolph is not all that he seems.'

My eyes narrow. 'What do you know of Rudolph?'

'I know that you trust him implicitly, but would do well to distance yourself from him.'

Her words sink in and I think about the conversation we had at the market recently. She must be confused. Rudolph is no threat to me.

'Saxon, you should probably kiss me before my friends get suspicious.'

I hesitate. Anastasia reaches her hand up around my neck, urging me along. I follow her lead and lean in. I kiss her with a slow, lingering kiss, full of confusion and questions. As I pull back, I notice Lia is watching us. She turns her head back to the screen just as I look up. I hope she didn't overhear us. Anastasia might be trustworthy and want change, but I doubt her friends feel the same way.

Chapter 12

Kerina

The sun beats down on me. My drink bottle has been empty for two days. A water source is my top priority, but I know it will be hard to come by in the wasteland. My companion's body slumps beside me. Her body is unwilling to go any further.

'Get up, Lariel. You can't stop now.' I pull my friend to a seated position. Her head flops forward, but she doesn't respond. 'You can't give up. We have to keep moving or they'll find us.'

Lariel makes no sound. I shake her, but still nothing.

I scream, thumping the ground. 'Arrgghh.' I sob, but no tears form.

I drag Lariel toward the tree for what little shade there is. She groans as she leans against it. A sign that she is not dead, at least. Her lips are cracked and her face is blotchy and peeling.

'Lariel! Stay with me. You can rest soon.'

'Leave me, Kerina. I'm done for.'

'No, you stay with me. We will get through this together.'

A noise by the bushes distracts me. A trickling sound. One that echoes loudly through my ears. I leap up and stumble toward the noise. I crash through the bushes and tumble down the hill on the other side. I smash into the slow flowing creek behind it. The coolness makes me laugh. I waste no time slurping up the clear liquid, coughing as I try to swallow without choking. I fill my drink bottle and rush back to Lariel with it.

'There's water, Lariel. You found it!' I tilt Lariel's mouth upward and pour the lifesaving nectar in the hole. She splutters to life and reaches for the bottle.

'There's plenty. Drink it all.'

Lariel gulps so fast it dribbles down her chin. She pours the refreshing liquid over her head.

'I'll get more.' I crash back through the bushes, laughing as I go.

I open my eyes and find myself back in the bedroom. Giggles burst from within. The noise is loud to my ears. I cover my mouth to stop them, but the sudden movement gives me a fright and makes me laugh more. My senses must be heightened from the relaxation session.

'Kerina, are you okay?' Janoah's striking green eyes stare down on me.

'Yes, I'm wonderful.'

'You found some memories?'

Constance appears beside the bed. 'What did you remember?'

'My friend, Lariel! I wasn't alone after all. I was travelling with her. We were both so thirsty. Lariel had almost given up when we found the creek.'

'You remember your friend, Lariel? That's wonderful, Kerina, well done,' says Janoah.

'What happened to her?' asks Constance.

The smile wavers on my face. 'I don't know … I mean … I'm not sure …'

'Kerina, that's okay. It's your first memory to return. We might learn more next time,' says Janoah.

'Except I'm here, alive,' I say, panicked. 'But she's not with me.'

'Hush now, it's been a big day. You've been in here with Janoah for over two hours.'

'Make me unconscious again, Janoah. I have to know what happened to her.'

'Shhh, you must rest.' Constance tries to adjust the bed cover.

I push her hand away. 'No, I have to remember. Janoah, what else can you do to help?'

Janoah blows out the candles and collects the sprigs of lavender. 'You did well, Kerina. You must sleep now. We can't push this. The brain is an unpredictable organ. It can't be rushed and it won't be forced.'

'But I need to know, don't you understand? What if she's still out there?' I try to stand up, but my body sways from vertigo, sending me sprawling back to the bed.

Janoah reaches for me and grips my hands. 'I will help, but you must trust me.'

I picture Lariel in my mind again and see her smiling face as she poured the water over her head. I have a feeling I woke up at that moment for a reason. A bad reason. I must know what happened.

'Kerina, will you let me help you? Can you allow yourself to trust me?'

If we found water, it must have helped us, but why are we now separated? I need to learn more. But to do that, I need Janoah's help.

'I will trust you, but you must promise to do everything in your power to get my memories back.'

'I promise.'

Janoah collects up her things, and she and Constance leave me alone in the room. Darkness surrounds me. There is no moonlight through the window tonight. My body feels like lead. The rush of excitement has zapped my strength. I try to roll over, but the effort is too much. I stay in the same position and close my eyes, waiting for sleep to find me. Instead, Lariel's face appears. Her accusing glare haunts my dreams all night long.

Chapter 13

Saxon

The crowd spills out on to the street after the screenshow. The lights will stay on for thirty minutes before the area becomes dark. The screenshow runs once a week with a different show each time. It uses up a lot of power, so they shut everything off soon after it finishes. Even with solar panels installed on rooftops, the community is still conscious of conserving energy.

'Hey, Saxon! I didn't know you was here, mah friend.' Elgee grips my shoulder, then punches his fist against me in greeting.

I grin at my childhood friend. 'I didn't see you in there.'

Elgee looks between me and Anastasia. 'Problee too distracted.'

Anastasia stands on her tip-toes and kisses my cheek. 'Thanks for the bubbles. I'll see you later.'

We watch Anastasia walk away to join her friends. The group of young ladies move without haste, poised and confident as they return to their comfortable homes, surrounded by neighbours of similar wealth. None of them wear clothes handed down from older siblings. Nor are their clothes ripped or full of holes. Their outfits are tailored from Witon to fit perfectly. Anastasia turns back briefly, sending a wave over her shoulder.

Elgee punches my arm. 'Watcha doin'? She's way outta your league.'

'It ain't like that. We're just friends.'

'Does she know that?'

'She knows I'm not interested in having a girlfriend.'

'How come I ain't seen you lately? Mumma Bear saw you

yesterday. Said you tore through like a demon was on yer tail.'

I scope out who is nearby. It looks clear, but I can't be too sure. I grab Elgee by the elbow and lead him out on the street, away from any ears that might be listening in.

'We found a rambler.'

'*What*?'

'Shhh.' I drag Elgee further away. 'Me and Manny found them. Thought they were dead.'

'So where is he now?'

'*She* is still at our house.'

'Get outta here. Are you serious?'

I nod, checking for any Agents nearby.

'She wild? Crazy? Can she even speak?'

'Shut up, of course she can speak.'

'She must be crazy den.'

Something flares in me, a protective instinct to defend Kerina. 'She's normal, Elgee. She's just like us, but …'

'Oh, I *knew* there was a "but".' Elgee rubs his hands together, grinning.

'She's got no memory. Could barely remember her own name.'

'For real? She ain't bangin' it on?'

I shake my head. 'If she's faking, then it's a really good act.'

'*Saxon*!' Bayley runs toward us. 'You gotta come quick. It's Manny.'

I don't wait for an explanation as I follow him down the street. The crowd thins out as we move further away from the screen-show. People have dispersed and begun the walk home. Agents ensure there's no loitering on the streets after dark. Bayley leads us toward a darkened building. The windows are painted black so that anyone passing by would think it was empty, but I know better. I follow Bayley down the side. It hooks around to the back of the building. A groan comes from the dark.

'Manny?' I try not to panic. 'Where are you?'

Elgee shines a solar-powered torch around the space. The

light is dim and he frantically points the light about in different directions.

'He's over there,' yells Elgee.

A crumpled body lays curled up on the ground.

I run toward him. 'Manny, I'm here. You're gonna be okay.'

Manny tries to speak, but barely manages a moan.

'They beat him pretty bad,' says Bayley.

I shove him. 'What the hell happened? Where were you?'

'I was only gone twenty minutes, I promise. When I came back, I couldn't find him. Then I saw Zeb and some of his crew comin' in through the back.'

I squat down and try to turn Manny over. 'Manny? Are you with me?'

He doesn't respond. I shake him. 'Manny!'

He manages to open an eye.

'You damn tinker, what happened?'

'I lost,' he slurs.

'He's drunk! Damn it! Elgee, help me get him up.'

Elgee comes around and secures Manny under the armpit while I grip the other side. We hoist him up and hook his arms around our necks.

'Is he gonna be all right?' asks Bayley.

Manny's lip is split with one eye already swollen shut. His top is ripped and a graze covers his cheek.

'Don't … tell Constance,' Manny slurs.

Elgee chuckles. 'He gonna be fine.'

'Not when Constance finds out,' I say.

Chapter 14

Kerina

'Good morning, Kerina. How did you sleep?'

Constance tugs the curtains all the way open. Sunlight streams in, brightening the room.

I shield my eyes from the morning glare.

'I slept some. It just wasn't very restful.'

Constance smiles. 'Keep trying. It's going to get better.'

I want to believe Constance but am unsure of the truth to her words. I sit up, and for the first time my body doesn't creak from the effort. In fact, I feel stronger than I have before. The memories with Janoah, while worrisome, have me wanting to learn more. I pick at the invisible lint on the purple bedspread.

'Was there a problem this morning?' I ask, changing the subject.

Constance pauses. 'You heard us arguing?'

'Just voices. I couldn't make out what you were saying.'

Constance sighs. 'No problem. Just my husband being … stupid and impulsive.'

'Nothing serious, I hope.' Constance has been nothing but kind to me. I wouldn't want to be the cause of any problems for her.

'Nothing for you to worry about.'

She pulls some clothes out of the wardrobe and lays them on the bed.

'I fit into these not so long ago. Before we were blessed with this growing little miracle.' She rubs her belly. 'So, this morning I thought we would get you up on your feet and—'

Knock, knock, knock.

'Ahh, perfect timing.' She winks at me. 'Come in.'

The door opens and Saxon steps in. 'I can help this morning, but then I have jobs to do.'

'What's going on?' I say.

Constance hugs her stomach. 'We thought it was time to get you back on your feet. For a short time anyway.'

'Yes, good! I would like that.' I throw back the sheet, ready to begin.

My nightshirt has shifted and my bare legs are exposed. Saxon quickly turns away when I catch him staring.

'Saxon, don't pretend you haven't seen a pretty girl's legs before.' Constance slaps him over the head.

Saxon looks at me, then averts his eyes again. I swing off the bed and prepare to stand.

'Wow! Your legs are nearly healed,' says Constance.

'What do you mean?'

'When Manny and Saxon found you, those legs were covered in scrapes and cuts. It's only been a week. You should at least have some bruises left behind, but there's nothing.'

I shrug. 'I must heal quickly. What about some privacy to get dressed?'

'Of course.' Constance hovers while Saxon scurries out of the room.

'I'll call out if I need help.'

Constance closes the door behind her and I'm left alone. My legs are smooth and blemish free, apart from the purple rings around my ankles. But even they seem lighter than when I looked the first time. I push myself off the bed. The solid floor feels strange against my bare feet. The dizziness from last night has gone. My legs feel strong and my balance has improved. I look at the garments carefully laid on the bed. A pair of dark-green pants and a long-sleeve black top. I rub the soft fabric between her fingers. An unexpected material. I wonder how Constance came to have clothes made from Witon.

'Why do I have to wear the same type of clothes?'

'Because it's expensive, child, and moving often means we can't take much.'

My head spins from the memory. I freeze, not willing to shift an inch should I lose the image in my mind. I see myself walking along a dirt road as a young girl. There are a series of images of towns, buildings, and barren landscapes flashing by. How many places have I lived?

'Are you okay in there?' Constance calls out.

The images disappear.

'I'm fine,' I say, annoyed by the interruption.

I manage to dress myself without assistance.

'Those undergarments are new, by the way.'

I cringe. Saxon will be listening to the conversation, and I certainly don't want him to know about my underwear. I adjust the attire. The clothes are a little big, but good enough for me to wear.

I shuffle my way across to the wardrobe. The door has swung open and there is a mirror on the inside. A stranger's face looks at me from the reflective surface. I reach out to touch it as I peer into my own blue eyes. Standing sideways, I see that my dark hair falls halfway down my back. It is not straight and silky like Janoah's, but thick and wavy. I will speak to Constance about cutting it shorter. A new style for a new Kerina.

I run my finger over the necklace clasped around my neck. The ruby stone stares back at me. It taunts me with my lack of knowledge about it. Dare I hope I was loved by a family who gave it to me? I lean closer to my reflection, wondering who the person is looking back. What kind of person am I? What things have I endured? The image in the mirror gives no clues to the answers.

Chapter 15

Saxon

Kerina emerges from the room dressed. The clothes are a nice change to the nightshirt she's being wearing for days. They make her seem like any other community member around Nevertyre. Not a rambler lost in the wasteland.

Kerina moves past me and uses the walls to assist. I give her some space and follow her down the hallway.

'Take it easy,' I say. Her muscles must be screaming from a lack of use, but she doesn't let on. Manny's pumpkin soup has helped get her healthy again. And we have been sharing our nutrient drinks to try to build her strength back up. Constance can't spare much of hers in her current condition. She needs to consume all her nutrients to keep herself and the baby strong.

'She's up.' Manny stands behind the bench. His blackened eyes are out of place in the kitchen. 'Had a misunderstanding last night,' he says, by way of explanation.

'Had a moment of stupidity, more like. That *won't* happen again,' says Constance.

Manny scowls at his wife, and I know they haven't finished with that conversation.

I walk toward the back door. 'Think some fresh air will be good. Are you coming, Kerina?' I reach out to guide her through the doorway, but she shakes me off.

'I can do it.'

'Just trying to help.' I knew she wouldn't accept it, but I wanted to see what she would do.

Outside, Kerina leans against the house and inhales the fresh air. She closes her eyes and turns her face toward the sun. After being trapped indoors as long as she has, the fresh air and sunshine will be good for her.

'The veggie patch is down there. Do you want to see it?'

I offer my arm, but again she refuses any help; instead, she sets the pace. It's slow going, but I don't complain. This is a good test to see how well her strength has returned. She continues with one step in front of the other, steady and determined for the next thirty metres. The ground is uneven, but Kerina manages well and makes it to the edge of the veggie patch. She puffs, exerted from the short walk. Beads of sweat have formed on her forehead.

'I think that's far enough. You should rest.' I return to the house and retrieve a chair from inside.

'Thank you.' She slumps on it.

A strange-looking stuffed figure faces us. It is strapped to a pole. The clothes are faded and full of holes.

'What's that for?' asks Kerina.

'It's a scarecrow. People used it long ago to scare away birds from the food growing in the fields. We don't really need it anymore because not many birds fly around these days.'

'I've seen an eagle once.' Kerina squints up at the sky.

'What was it like?'

'I remember the span of its wings caused a shadow to fall over the ground. I was terrified it would pick me up and carry me away.' She falls silent, lost in her thoughts.

Questions gather in my mind, but I push them to the back for now.

'These clothes are comfortable, but I'm worried I might ruin them.'

'Don't be. Constance came with quite a wardrobe.'

'Really?'

I nod. 'Her upbringing was different to ours, maybe even yours.'

I can tell she wants to ask more, but it is not my story to tell.

'You know, you don't have to push yourself too hard,' I say, changing the subject. 'Who knows how long your legs walked before we found you.'

'My friend Lariel was with me,' she says quietly. 'I remembered her last night, but I don't know what happened to her.'

My eyebrows draw together. 'You were alone when we found you.'

'I was so happy when I first remembered her, but then … I felt guilty.'

'Why?'

'Because I'm here and she must be out there somewhere. Dead or alive, I don't know. It makes me feel guilty.'

I know something about survivor guilt. When my parents died, it was consuming.

'So, dis is yer rambler?' Elgee's footsteps crunch toward us.

Kerina tenses at the towering figure before her.

'It's okay, you can trust him. This is my good friend Elgee.'

'Nuh uh, I his *only* friend. No one else puts up with him.'

'Elgee, this is Kerina. This is her first time out walking since … we found her.'

Kerina watches Elgee, who often bounces while he talks. It makes his dreadlocked hair bob around. His skin is dark as night and his teeth shine brightly when he smiles.

'Now I know why he kept quiet 'bout you. Ain't such a scary rambler, is yer?'

'Are ramblers supposed to be scary?' says Kerina.

Elgee laughs. 'Well, they sure ain't sane. Nobody wants to go walkin' alone in that dustbowl out there.'

'Have you been out there?' she asks.

Now it's my turn to laugh. 'Elgee doesn't venture far from home.'

'Don't need to. Got all I want where I am.' He squats down so his eyes are level with Kerina. 'But I'm tellin' yer. People who wander around out there. They either crazy. Or desperate. Which one are you?'

Kerina looks between us and stands once again. 'Guess we'll find out.'

Chapter 16

Kerina

It's evening, and Janoah lights the incense from last night. She places sprigs of lavender on either side of the bed.

'We're going to try something different this time. Your body has been through a great trauma. It is holding much tension that we need to release. I'm hoping if we can release it, your memories will be free to return.'

She lights the candles, then pulls the curtains closed.

'I need you to close your eyes, Kerina. You will soon feel a repetitive tap on different parts of your upper body, mostly your face. Keeping your eyes closed, I want you to look toward the point of pressure. Do you understand?'

'Yes.'

Janoah places her hand over mine. 'I need you to focus on your memory loss. Focus only on this and the pressure of the taps. Okay?'

'Yes.'

'Let's begin then.'

I feel the first tap near my heart. It was so light I barely noticed it. The tap on my eyebrow is stronger and reminds me of a heart beating. Janoah moves the tapping to the side of my eye. I cringe from the pressure beneath my eye, worried Janoah might poke it. The pressure is light and repeated several times. I keep my eyes closed, but focus on the tapping, moving my eyes toward each sensation. The next tap is beneath my nose, light fingertips almost tickling my top lip, but the repetition stays the same. My chin is tapped but dull and with more pressure, like a knuckle. My collar-bone is tapped several times, the action light for such a solid bone. My eyes continue to follow the pressure while still keeping the lids closed. I chant a silent mantra.

'My memories will return. My memories will return.'

Janoah moves the tapping to the top of my head. Again, it feels like knuckles against my skull. Not uncomfortable, just strange as the tap vibrates through my body. I almost miss the lighter tap of the top of my thumb. It's followed by my index, middle, and baby finger. The pressure is so light. Suddenly, a sharp thumping is applied to my mid-section. It covers a wider area and must be the side of a hand, not fingertips.

I block out any other sensory thought and concentrate on the tapping. It moves back to where it began and continues like a heart beating. Janoah moves through each area a second time. I concentrate only on the tapping and my determination to retrieve my memories.

'There's water, Lariel. You found it!' I tilt Lariel's mouth upward and pour the lifesaving nectar in the hole. She splutters to life and reaches for the bottle.

'There's plenty. Drink it all.'

Lariel gulps so fast it dribbles down her chin. She pours the refreshing liquid over her head.

'I'll get more.' I crash back through the bushes, laughing as I go.

Suddenly, from the bottom of the hill, I hear Lariel's screams. I drop the bottle and run toward her. I scramble up the hill, tripping and sliding as I climb. A gunshot echoes in my ears and freezes my ascent. Voices float over the ridge as I creep toward them. Three men sit on horseback, each dishevelled and dirty. A cart is hooked behind one of the horses. Slumped inside is Lariel.

'We'll get our reward for this one 'n tell 'em the other was dead. One's better 'n none.'

'Damn it! The other was worth twice as much.'

My body is coiled tight. I am ready to spring from the bushes and help my friend, but something holds me back. The man closest to me searches the area. His gaze falls on the bush that conceals me. He must make the decisions, as the others wait for him to speak. I dare not breathe, certain he will hear me. He spits on the ground and kicks the horse.

'Let's go, fellahs. One big fat reward for an Okodee girl is certainly better than none.'

The men laugh as the dust kicks up behind them. I watch on with anguish as Lariel is dragged away. I do nothing to save her.

My eyes snap open. Sweat covers my forehead and my breathing is ragged.

Janoah watches over me. 'You are safe, Kerina. You are not alone.'

I sit up, panicked, dazed, scared. Curtains flap from a small breeze. The purple bedspread covers my body and I remember where I am. The knowledge calms me.

'What do you remember?' says Janoah.

A gunshot rings out in my ears. Three men waiting, watching, searching for their prey. The man on horseback with long hair, spitting on the ground, looking for me. Lariel's body slumped in the wagon.

'Kerina! What did you see?'

Janoah pushes my hair away from my face and grips my hands. I want to scream, but my voice won't work. A strangled sob come out.

'Lariel. I saw Lariel and they took her and it's my fault. It was me they wanted.'

I want to slump against Janoah and feel comfort from her, but I don't deserve such solace. If I abandoned my friend, then grief is my punishment.

Chapter 17

Saxon

'You're up early,' says Manny, cutting carrots for the soup.

'I'm going out to look for Rudolph. I haven't seen him for a while,' I say vaguely. I remembered the way the Agent looked when Rudolph tried to distract him. A heavy feeling weighs down on me.

'Don't worry about the old man,' says Manny. 'He can take care of himself.'

'I won't be long.' I collect my bag and walk out the back door, colliding with Kerina. 'Woah, watch it!'

'Sorry,' she mumbles.

'Were you out walking alone?'

'I needed to think.'

'Did anyone see you?' I say.

She shakes her head. 'I didn't go far.'

I pinch the bridge of my nose. 'It's not safe for you to walk around by yourself.'

'If I can survive the wasteland, Nevertyre should be easy,' she quips, trying to pass me.

I block her path. 'This isn't a joke. You need to be careful! You're a rambler and ...'

'And what?' She glares at me. 'I know my being here is a risk. I might not know who I am, but I'm not a fool.'

I create some space between us. 'You're angry.'

'Yes, I am angry! I'm sick of these half memories that only confuse me.' She shoves her wrists toward me. 'I know how I got these marks, but not who did it to me.'

'So, you remember how you got them?'

'Those dreams I wake from, screaming …' Kerina turns away embarrassed. 'I don't think they are just nightmares.'

I swallow, warning myself to be careful with my tone. 'What happens in the dreams?'

'Awful things. But I don't know what they are, I just hear them.' She won't look at me. 'There are others in the dream and their screams don't stop. I try to block out the sounds, but I can't. My wrists are tied to the wall and my ankles are chained to the ground.'

She lifts the material of one pant leg and removes the sock. Her ankle is circled by a purple ring. 'It's the same on the other.'

My fists curl with rage at those who have done this to her. 'Those people can't hurt you anymore, Kerina.'

'In my dreams, I fight the restraints, but there is not enough length for me to even lie down. I stay upright and try to block out the cries for help.'

'Who calls out?'

She shrugs. 'I always wake up just as someone enters my prison room.'

She fidgets with the door, not entering, but not looking at me.

'Come with me,' I say.

'Where are we going?'

The change in conversation makes her wary. I can see it in her face, but I grab her hand and pull her behind me.

'I can teach you to fight and help you get stronger. I think you were strong once.' I stop and grab her by the shoulders. 'Kerina, you should be dead! When we found you, that's exactly what we thought you were. Manny had already turned to go home, but you weren't dead. You frightened the hell out of me when your eyes opened.'

She smirks at my admission.

'Don't you see, Kerina? You're a fighter already. You just need to learn some basic skills.'

'And you can show me these skills?'

'Yes, I can teach you.'

'Good, because I'm ready to fight back.' Kerina stands taller. 'I don't want to be afraid anymore.'

'There's just one rule.' I cross my arms. 'You can't tell Constance. She won't think you're ready, and I'll never hear the end of her badgering. Deal?' I extend my hand toward her.

She grips it without hesitation. 'Deal.'

'Let's go then.' I walk toward the shed near the veggie patch. 'First, I'll show you some blocks.'

I stand with knees bent and arms raised, fists covering my face. She mimics my position.

'When I strike, you deflect.' I punch toward her in slow motion and she swats my arm away with her forearm. 'Good reflex.'

I repeat with the other hand. We start slowly and Kerina responds immediately every time. I pick up the pace and *Wham!* Kerina deflects with a speed I've not seen before. I raise an eyebrow in question.

'Must be a quick learner,' she says.

'Quick healer, quick learner. There's much we don't know about you.'

She stares at me, bouncing in her bent stance with fists protecting her face. I begin punching slowly at first, then faster and faster. Kerina deflects every punch until suddenly she responds with a hook to my temple. The force sends me sprawling on my backside.

'Told you I'm a quick learner.'

'Not that quick. You've done this before, haven't you?'

Kerina grins. 'I had forgotten until we started.' She reaches down and pulls me up.

I step toward her, dusting myself off. 'Who are you, Kerina the *rambler*?'

She puts her fists up again, ready for combat. 'I am a survivor.'

Chapter 18

Kerina

Saxon left for the market a while ago. He had me punching repeatedly against a sack of sand after our sparring session. My hands hurt after five punches against the solid surface, but I refused to quit. Instead, I did everything he asked and more. Saxon even showed me some self-defence kicks. Just like the punches, the kicking action returned to me quickly. Combat training is something I have been doing all my life. The question is, why?

I told Saxon I would rest after he left, but I am sick of resting. Resting and waiting for memories that might never return.

'Strong body, stronger mind.' Somebody told me that once. Perhaps one day I will remember who it was.

I have regained much strength from these people's care. Mostly through Manny's homemade soup. Some families, like Saxon's, grow vegetables that can be traded at the market, or cooked in soups and stews. Constance explained that if the community members are self-sufficient, they can scrape together their tokens for other things, like nutrient packs during the harsher months.

There is little land worth farming for crops or animals since the Burn. The nutrient packs are two liquid meals per day. They are scientifically calculated to give the body everything it needs to survive. The packs don't expire, they don't curdle in the hot weather, and they don't need cooling to keep them drinkable. There is no longer the gluttonous waste from before, except, of course, if you can afford it.

'There has always been a battle for wealth and power. The wealthy get powerful and the powerful get wealthy.'

'But what about people like us, Daddy?'

'People like us are rich with love, but poor with opportunity. That is, until somebody special comes along.'

'Like me?'

'Exactly like you, Kerina. Come, or your mother will begin to worry.'

This conversation pops into my mind without warning. I try to freeze details like my father's face, but I can only hear his voice. Do I look like him? The holes in my memories are frustrating. I grip the necklace hanging from my neck. It must be of great value for me to have kept it. If I was taken prisoner, why wasn't it taken from me? I must have kept it hidden somehow.

I unclasp the chain and look over it for a clue. There is no engraving, nothing except the ruby stone sitting in the middle. I hold it closer to my eye, squinting as I peer into the stone.

Suddenly the red stone merges from fuzzy to words. 'No way!'

I polish it against my top and hold it close. Words appear again, magnified words hidden inside the stone.

Time lost, time true.

Now is the time to do.

'These words make no sense,' I say to myself.

I look around the yard to check I am completely alone. Anyone who passed by would think me quite mad, squinting into a tiny necklace. I look again.

Time lost, time true.

Now is the time to do.

'Kerina? Are you out there?' Constance calls from the back door.

'I'm coming,' I say, clipping the necklace back on.

The back door slams and Constance meets me halfway along the path. For a very pregnant woman, she moves fast.

'I hope you haven't been overdoing it,' she says. Her tone is playful, not scolding.

'No,' I lie, remembering the deal Saxon and I made not to tell

Constance. 'I was just doing some breathing exercises like Janoah taught me.'

She looks pleased. 'Are they helping?'

'A little.'

The breathing techniques are helping, that part is not a lie.

'Constance, what if I never remember? I can't stay here forever.'

'Why not? We have room.'

I smile at my new friend. There's no doubt she means it.

'You won't have room for much longer.'

Constance's expanding belly fills the space between them.

'Saxon tells me your child will be here soon.'

Constance caresses her stomach. 'That's true, but a baby takes up hardly any room. We have plenty for you. Besides, I think Saxon enjoys having you around.'

'Manny doesn't like me being here.'

'Manny worries too much.'

'I am a threat to his family. It's his job to worry.'

Constance rests her hands on her growing bump. 'Our family takes care of each other, so you can stay as long as you like.'

I nod, grateful for her offer. But I am under no illusion that my time here must come to an end. I have put these people in danger for too long. Besides, I need to find answers to my questions.

Chapter 19

Saxon

The market is quiet today. There are not as many people bustling around. The grey clouds overhead could be the reason. The days are getting longer and that means the rainy season will soon be upon us.

I think about Kerina and her self-defence moves. She was sluggish to begin, but once her body remembered what to do, there was no stopping her. Not only did she make no mistakes, she packed some power behind her punches that would put Elgee to shame.

I stop at my friend's stall. 'Elgee, where is everyone?'

He shakes his head and lowers his voice. 'Ain't yer heard? The Agents been takin' people away for questions.'

My thoughts go immediately to Rudolph. 'For what?'

'No one really knows, 'cause they don't give no reason. The Agents just been marchin' people in for questioning.'

'Come on, Elgee, you know everything. Say what you know.'

Satisfied there are no Agents nearby, he leans closer to me.

'I heard the Agents is lookin' for someone. That the person has somethin' they want and that somebody round here is hidin' them. Don't know more n' that.'

The air is sucked from my lungs and I stagger, lightheaded from Elgee's intel.

'How could they possibly know about Kerina? It's gotta be a coincidence.'

'Pretty big coincidence, don't yer think?'

I pinch the bridge of my nose as I put all the information

together. How could the Agents know about Kerina? She has no memory, so she's hardly a threat. They can't possibly know about her mark. No, it can't be her that they seek.

'Did you tell your girlfriend the other night? About Kerina?'

'Anastasia? I did, but she wouldn't say anything.'

'Saxon! She's the Dictor's daughter! What were you thinking telling her?'

'She's not like the rest of them.' I remember our conversation, her vehemence to trust her. Was it an act? 'No, I trust her. She won't have said anything.'

'You better be sure that pretty face can keep her mouth shut.'

I will have to deal with Anastasia later and find out for sure. But for now, I have to find my white-haired friend.

'Have you seen Rudolph lately?'

Elgee rubs his chin. 'Come to think of it, I ain't. He's usually round here.'

'If you see him, can you tell him I'm looking for him? Better still, tell him we got fresh veggie soup and Manny invited him over.'

'Will do. You take care, mah friend,' Elgee says with a fist bump.

I wander off to look for the eccentric old man. Most people passing by Rudolph pay no attention to him. They think he's just a poor street man, but they don't know a thing about him. He was once a respected scientist who worked on the evolution of the nutrient packs. He also worked on the development of oxygenation treatments to help the body breathe better and less often to help cope with the poor air quality. Rudolph was a wealthy man who lived a privileged life. For some reason, he gave up that life many years ago. But he never gave up on me and Manny. He always checked in to see if we were okay. He even made sure we had extra nutrient packs to help us through the cooler months. We never knew when he would show up, but somehow it always seemed to be when we needed him.

I cross the road and spot the Agent from last week. He is walking amongst the crowd as though he's part of it and just like the rest of us. Pity his uniform makes it obvious he is definitely not one of us. I pretend to scratch my cheek, hoping it will hide my face. Something about that Agent has my gut instinct prickling.

'Arrgghh.'

A woman screams from near the undercover section. The crowd moves fearfully away from the high-pitched noise. There is a man collapsed beside her.

'Help! Somebody, help me!' she yells.

The Agent runs toward her. He pulls up short as he approaches and holds his hands out wide without threat. He leans toward the woman, but I can't hear what he says. I jostle closer for a better view. That's when the collapsed man jumps up and grabs the Agent's gun.

'Don't come near me. I will shoot.'

'Give me the gun,' says the Agent.

The man shakes his head, an emphatic no. He must have a death wish. Nobody challenges the Agents. They are the law enforcers. You don't question them, you don't provoke them, and you sure as hell don't grab their weapons and threaten them.

I try to move closer, but somebody grabs my jacket and pulls me back.

'Stay here,' Rudolph hisses.

'Where have you been, old man?'

'Around.'

A gunshot rings out. Screams fill the space and everybody scurries away. The man is splayed out on the ground. Blood stains the area around him. The woman is restrained by a different Agent, his gun poised at her head. She is forced to her knees, the anguish clear on her face. The Agent forces her hands behind her back and shoves her on the ground. Her fate was sealed the minute she went along with the hoax calls for help.

The first Agent on the scene is hunched over the dead man. His head hangs, seemingly remorseful for his actions.

'That is no ordinary reaction for an Agent,' I whisper.

The Agent must realise his mistake as he stands tall, pushing his shoulders back. He searches the crowd when his eyes stop on me. There is a glint of something, recognition perhaps, before he turns away.

'Move it, boy.' Rudolph tugs at me and we flee before the Agent has a chance to look back again.

Chapter 20

Kerina

I creep along the hallway toward the kitchen. I slurp the water from my cradled palms, then splash the cool water on my sweaty face. The relief is pleasant but short-lived. My hands tremble from the dream, so vivid it had to be real. I close my eyes and allow it to replay in my mind, hoping to pick up a clue I might have missed.

'Come on, Kerina. Don't be scared.'

Lariel runs to the water's edge. A rope is attached to the tree and she reaches out for it.

'I'm not meant to play down here,' I say.

'You're not meant to play anywhere,' says Lariel. 'Enjoy yourself for a change. I dare you!'

We are both younger, but I know it is Lariel from the other dream. My hair is much shorter than I wear it now, but my face is mostly the same.

Lariel grabs the thick rope hanging from the tree and runs toward the edge. She squeals before letting go. She splashes into the deep water below and I hold my breath, waiting for her to resurface. Just as I can barely hold it any longer, she bursts through the surface, squealing and splashing about. I grip hold of the rope.

'Come on, Kerina, jump!'

I hesitate before following my friend. It looks like so much fun and I don't want to miss out. I run, swing, and release my grip. The freedom of flying through the air feels wonderful.

The dripping tap breaks my trance. For the first time since my memories began returning, I feel happy. This memory was a pleasant one. It tells me I have had good times as well as bad.

I think about the details of the dream. The watering hole was surrounded by scribbly gum trees. The smooth pale trunks were covered in patterns, making it look like a child's scribble drawing. It is a strong tree because only the heartiest trees survived. They regrew from charcoal trunks and seeds regenerated after the Burn. The location doesn't look familiar though, and the flora doesn't help either. The eucalypts in the background are common plants, scattered throughout the wasteland. This memory from my childhood could be from anywhere outside a community that has been rebuilt from fallen cities.

A soft moan comes from the front room, stealing me away from my thoughts. My body tenses. There is a grunting noise followed by a deep, gruff sound. I tiptoe toward the main bedroom and find the doorway half open. Another moan comes from the room. It's female and louder.

'Manny,' Constance says softly.

A dull thump sounds against the wall. Thud, thud, thud.

I see Manny's back, naked. He shifts and there are arms circling his neck. Manny rocks backward and forward. I realise Constance is beneath him, their bodies entwined.

'Kerina?'

I turn toward the voice down the hallway. Saxon stands in the doorway to his bedroom.

I hurry toward him. 'I heard noises. I thought Constance was hurt.'

Saxon's eyebrows rise, then fall. 'She's not hurt.'

I shuffle uncomfortably. 'I wasn't … spying. I was getting a drink.'

'You do know what they're doing, don't you?'

'Of course, I know!'

'It's okay if you don't. Surprising, but okay.' He watches me intently.

'You're sure Manny's not hurting her?'

His face softens. 'I promise you he's not.'

I turn back toward the bedroom, but the noises have stopped.

'You need to get some sleep, Kerina. These questions you have can be answered in the morn.'

My face flushes, embarrassed, but unsure why. 'Goodeve, Saxon.'

I return to my room and try to put the noises I heard out of my mind. I know about sex. That is, I know how a baby is made. But Constance already has a baby growing inside of her, so I am confused by her and Manny's actions. I open the window and warm air flows inside. I stare out across the backyard. Shadows in the moonlight fall across the space.

Lariel's face fills my mind. Memories of us playing together when we were younger mix with the images from my dreams. We must have been friends for a long time, and I just left her on the side of the road. I let those men take her and made no attempt to stop them.

I press my palm against the glass window. 'I'm sorry,' I whisper to the night sky.

I climb into bed and try to clear my mind like Janoah taught me. Deep breaths and wriggling toes, relaxing my body as I go. If only I could remember why I was out in the wasteland in the first place. Who were the men that took Lariel and why did they want her? I dare not consider Lariel's fate, but the truth is that she is most likely dead. My heart aches at the thought, but I can't waste more time on the unknown. If I can learn why the men wanted us both then, hopefully, what I need to do next will become clear. For now, I have no idea. The thought is just as frightening as having no memory.

Chapter 21

I lie on top of the bedsheets, unable to return to sleep. Since we found Kerina, I have been sleeping in the spare room. It is smaller than mine and will become the baby's room once it arrives. I try to give Constance and Manny privacy, but living in a small house can be difficult at times.

The thought of my brother becoming a father makes me wary. Not because I think Manny will be a bad father. I know firsthand how fiercely protective he can be. The wariness comes from the fact our parents won't see their grandchild. Their absence is often felt, but when the baby arrives it will be amplified. Especially because Constance has no contact with her own parents. They disapproved of Manny and didn't hold back in sharing such views. They judged him before they knew him. They tried desperately to break up Manny and Constance, believing Manny only wanted someone to help take care of his brother. They gave Constance an ultimatum and she chose Manny. She's not spoken to them in years.

My mind spins from the events of the past couple of days. I'm almost certain Kerina didn't know what was going on in the main bedroom. Kerina's innocence just now compared with her ferocity when boxing confuses me. The shooting at the market, the reappearance of Rudolph, Kerina and her memory lapses. The three are unrelated, and yet I can't help wonder if they are linked. Especially after what Elgee told me. Agents looking for people with information can be a dangerous situation. Those with information rarely speak, while those without information—lagers—often sprout their make-believe tales. Some folk are desperate and will say any-thing for the promise of extra tokens. I have been on the receiving end of such tales before. I've been hauled into chambers and questioned without any evidence based on lies spoken about me.

It is a mild night with warm air coming through the window. Sweat lathers on my brow, so I decide to sit outside for some reprieve. Walking along the hallway, I listen to the sounds of the house, confident everyone else is asleep. Gently, I open the back door and slip out. I take in the night sky with the stars scattered above. I replay the conversation with Rudolph from yesterday.

'You need to be careful, Saxon. The Agents are looking for people. Ramblers that arrive, changes to people's routine, anything they think is more suspicious than normal. They will take people in for questioning. They will not hesitate to get answers in any way possible.'

'How do you know all this?'

'Never mind that. I still have some reliable sources in high places.'

'But why are you telling me?'

Rudolph tilts his head to one side. 'Come on, boy. You think I'm not aware of the visitor staying in your house?'

I narrow my eyes, surprised at what the old man knows. 'She's no threat.'

'Are you sure?' Rudolph places his hand on my shoulder and grips it tight. 'If you know anything about this girl that might put you or your family in danger, you need to come up with a plan.'

'What do you know, Rudolph?'

'I know the Okodee people are real. And anyone who helps them is in danger.'

Does the old man know about the mark on Kerina? Impossible! All my questions are making me paranoid.

'How do you know all this, Rudolph?'

'Because I helped my sister, Shianne, by working for the government. Then they took her away and I haven't seen her since.'

'Why?' I say, knowing the answer but hoping I'm wrong.

The old man's face crumples. 'She was Okodee.'

A rustle in the dark draws my attention. *Snap!*

'Is someone there?' I reach for my pocket blade before remembering I'm only wearing sleepwear. 'Hello?'

I squint into the darkness, searching the shadows for anything out of place. I miss them the first time, but as I look again I see a figure squatting near the bushes.

'I know you're there. I'm not armed. You'll not be harmed if you come out now.' I hold my arms high in surrender.

The figure stands up slowly, hesitates, then runs. I chase after them. The figure is shorter than me. With my long legs, it should be easy to catch them. But I have the disadvantage. I have little protection covering my skin and wear no shoes. The figure disappears along the path as quickly as they appeared. Damn, they were fast! I was no match for them and wonder if I could have caught them even with shoes.

I stop chasing and, with hands on my hips, try to catch my breath. I'm a fast runner, but they were much faster. Who was that? A prowler near our house at the same time I learn about Rudolph's sister, people being questioned by Agents, *and* discovering Kerina's birthmark. It can't all be a coincidence. I must find out more about Shianne, especially because I never knew she existed until yesterday. All the stories over the years and Rudolph never once mentioned he had a sister. An Okodee sister.

Chapter 22

Kerina

Constance leads me to the track behind their house. It winds along behind the other homes toward the river. It is easy to imagine the animals that must have frequented this place once. Ducks, birds, swans. Most of them are extinct now.

Sweet smelling acacia plants and xanthorrhoea grasstrees sit along the river's edge.

'Did you know the nectar from these flowers can be used to create a thick, alcoholic drink?' says Constance, breaking the silence. 'Many people have tried, most with limited success.' She laughs.

I stop to smell the plant. The scent is fresh and reminds me of twilight on a hot day.

'You are getting your strength back so fast,' says Constance.

'It must be Manny's soup.'

A bench seat forms from a fallen tree. It allows a perfect view of the river as it meanders past. Constance rubs her stomach and sits down.

'This baby is strong, so I think you are right. It must be Manny's soup.'

'Constance, you can't keep sharing your nutrient packs with me. You need them for yourself and the baby.'

'I'm growing at a normal rate, so there's no need to fret.'

'Do you think it will be a boy or a girl?'

'A boy. I am sure.'

'Why?'

'Janoah told me, but only after I begged her to. You mustn't tell

Manny though. He wants it to be a surprise.'

A comfortable silence falls between us. The more time I spend with Constance, the more relaxed around her I feel. She is kind but firm, tough but compassionate. All great traits to have.

Constance clears her throat. 'Saxon tells me you heard some … noises … last night.'

Heat rises up my neck. 'I thought you were hurt. That maybe the baby was coming along.'

Constance giggles. 'Well, last night is how the baby got here in the first place.' She tugs me to sit on the seat.

'I know how babies are created,' I say. 'I know about sex.'

'Sex and creating babies are one thing. But making love is different. One day you will meet someone. They will make you smile for no reason. Their touch will warm your skin and cause your body to ache. You will develop feelings so strong, the only way to ease them is to be with them. You will connect with them not only emotionally and mentally, but physically as well. What you saw last night was our physical attraction. Manny is my mate and together we are whole.'

'Is that why you're having a baby together?'

'Of course! Plus, Manny has always wanted to be a father to his own child. He was only a young man when he took on the role for Saxon. He was much too young for such a responsibility.'

I hesitate before asking, 'What happened to their parents?'

'They were killed in an accident. Both of them died at the same time.'

'That's unimaginable.'

'Sometimes it is harder for Saxon. He was only a boy, and his memories have faded more than Manny's.'

'You love Manny?'

'Oh yes, very much. One day you will feel the same way about someone and perhaps want a family of your own.'

I doubt it, but stay quiet about such thoughts.

Constance taps the end of my nose. 'Don't look so worried, my friend. These feelings, this love between two people, it is a good thing. It's a wonderful thing. You'll see.'

She pushes herself to her feet. 'There is more to the attraction between two people, but I think that is best saved for another day.'

We wander back toward the house. I look into the backyards of the homes along the way. Most look the same. Whatever space there is has plants and vegetables growing within.

'Constance, I was hoping you could do something for me. All this hair weighs down my head. Would you cut it for me?'

'No!'

I stop, startled by her response.

'What I mean is, no, because it is too lovely and long to cut.' Constance smiles. 'But I will teach you some ways to fix it so it won't bother you.'

'But wouldn't it just be easier to cut it?' I say, confused by her suggestion.

'Well, we could, but how about a compromise? Let's cut some off but keep it below your shoulders.'

I nod, agreeing to her suggestion.

Suddenly the hairs on my arm stand up. I look around, alert.

'What's wrong?' says Constance.

'I'm not sure. I just got the feeling that ... nothing, it's silly.' I shiver.

'Kerina?'

'I think we should go back. I feel like we are not alone out here.'

We return to the house. The feeling of being watched doesn't leave me.

Chapter 23

Saxon

'We need to talk. Alone.' I shove past Manny to get to the shed. The sandbag still hangs from the last session with Kerina. I give it a thump on the way past.

'What's up with you, Saxon?'

'We've got a problem.' I pick up the shovel and lean against it. 'Did you know Rudolph had a sister?'

I continue when Manny doesn't respond. 'Shianne. She was younger than him and she got taken—'

'Taken? What do yer mean taken?'

'Just shut up and let me finish! She was taken for a reason, and Rudolph hasn't seen her since. Manny, she was Okodee.'

'That's rubbish. There ain't no such thing.'

'Why would Rudolph make up such a story?'

Manny shrugs. 'Most of his tales are made up, Saxon. He only told them to entertain us. Besides, the old man's been losing it for years.'

'Well, that isn't all. Last night there was somebody outside our house. Right there in the yard.' I point to where the figure had hidden in the dark. 'I chased them, but couldn't catch them. They were fast! But I'm telling you, somebody was watching our house last night.'

'You think we had a prowler?' Constance walks into the shed unannounced.

Manny sighs. 'Saxon's freakin' out 'cause he thinks there was someone in the backyard last night.'

'I don't think it, I know it.'

'That's strange. This morn, Kerina made us return to the house from down near the river. She had a sense we were being watched.'

'You see, Manny. Some tinker is sneaking around! Plus, Rudolph told me some other things.'

'You saw Rudolph?' Constance asks. 'What did he say?'

'Saxon says Rudolph had a sister. Problem is, we never knew he had a sister. He reckons his sister was born Okodee.'

Constance covers her belly protectively. 'Okodee people are a myth. They're stories made up to scare communities. What else did he say about this sister?'

'Said her name was Shianne,' I say.

'But you're sure neither of you have never heard him mention her before?' Constance persists.

'The old man's been losing his marbles for years, Constance,' says Manny. 'Sleeping rough rather than being in his own house. He's got money, but he might as well be dirt poor the way he lives.'

'Exactly!' I say. 'Perhaps there's a reason he lives that way, Manny. Ever think of that?'

'Oh gawd, here he goes with his conspiracy theories again.' Manny throws his arms up in the air. 'Not everyone's got a hidden agenda, Saxon.'

I withhold my knowledge of the mark on Kerina's neck. I can't bring myself to share it just yet. Not until I'm sure.

'But what if it's true, Manny?'

Manny laughs. 'Okodee? Humans with extra strength and powers? Like superheroes from old stories?'

'Not superheroes, but yeah, extra abilities normal people don't have.'

'Do yer hear yourself?'

'They could be real, it's possible.'

'How do you know, have yer ever met one?'

'Would *you* know if you met one?' I challenge Manny.

'Cut it out, you two,' says Constance. 'There's only one way to be sure.'

I cross my arms. 'How?'

She rubs her belly. 'You have to check the birth records.'

'But I'd have to break in to the town hall first.'

'That's true. Unless you knew someone who could get you access.' A sly smile creeps across her face.

Manny snorts. 'Who do we know that would have such access?'

Constance taps the side of her head. 'Think about it, Manny. It's not so hard to come up with somebody.'

Manny grins, rocking back on his feet. 'Of course! Anastasia.'

Constance smiles. 'And she'd do anything for our Saxon.'

'Yes, she would,' I say, grim.

'You want to find out if Rudolph had a sister? That's how you'll learn the truth.'

Guilt creeps in at having to use Anastasia, but I push it away. I can't let my fondness for her cloud my judgement. Besides, I need to check with her and make sure she has kept her knowledge of our rambler to herself.

Anastasia is the easiest way into the records office. As the Dictor of Nevertyre, her father's office is in the same building. Besides, Constance is right. Anastasia would help me, so long as I asked nicely.

Chapter 24

Kerina

I move along beside Constance at a slow pace. She wobbles from side to side as she walks. She was complaining of swollen ankles earlier, so I am sure it is difficult for her to walk, but it won't stop her. My head flits around the street, taking in the buildings and people. It is my first time leaving the house and going where other members of the community will be. The thought excites and horrifies me all at once.

Containers with warbles sit out the front of the buildings trying to grow plants in them. They help add colour to the drab, darkened buildings. Some are well maintained, but most are left to battle the elements alone. We haven't passed many people yet, but I can see more people ahead, closer to the market.

'Are you sure it is safe for me to be walking around?'

Being in such an open environment makes me nervous. But the people passing by take no notice of me. Too busy with their daily lives to care about a pregnant lady and a young lady who appears the same as any other.

'Just keep your head high as though you have nothing to hide. I won't be long at the doctors. It's just a check-up to ensure my nutrient intake is right.'

I stare at her growing waistline. Her pregnancy was not as obvious when I arrived. But now there is no confusion.

Noises grow louder and smells get stronger as we approach the town centre. Constance stays close to me, but I do not feel comforted by it. Instead, voices ring in my ears and heat warms my skin. My senses are on high alert, like hackles on a dog. This all seems strangely familiar. As though I have been somewhere like this before. I try not to panic. I don't want Constance to worry, especially after all she has done.

We arrive near a building with a green cross on the outside. 'Do you want to come in?' she asks.

I shake my head. The open space frightens me, but the cramped quarters scare me even more.

'I will be quick. Take in the view around you and inhale the smells. It might loosen some memories for you. Janoah said that might happen with new experiences.'

I force a smile and turn to watch the crowd. I don't want to admit I am afraid of my memories returning.

An older man with white hair walks on the other side of the street. His gait is slow and strange as he moves. His arms remain by his side when they should swing as he walks. He holds a grimace as he shuffles a bad leg along. I turn away when he catches me staring. When I look back, he is still watching me.

An eruption of laughter and jeering emanates from a group nearby. The sounds trigger a memory and I am swamped by a moment in time.

People are crowded around me as I am jostled about. Hands push me through the crowd, shoving me from one to another. Guards do their job and herd me along. They push the crowd back, but with little effort. They seem to enjoy the abuse directed at me. Chains surround my ankles, pinching the skin as I walk. A rock hits me in the head and skin is ripped from my scalp. I fall to the ground and blood trickles down my cheek.

My head spins as the present day rushes back to refocus me. I sway and the white-haired man steadies me. 'Easy there, girl.'

I shrink from his touch, but he doesn't release his grip. He is stronger than he looks.

'You don't want to draw attention,' he whispers. 'Deep breaths. Keep it together.'

I do as he says, concentrating on the man's well-kept shoes. They are so out of place compared with the rest of him.

'You shouldn't be in town. I warned Saxon about you,' he says.

'You know Saxon?'

'Yes. Have done for a long time.'

I look at the man. White hair sticks out at all angles. His beard covers most of his face, but his brown eyes stare at me. Something haunted and angry sits within the pupils, yet I'm not afraid of him.

Constance emerges from the clinic. 'Rudolph! What a nice surprise.'

'Constance, you need to get this one home.' He jerks his thumb at me. 'Keep her out of sight. I told Saxon this.'

'He never said anything to me.'

'Please trust me and do as I say. Go!'

Constance grips my elbow and follows the path away from the centre. We rush along the road as fast as we can move in Constance's condition. I realise she is still holding my elbow to steady me.

'You can let go. I feel fine now,' I say.

'What happened back there?'

'I had a memory return and I became faint. Rudolph caught me or I would have landed face down on the road.'

'You can rest when we get home.'

'I'm sorry I've put you in danger.'

'I'm sure it's nothing,' says Constance. 'Just an old man overreacting.'

I turn back to look at Rudolph, but he has vanished.

Chapter 25

Saxon

I ready myself before knocking on the clean, white door. My knuckles have barely lifted when Anastasia answers.

'Saxon? I was just going out.'

'I'll walk with you.'

She smiles and links her arm through mine. 'That would be wonderful.'

Anastasia is confident, blunt, and even bossy at times. But she is still kind and caring. She has not been corrupted by the class division that runs through the community. The divide is obvious from the homes we live in to the clothes we wear.

'Where are you headed?' I say.

'My mother asked me to drop some documents off to my father.'

I swallow down the excitement. The timing couldn't be better. I must be careful and not give my intentions away. Anastasia is also very smart and perceptive. Her confessions at the screen-show made me realise how alert she is. If Anastasia thought for a moment I was using her, she would not be so kind. What she lacks in temper she makes up for with an acerbic tongue. I should know. I've been on the receiving end of her remarks before.

'So tell me, Saxon. Why were you knocking on my door?'

I panic. I had not thought my story through, and Anastasia will sniff out my lies in no time.

'I just hoped you would … hang out with me.'

My reason is flimsy, but Anastasia doesn't question me further. I swallow the guilt of my lie. I know what I must do to find the truth, and the less she knows the better.

The walk is short, only four blocks. We walk in silence for a while. I try to get my thoughts and plan straight. Anastasia is no fool.

'So, dear Saxon, I had thought you might have come to get me so I could meet your rambler.'

'Quiet! Keep your voice down.' I remember the Agents asking questions around the market. I needn't worry; we are alone on the street.

'Have you told anybody about her?'

Anastasia stops abruptly. 'Of course not. I told you that you can trust me and you can.'

'I'm sorry, I do trust you. It's just there is a lot at stake if she were to be discovered.' More than I plan on sharing with Anastasia at this point. I take her hand as a peace offering. She accepts and we continue walking.

Soon we arrive in front of the official building. The town hall is big and imposing and surrounded by security Agents and cameras.

'Wait here, I won't be long,' says Anastasia.

'Can I come in?' This might be my only chance to get in the records office. 'I've never been inside, but I always wanted to have a look.'

'Why didn't you tell me sooner? I'll give you the grand tour!'

We walk up the stairs and security allows Anastasia through the checkpoint without question. Their stunners block my entry.

'It's fine. He's visiting my father with me,' says Anastasia.

Her voice holds a tone of authority, yet they hesitate.

She sighs. 'My father will *not* be happy if he is kept waiting.'

The threat of an unhappy Dictor is enough for them to lower their weapons and allow us both entry to the town hall.

I force a smile at the guards. 'Thank you, gentlemen.'

I follow Anastasia, awed by the height of the ceilings and grandeur of the foyer. Her shoes click-clack across the floor.

'I will deliver this first and then we can take our time looking around.'

'Your father won't mind?'

'Who said I was going to tell him?' She winks and pulls me along behind her.

The workers take no notice of us, confident security has done their job. I follow Anastasia up a shiny, curved staircase. The wood is a dark mahogany. A sign of power and wealth for it to still be in such good condition. At the top of the stairs, I hesitate to walk across the white-tiled floors. They are so clean and bright; my dust-covered shoes will stain them for sure. Closed doors surround the grand staircase while a hallway leads to the left.

'Wait here,' says Anastasia. She walks off, then hesitates. 'On second thoughts, perhaps I should hide you, just in case.' She drags me toward a door marked *Storeroom*.

'Nobody should be around today, but it's more exciting this way,' she says. 'If my father knew I'd brought you inside, he would make it his business to know everything about you. We don't want that, do we?'

I get the feeling she knows more about me than she lets on. Perhaps more about everything and the goings on of Nevertyre.

Inside the storeroom, I wait in the dark. The space is cramped with some shelving, mops, and other cleaning items. If somebody else were to open the door, there would be nowhere for me to hide. I press my ear against the door, but can hear nothing through the wood. My first time in the Dictor's chambers and I am locked in a cleaning cupboard. Suddenly the door is pulled open. I brace myself, ready for whoever is waiting.

Anastasia laughs. 'Who did you think it was going to be?'

I relax my stance. 'You can never be too careful.'

She offers me her hand. 'I'm all done, let's go!'

I allow her to drag me from the cupboard. I must think quickly and use the first opportunity to gain access to the records room. This might be my only chance to seek the truth. I cannot let it pass me by.

Chapter 26

Kerina

I follow Constance through the backyard as she storms toward the back door.

'Manny, where are you?' Constance yells, entering the kitchen.

He emerges from their bedroom. 'I'm right here. Is somethin' wrong with the baby?'

Constance waves him off. 'The baby's fine. It's your brother.'

'Saxon? What's he done now?'

'What else did he say Rudolph told him?'

Manny looks at the ground and tugs on his ear.

'Manny, my love,' she says through gritted teeth. 'Just tell me.'

'Rudolph said the Agents are lookin' for ramblers, and that we should be careful.'

'But you didn't think that was worth mentioning when I told you I was going into town.'

'You didn't take Kerina, did yer?'

'Of course, I did!'

'Aww, damn it.' He scratches his stubbled cheeks. 'I didn't know you were takin' her. I thought she was in her room.'

'Can someone—' I try to interrupt the conversation playing out as though I'm not standing right next to them.

'Manny! We don't keep secrets, remember?'

'It weren't no secret. I just thought Saxon was overreacting like he does.'

I try again. 'Would you mind—'

'Besides, you know how Rudolph is, tellin' stories to impress

Saxon. Always has since we were boys.'

'Manny, this isn't good. Something about Rudolph scared me today. Made me think he might be speaking the truth.'

'*Hey.*'

They both stop and look at me.

'Sorry,' I say without meaning it. 'But don't talk about me as though I'm not here. It would be nice to know what's going on.'

Constance pulls a chair out from the kitchen table and sinks down in to it. 'Yes, it would.'

I remember the warning Rudolph gave Constance. '*Keep her out of sight.*'

'I am a *rambler*, therefore you are all danger just by me being here. Is that right?'

Manny nods. 'We don't get many newcomers to the community. Most people stay where they're born these days.'

'It's too difficult to travel unless you can afford the solar-powered vehicles. So, if a new person turns up, townspeople are wary of them because trouble often follows,' says Constance.

'What happens if you're caught housing a rambler?'

'The Agents, the enforcers, make sure we're all followin' the rules and doin' the right thing. They're suspicious of everyone, 'specially ramblers. That means anyone aiding one becomes a target of suspicion too,' says Manny.

'Then I can't stay here any longer. I won't put you in such a position.'

'Kerina, I admit I didn't want yer to stay here at the start after we found yer. Saxon talked me into it and I said one night only.'

Constance squeezes his shoulder. 'Looked how that turned out.'

Manny sighs. 'The point is that nobody knows yer here.'

'Then how did Rudolph know?' I say.

'Saxon must have blabbed. He told Elgee, so it makes sense he told Rudolph as well. He was probably showin' off to the old man.'

'Both of them can be trusted though,' says Constance. 'So, there is no problem with you being here.'

I know she is trying to reassure me, but I can't be responsible if anything were to happen to them. I suspect I am responsible for too many things already.

'Maybe you should just report me and see what happens? They might agree for me to stay in Nevertyre.'

'It's not that simple,' says Constance. 'You would be locked up indefinitely until a decision is made.'

'I can handle that.'

'But what if they send you back out into the wasteland? Could you handle that?'

'Oh damn! What about the tinker Saxon said was creepin' around last night?' says Manny.

'There was somebody here?'

'Manny!' scolds Constance. 'Now you're sounding as paranoid as your brother.'

'What if it was them this morn when we were talking by the river?' I say. 'It felt weird, like we were being watched.'

'I'm sure it's nothing,' says Constance. 'As soon as Saxon gets home, we'll find out exactly what is going on.'

'We ain't gonna kick you out on the streets,' says Manny.

His gruff exterior softens and I am overwhelmed with gratitude to them both. But, regardless of what they say, I know it is no longer safe to stay here. This family has already done so much for me. I can't be the cause of any further trouble for them. I must leave. For some reason, the thought saddens me.

Chapter 27

Saxon

Anastasia shows me around the town hall. There are some impressive rooms, particularly the grand ballroom, meeting room, and the Dictor's private bathroom. She leads me up another flight of stairs toward the back of the building. This one is not as exorbitant as the first.

'Do you know what is up here?' says Anastasia.

I shake my head, but my mind races with the possibility.

'The records room,' she whispers. 'Nobody is allowed in there though.'

I swallow my disappointment. I can't let this opportunity pass. There has to be a way to get in there. It's my only chance of finding out what I need to know.

'Have you ever been in there?'

'Saxon, I know my way around every inch of this place.'

I lean close to her. 'It would be great if … you and I … could sneak in there.' I nuzzle her hair and inhale her perfume. Sweet, like the caramel tarts my father used to make.

'Anastasia,' I whisper.

She inches toward me, our lips almost touch. 'What would we do in there?'

I know the next thing I do will determine whether I go home with answers or unanswered questions. It is a dangerous balance, but I have looked out for myself from a young age. Today is no different.

I kiss her, tentatively at first, then again, with more pressure.

She responds, just like I knew she would. I place my hands on either side of her face, gently caressing her cheek.

She pulls back, breathless. 'Let's see if we can get in.'

She tries the handle, but the door is locked. She pushes against a panel. It pops open and a simple keypad waits for the correct code to be entered.

'That's all the security there is?' I say.

'Well, someone would have to get in the building first and that is virtually impossible with the electronic sensors all over it.'

'So how are we going to guess the code?'

Anastasia taps my nose. 'Luckily my father has little imagination and only one daughter.'

A.N.N.I.E. 'It's the nickname my father calls me, in private, never in the public realm.'

Click. The door opens and she grins at me.

'I'm impressed,' I say and mean it.

We enter and row upon row of filing cabinets fill the room.

'In another time they kept paper files. Can you imagine all that wasted paper? Now it is still stored in the cabinets, but everything is electronic. You pull out the electron file and load it onto the system for viewing. It's efficient and has much more storage capability.'

'How would you find someone?'

'It still uses an alphabetical order.' She walks down the back and stops. 'If I wanted to find out more about you, *Saxon Vespa*, I would find the V file.'

She opens the drawer and fossicks until she finds the correct electron card. 'Shall we?'

I follow her back to the screen, intrigued by what it might say about me. Anastasia inserts the card into the slot and we watch the information appear. She locates my name easily.

'How many times have you snuck in here?'

She shrugs. 'What can I tell you? I'm curious about the people around me.'

I can't help but admire Anastasia for her resourcefulness. She will make a good Dictor one day. She will be a formidable force for anyone who goes up against her. The thought makes me swallow my own guilt for using her.

Anastasia enlarges the information about me.

Name: Saxon Vespa
Parents: Shayne Vespa (deceased) #36577PED, Marlane
Vespa (deceased) #36578PED
Siblings: Manny Vespa

'That's strange,' says Anastasia.

I stiffen. 'What's wrong?'

She taps a few keys and leans closer to the screen, ignoring me. Different information pops up. Her fingers flick over the keyboard and the pointer on the screen moves quickly, click, click, clicking.

'How did your parents die?' asks Anastasia.

'Why?'

'Tell me now, Saxon.'

'It was an accident. A building collapsed on them and several others.'

The colour drains from Anastasia's face. 'That's what I thought. So, it should be ADO – Accidental Death Occurred. But see this code: PED?' She points at the sequence after the names. 'That code doesn't mean an accidental death. It means Public Enemy Directive.'

'I'm not following you.'

She taps a few more buttons and brings up the files of both my parents. They have been tagged PED just as they were on my file.

'Public Enemy Directive. What does that mean, Anastasia?'

Her eyes grow wide and she steps away from the screen. 'It must be a mistake. Somebody has typed in the wrong code.'

'Anastasia, tell me what it means.'

'It means their deaths were no accident. Saxon, your parents were murdered.'

Chapter 28

Kerina

We sit in silence, waiting for Saxon to return. I try to plan my next move, but it is difficult to know which way to go when I don't know which direction I came from. The one thing I know for sure is that this family has already done more than I can ever do to repay them. It is time for me to go and discover my past in order to live my future.

Suddenly the front door slams shut, making all of us jump.

'Saxon? Can yer come here?' says Manny.

Saxon's footsteps are heavy as he thumps down the hallway.

'Saxon!' says Manny.

He thunders past us and heads straight out the back door, leaving Manny ignored in the kitchen.

'Oh no, he's not avoiding this,' says Constance, getting up from the chair. 'Go after him, Manny.'

I follow behind hesitantly. Saxon is punching the sandbag, avoiding everyone around him. His face is contorted and he pounds the target. *Thud, thud.*

'Maybe we should give him a minute,' I say.

'Saxon is known to overreact,' says Manny. 'His charm prob'ly fell flat on Anastasia.'

I am unconvinced. That is rage on his face, pure and simple. Anastasia can't be responsible for that.

'Saxon, stop. We wanna talk to yer.'

Saxon charges, gripping Manny by the shirt and shoving him backward, half shuffling, half dragging him along. 'Did you know?'

'Know what?'

'*Saxon!*' Constance screams.

'Did you know about our parents? How they died?'

'The accident?'

Saxon shakes him about. 'It wasn't an accident, Manny. My whole life, everything I've known about their deaths has been a lie. So, the next words that come out of your mouth better be the truth.'

Manny falls limp in Saxon's grip. He squeezes his eyes shut, as if blocking out Saxon's words.

'Do you know what a PED is?' says Saxon.

'What's he talking about, Manny?' says Constance.

Manny shoves Saxon off him. He staggers out of his brother's reach. 'You weren't meant to find out.'

'Have you known all this time, Manny?' Saxon's voice breaks.

Manny doubles over and covers his head with his hands. Saxon roars and charges toward his brother. Manny is flattened to ground, but he doesn't stay down for long as the two brothers roll about. Saxon swings and connects with Manny's lip. Blood spurts from the cut. Manny rolls over to sit on top, trying to fend off more blows. Saxon lifts his knee upward and Manny grunts in pain as it connects with his groin. Saxon shoves him off, rolling on top again. He punches Manny, once, twice.

'*Stop it*! You're brothers!' I try to rip Saxon off.

Saxon stumbles about before slumping to his knees. 'You've been lying to me … all these years?'

'Lying about what?' Constance says. 'Manny?'

Manny shakes his head, defeated. 'Our parents. They weren't killed by accident. They were … murdered. PED. Public Enemy Directive.'

'No! That can't be,' says Constance.

I watch as this kind and caring family falls apart from this revelation. I can barely remember my parents, but can't imagine knowing they were murdered.

'Why didn't you tell me?' Saxon says. 'I had a right to know the truth.'

'Rudolph told me not to. Said I had to be both mum and dad to yer now they were dead. He drilled it into me. I had to step up and take charge. Not worry about somethin' that couldn't be changed.'

'You never looked into it? Demanded justice?' says Saxon.

'I couldn't go off on a vendetta hunt. Don't you think I wanted to? It killed me knowin' the truth and keepin' it from you. But Rudolph said it was better that way and he was right.'

Saxon shakes his head. 'That's where you're wrong, Manny. The truth is always better.'

'Not always,' I say.

The brothers turn in surprise, as though they had forgotten I was a witness to this family secret.

'I had a memory today. People were calling me a traitor and saying I was evil. They were calling me a murderer.'

Constance gasps. 'That can't be true.'

'What if I am? Am I better off not knowing the truth?'

I stare directly at Saxon. He is the first to turn away.

Chapter 29

Saxon

After a restless night, I set off to find my best friend. Elgee has many connections around the town and will be able to get the things I need. He is discreet and trustworthy. I didn't speak to Manny after our fight yesterday. I avoided him again this morning by leaving early. Constance came to speak with me during the night.

'I don't want to talk about this, Constance.'

'Manny was just trying to do his best with both your parents gone.'

'I know, and I'm grateful for everything he's done. But I can't understand how Manny can live with it.'

'Which part?'

'Knowing they were murdered. The thought is killing me.'

I know it wasn't her fault, but part of me is mad at her too. He lied to her as well, and she was trying to defend him.

I spot Elgee in the distance. He stands near the market stall he runs with his family, setting up for a day of trading. They sell herbs and plants kept in warbles. Customers select items fresh from the pot.

'Elgee, yer got time for a walk?'

'I always got time for mah friend.' He grips my shoulder.

'Saxon?' Elgee's mother screeches. 'Dat you?'

'Sure is, Mumma Bear.'

I should have known I wouldn't be able to pass through without her catching me. An older woman, short and wide, squeals as she comes around the front of the table. She draws me in for a long hug.

'Ain't been round to visit for too long,' she scolds, cupping my face with her hands.

'I'm sorry, but I've been busy.'

'Mmm hmm. Been turning that dirt like I taught yer?'

'Of course. Manny just cooked up a batch of his famous pumpkin soup with some of our crop.'

'Good boys. Just like I showed yers.' She ruffles my hair. She has to reach high these days, unlike when I was younger.

'Let him go, Ma! We gotta go and see about some things.'

'You come visit next time, Saxon, yer hear me? And don't wait so long between visits.'

I untangle myself from her grip. 'I promise I will. Just as soon as I get a chance.'

We leave the stall with the old woman watching us. Elgee must sense something is up with me. He stays quiet the whole time for a change. I lead him toward the river that borders the outskirts of the market area.

'I need your help, Elgee.'

'Anythin' yer need, I'll get it.' His dark dreadlocks bounce around as he speaks.

'A gun, bullets, high energy nutrient packs, thermal ponchos, sterile water strips.'

Elgee lets out a low whistle. 'Dat sure is some list.'

'Can you get it all?'

Elgee crosses his arms. 'Sound to me like yer plannin' a trip.'

'I am. Might be a long one.'

'Sound to me like yer might need some company.'

'No! Absolutely not, Elgee. This doesn't involve you.'

'Now listen here, ya tinker. I'm involved now and yer my friend, mah best friend. Ain't no way I'm gonna let you go off alone.'

I stare at my oldest friend. When we were boys, Elgee always stuck up for me when the other kids teased me. I was quick-tempered and never failed to swing a punch. Didn't matter if it was one or six kids I took on, Elgee always jumped in to help. He accumulated many cuts and bruises because of it. I won't lead him into danger by allowing him to come along. I can't take on that responsibility.

'Elgee, I can't ask you to do that.'

'You ain't askin'! I'm tellin' yer and there ain't no point arguing with me.'

Elgee is as loyal as he is honest. That means Elgee is coming with me, whether I like it or not.

'How long till you can get it all together?'

'Give me a few days. Week at da most.'

I nod. After what I learnt at the records centre, there is no way I'm just going to accept it like Manny did. I need to find out who put that directive out about my parents and why.

'Thanks, Elgee.' We fist bump, sealing the arrangement.

'Saxon? What we doin' exactly on this trip?'

I grit my teeth. 'We're going on a manhunt.'

Chapter 30

Kerina

'*Kerina, you're not allowed to play with just anybody. We have to keep you safe,*' the lady with the pretty smile says.

'*But why?*'

'*Because you're special. You are so precious that not everyone likes your kind.*'

'*What do you mean, Mumma?*'

My mother holds a mirror up to my neck. I see the reflection in the glass.

'*You see that sign? That is the birthmark of Okodee. Many people believe in its power, while others fear it. Either way, nobody can know about it until you're ready. You have a very important role to play in the future. Do you understand?*'

I nod, but only to please my mother. None of it makes much sense to me.

'*Now this is going to hurt, but I need you to be brave.*'

A man comes toward us. He holds a large knife that glows red. He pushes the knife against the birthmark on my neck.

I wake screaming and thrash about, trying to fight off the man in my dreams. Light fills the room and stuns me.

'Kerina,' says Saxon, shaking me.

I sit up, dazed by the brightness. Saxon comes into focus.

'Take it easy. You're safe,' he says.

'I had another dream.' My sweat-soaked nightshirt clings to me. Saxon releases his grip. 'I heard you scream.'

I clutch my chest as my heart pounds against it. My neck burns as though it's on fire. I wrap my hand around it. Heat radiates outward, but the touch is smooth against my skin.

'I need a mirror.' I leap out of bed and move toward the door.

My legs are strong beneath me. All stiffness has disappeared and the bruises are gone. My body is healed; the only thing still broken is my memory. But even that is returning in frightening bursts.

I wait in the bathroom for Saxon. He appears with a smaller hand mirror. Our reflections face each another in the bathroom mirror.

'Hold it behind my head so I can see.'

Saxon hesitates before doing as I ask. I pull my long, dark hair into a ponytail and move it off my neck. It reveals a patch of reddish-purple skin, blemished but smooth. There's no mistaking the birthmark from my dream.

'Okodee,' I say, caressing the mark.

Saxon watches, concerned, but not surprised.

'You knew?'

'I suspected,' he says. 'That first time I brought you soup.'

I remember the fear and shock on his face when I choked on the soup and he tried to assist me.

'But you never said anything.' I turn to face him. 'Why not?'

The bathroom is small, especially with both of us squeezed in.

'You needed to remember on your own. Besides, I've never met a person who was Okodee before. I thought they were just stories.'

I look at the strange mark, faint on the skin but dark enough it can't be missed.

'How did you remember?' says Saxon.

'I dreamt it.' I don't explain the smell of burnt flesh as the knife touched my skin. The burning sensation as it branded the mark. 'What is Okodee?'

'Okodee people are like old fairy tales, some versions are scarier than others. Townsfolk talk about them in whispers, but nobody admits to knowing one or being one. I wasn't sure what to think when I saw your mark.'

'What does the mark mean?'

Saxon reaches for my hair and adjusts it back into place. 'It means you're in danger.'

I am close enough to Saxon that I can see specks of hazel in his green eyes I hadn't noticed before. His dark hair hangs in such a way that I have the urge to push his locks away to see him clearer.

Crash, bang, thud!

'Stay here.' Saxon rushes toward the sounds from my room.

I follow and find him grappling with a person halfway through the window. A hood covers their face. He yanks the intruder backward and spins them around. They fight him off, but he hurls them onto the bed. They grunt and lash out, but Saxon has height on his side. The intruder battles to get up, but he straddles the offender and pins them down.

'Get off me,' a girl yells.

She is strong and fights like a trapped animal. Saxon flips her over. She swings wildly, but he is bigger and stronger. Her fist connects with his cheek. He roars and grips her wrists to fend off the punches.

'Let me go!' The hood falls back, revealing her face.

I look down at the friend from my dreams. 'Lariel?'

Chapter 31

Saxon

Manny crashes through the doorway. 'What in Nevertyre is goin' on in here?'

I ignore him. 'Kerina, do you know this person?'

She nods, eyes wide, her face full of anguish. 'I thought you were dead. I thought I'd let you die.'

'Are you sure she's no threat to you?' Saxon persists.

'She's no threat. Let her up,' I say.

I release the girl cautiously. Kerina has had fractured memories since she came here. Who knows where this girl fits into the story? I'm not trusting her just yet.

'Hello, Kerina.' Lariel appears neither friendly nor hostile.

'It's really you,' Kerina says. 'I had these broken memories of you. Snippets from a time I can't remember, but you're alive.'

Lariel stands up and they embrace. Both tremble from the unexpected encounter. I step back to give them some space as they fight to control their emotions.

Constance enters the room. She raises her brow in question and I shrug. We wait patiently while the reunion plays out. Eventually the girls release one another. Kerina grabs the intruder's hand and turns to us.

'This is my friend Lariel.'

'From your session with Janoah?' says Constance.

'Yes. I recognised her face from my memories.'

'Hold on a minute, what happened in the session?' I say. 'You say you remember her from one memory?'

'That's right. The last thing I remember is Lariel being taken by three thugs on horses. I heard them speak about a reward and wishing they had found me because I was worth more.'

'Your memory is right. They did kidnap me and take me with them. They were going to hand me over for a reward, but I escaped, again,' says Lariel.

Her face pales and nobody asks how.

'Were you here the other night?' I ask.

She nods. 'You chased me off.'

'Why didn't you just knock on the door?'

'I was afraid! I didn't know what kind of people you were or if Kerina was being treated right. I can see now she has been in good hands.'

'How did you even find Kerina here?' I say.

'Saxon! Enough with the questions,' says Constance. 'This girl has been through an ordeal, the same as Kerina.'

Lariel turns back to face her friend. 'I know why they kept us, Kerina. I know why they want us. We can't let them catch us again because this time they *will* kill us.'

'Who wants yer?' says Manny.

I already have an idea, but it's not for me to say. Both girls reach for their hair.

'You know?' says Lariel, hesitating.

'Yes, but I only just discovered what I am,' says Kerina.

'Discovered what?' says Manny.

The two turn around and lift their hair to reveal their necks. Both show the same birthmark: one straight line crossed by three smaller ones.

Constance gasps. 'You're both Okodee?'

'I told you the stories were true, Manny,' I say.

'Rudolph was right? I can't believe it. I always thought his stories were just made up tales.' Manny shakes his head.

I shove my brother. 'See? My conspiracy theories aren't always wrong.'

'Did you know about the mark, Constance?' says Kerina.

'I saw it when you first arrived. I've had heard the stories like most people, but I wasn't sure when I saw it. When you arrived, it was mottled purple and I figured I was mistaken or it was just a coincidence.' She steps forward for a closer look. 'Even now it looks different to when you first got here.'

'It's healing,' says Lariel. 'Soon it will be free of any blemish.'

'How did it get discoloured?' I ask.

'I think it was burnt off for concealment,' says Kerina. 'At least that's what happened in my dream.'

'Your father was always the one to do it,' says Lariel.

Kerina grimaces. 'He must be the man from my dream.'

'The burning hides it for a while, but it always comes back. Our ability to heal means it won't stay hidden for long.'

'You mean to tell us Kerina's father branded you both to hide the marks?' I say.

'It was for our own protection. If anyone discovered us, well, the men who hunted us are proof of what can happen,' says Lariel.

Lariel speaks the truth, but I can tell she is hiding something, holding back from us.

'Well, if we thought we were in danger before with one rambler, I guess we are in absolute peril with two,' Constance says with a laugh.

It breaks the tension in the room, but only for a moment. We all know this secret won't stay quiet for long.

Chapter 32

Kerina

I wake to see Lariel curled up tightly on the floor. Saxon gave up his mattress for her while he slept on the couch. Lariel looks peaceful, younger than when she is awake. Happy memories of her came trickling back through the night. Sharing stories, playing together, and doing school lessons with my father. He taught us history and reading, but he also taught us life skills. Things like starting fires and how to look for food in the wastelands. It was he who taught us self-defence.

Some bad memories resurfaced too. Both of us being marched through crowds and hit by guards. I know more answers will come soon and I am prepared to learn more, no matter how much the memory might hurt. I hope Lariel will help.

I rub the mark at the back of my neck. It explains why Constance wouldn't let me cut my hair. She mightn't have been sure, but she didn't want to take any chances either.

Lariel stirs and her eyes flick open.

'Good morn,' I say.

'It's nice waking up with you like this. It's much better than waking up on the dirt floor of a prison cell.'

'This family are good people, Lariel. They have been very kind to me.'

'Do you remember when we were younger, before we were taken? We would camp out for fun on the ground!' Lariel laughs, but I don't join in. 'What's wrong?'

'That's just it, I can't remember.'

Lariel sits up. 'What do you mean?'

'There are holes in my mind. Some memories have come back to me, but it's hard to know what's real. When Saxon and Manny first found me, I barely knew my own name.'

'But you knew me.'

'A little while later I dreamt of you. I remembered you were close to death. We had escaped and hadn't drunk water for so long. Finally, we found some, but when I came back, you were gone.'

Lariel's face softens. 'There was nothing you could have done to help me.'

'But I just let them take you. What kind of friend does that?'

'The best. The kind committed to our cause.'

Lariel's words do little to comfort me. The regret of not helping her is too strong.

She pushes the cover back and I see the matching purple marks surrounding her ankles. She climbs onto the bed beside me.

'After a couple of years of moving around, my parents found yours. It was only by accident we met. But we were raised as sisters from then onward. Neither of us had other siblings, so it was easy to pretend we were related.'

'I can remember some things about my parents. I see their faces in my dreams.'

'They were good people. Your parents let us stay with them. They said they would be able to keep us all safe. It worked for a long time, but then somebody betrayed our families.'

'Will you tell me what happened, please?' My voice wavers.

Lariel curls up into a ball and hugs her knees to her chest. 'We were found. They marched us through the town in chains. They forced us through the crowd.'

The memory from my walk into town with Constance returns.

There are people all crowded around me. I am jostled about as hands push me through the crowd. They shove me from one to another.

A new memory is added.

Two men and two women are tied to poles in the middle of the town centre. My father smiles at me, but my mother's eyes are blind-folded. A guard stands behind each one with a gun fixed behind their head.

'What happened to our parents?' I say, already sure of the answer.

'Are you certain you want to know?'

'Tell me.'

'They made everyone watch. They wanted witnesses to spread the word. Nobody can help the Okodee. If anyone does, they will be punished, just like our parents. You and I were also made to watch as an eye from each of our fathers was burnt. The stench of burning skin does not leave your nose for days.'

I try to process all that I've been told. 'But they weren't killed?'

Lariel squeezes her eyes closed. 'No, our fathers weren't. They got to live, to serve as a reminder, a warning.'

'And our mothers?'

Lariel holds my gaze. 'Each felt a bullet pass through the back of their heads.'

Bang! Bang! The bullet sounds in my memories. I don't see the action, but I feel the vibration of the gun through my bones.

'Why did they shoot our mothers? Couldn't they have just lost an eye as well?'

Lariel shakes her. 'Our mothers were killed to stop them from bearing any more babies. Any more *Okodee* children.'

Suddenly the room spins and I can't breathe. 'I need air.'

I run from the room, down the hallway, and burst into the backyard. I suck in as much air as I can before wrapping my arms around my centre. Saxon appears before me.

'Kerina, what happened?'

'It's true, Saxon. My dreams, the images. It's all true. I am a mur-derer. I just found out my mother was killed because of me.'

'That doesn't make you a murderer,' says Saxon.

'I might not have pulled the trigger, but it still makes me

responsible, so what's the difference?'

I walk away from him and Lariel and the truths I have just discovered. With me, I carry the heavy bundle of guilt.

Chapter 33

Saxon

'Hey Elgee! Haven't seen you here for a while,' says Manny, cutting up some fresh vegetables. 'How've yer been?'

'Been busy at da market. Mumma Bear's bossin' me round, like normal.'

Manny grins. 'Glad she was always on our side. She's one tough lady.'

'Sure is. Tough as wood outside, soft as warbles inside.'

'What have you got there?' Manny says, pointing to the bag.

'What's with all the questions?' I interrupt, throwing my arm around Elgee's neck and making a choke hold. 'Come out the back and I'll show you the crops.'

We leave Manny in the kitchen and walk toward the shed. Around the corner we nearly collide with Kerina and Lariel. They are both on alert, and Kerina looks between Elgee and Lariel.

'It's okay. Elgee can be trusted,' I say. 'This here is Lariel, a friend of Kerina's.'

Elgee laughs. 'Did yer just send out invites to all the ramblers?'

'What did you just call me?' Lariel says, guarded.

He holds his hands up. 'Relax, I didn't mean no offence. It's what we call people who ain't from around here.'

She walks right up to him, barely reaching his chin. 'I've had a lifetime of people who think they can call me names and label me. For the record, I don't appreciate it.'

'Noted.' He takes a step backward. 'With my apologies.'

I can tell Elgee is impressed with her confidence. I, on the other hand, am not as convinced of Lariel's intentions with her sudden reappearance.

'I was just showing Lariel some of those self-defence moves you taught me, Saxon.'

'That's probably a good idea.'

'Lariel don't need those defence moves. She can just stab 'em with her sharp tongue.'

She grins. 'You'd be first one stabbed because of your mouthy comments.'

'Now, that I would believe,' I say, laughing at Elgee's perplexed expression. 'Jokes aside, I thought you two would be reminiscing, not boxing.'

'Lariel already has some good moves, but we will need all the defence we can for when we leave. We need to be able to protect ourselves.'

'Hold up,' says Elgee. 'Saxon, you didn't say nothing about two extra folk comin' with us.'

'Coming where?' says Kerina.

'That's because they *aren't* coming with us,' I say.

Elgee rubs his chin. 'I'm confused.'

'We have to leave,' says Kerina. 'We can't keep putting Saxon and his family in danger.'

'Saxon ain't hanging around though,' says Elgee.

'Does Manny and Constance know about this?' Kerina crosses her arms.

I shake my head. 'I haven't told them yet. And neither will you.'

'You're up to something,' says Kerina. 'Where are you going?'

'It doesn't matter.'

Kerina points at me. 'Your parents! That's what this is about, isn't it?'

I don't deny it; instead, I turn the focus on her. 'Surely you understand more than most about uncovering the truth.'

Kerina flinches from my words. 'That's exactly why we have to leave. Our fathers are still alive.'

'What?' I step toward her. 'You're sure?'

Kerina nods. 'Lariel knows where we need to go.'

'Do you trust her?'

Lariel scowls. 'I'm standing right here. I can hear you.'

'Of course, I trust her,' says Kerina, dismissing my question.

Kerina has no reservations about her friend, but I certainly do. She arrives in the middle of the night, scares the household by breaking in, then claims she escaped from her captives and somehow managed to track Kerina down to our house. Something's not right with her story. I can't let Kerina go with her until I'm satisfied she is no threat to Kerina or to my family.

I turn to Lariel. 'So where do you plan on going?'

She challenges my question by remaining silent.

'You can tell him,' says Kerina.

Lariel sighs. 'Fine. We will leave for Middtown as soon as possible.'

Of all the places for them to be headed, it has to be the same place as me and Elgee.

I look grim. 'That's where my parents were murdered.'

'It seems like we will be travellin' together after all,' says Elgee.

This will be interesting. At least it will give me a chance to scope out Lariel and see if she really is who she claims to be.

'We'll help you find your father, Kerina,' I say.

Kerina asked me for help the first time I found her, and I always keep my promises.

'We don't need your help,' says Lariel.

'I wasn't offering it to you,' I say.

'You don't have to do that. I'm not asking you to help,' says Kerina. 'You and your family have already done so much.'

'A wise friend once said to me, you might not be asking, but I'm giving it. Agreed?'

I reach out toward her, a solemn promise to help her as much as I can. She hesitates before gripping my hand.

'Agreed.'

Chapter 34

Kerina

I pull the hood tight around my face. The air is cool tonight. Lariel promised to cover for me to avoid any suspicions being raised. I hate the thought of lying to my new friends, but I can't endanger them any more than I have to. I must do this alone. I need to get some answers. I might have agreed to travel with Saxon, but there are things I want to know and it seems I have a reliable source I can ask.

The sun drops below the horizon and the streets clear out. It will be pitch black in minutes with no streetlights. Once the stars shine through, there will be some faint light. I pick up my pace and walk quickly through the streets. I ignore anyone that passes, certain they will be able to tell I am a stranger to these parts. Light glows from within the windows. The solar power sustains the population, but people have learnt to use it sparingly. The panels soak up as much of the sun's energy as possible to draw power from. The wide silver panels cover many rooftops, the only area that is well maintained throughout the community.

I pass a window and see a family seated around a table. I stop to watch them. They talk and laugh, safe in their little world. The father passes a bowl of something to the small boy next to him. They are oblivious to my prying eyes. I wonder if I will ever feel that: safe. It seems a far-fetched fantasy at the moment.

I turn away from the family, remembering my mission, and make my way toward the river. Constance mentioned that's where Rudolph can sometimes be found at night, tucked away by his campfire. This might be my only chance before we leave.

'*Keep her out of sight.*' Rudolph gave Constance that advice, so what else does he know? If his sister was Okodee, he should know plenty. I have questions for him and I'm not leaving without answers.

The rush of the water flow gets louder. I must be getting closer. I veer off the main road and take the path toward the river. There is a glow through the bushes up ahead. That must be the campfire Constance spoke of. A smoky aroma curls at my nostrils.

Hushed voices whisper through the night air from near the campsite. I slow down, treading lightly, not wanting to alert them to my presence.

'You weren't supposed to warn them,' a male voice says.

'Would you have those other fools find them?' a deeper voice asks.

'No, of course not.'

'Then stop your whining. What's done is done.'

'But it's going to make it that much harder now.'

'Why? Saxon's no fool. He'd have come to the conclusion sooner or later.'

'Yes, but now they'll be more careful and cover their tracks.'

My eyes adjust to the dark. Rudolph's face is illuminated from the light. The other man has his back to me, but I can make out the uniform of an Agent.

'How do you think I've survived as long as I have?' says Rudolph.

The Agent rocks his head from side to side as though stretching out the muscles in his neck. 'Because you're lucky?'

'Because I'm careful,' Rudolph says. 'I cover my tracks. Nothing I do is unplanned.'

'If you're so planned, then why haven't I seen the girl yet? You tell me I can't go to their house. You tell me I have to be patient and yet you've seen her.'

Rudolph spits into the fire. 'That was a chance encounter.'

'Ahh, so not everything is as well-planned as you claim, is it old man?'

'Two more days is all that is needed. Then you will have what you desire.'

I lose my balance and a branch snaps. Both men turn in my direction. I freeze. The Agent is not familiar to me and even Rudolph looks different. Not as fragile as the day I saw him walking along the street. Another noise rustles further over.

'Just an animal. They come out once the streets are deserted,' says Rudolph.

The two men return to their conversation, their voices more hushed this time.

I back away slowly, not wanting to tread on more branches. I hold my breath until I reach the road, then release it in a rush. I turn to run just as somebody grabs me. They smother the scream on my lips. I wriggle and twist and kick their shin.

'Stay calm and follow me,' Saxon hisses.

I turn wildly to face him. 'What are you doing here?'

'The same thing you are. Seeking answers. Now, let's go.'

We turn and hurry along the street, away from the two men plotting to get me.

'Was it you who made the other noise at the river?'

'Yes. Good thing too, or they'd have found you.'

'Two days, Saxon. Two days before Rudolph hands me in.'

Saxon shakes his head. 'I can't believe he'd do such a thing.'

'You were there! You heard him tell the Agent.'

'No. It must be something else. Rudolph would never ...' Saxon falters with his words. 'He's no lager.'

'We've got to leave immediately,' I say. 'Your *friend* is now the traitor.'

Chapter 35

Saxon

After breakfast, I plonk the bag of supplies from Elgee on the kitchen table. I unpack it as Manny watches on. The air is thick with tension, but I refuse to break it. Part of me is still mad at him for keeping the truth about our parents from me. The other part is mad at myself for accepting their deaths were an accident and not looking into it sooner. I should have known better.

'Saxon, just stop for a moment, please.' Manny's words cut through the cloud of animosity.

I pause, but don't look up. His shoulders hunch forward as he grips the bag.

'I'm sorry, all right? I'm sorry I never investigated their deaths earlier.'

Manny's face is pale, his eyes sunken. Remorse and guilt are etched in his eyes.

'It's okay, Manny, I get it. You had to look after me.'

'It ate me up inside knowin' they were murdered. Murdered for a reason I knew nothin' about. I used to lie awake night after night tryin' to work out why and I don't want that for you, damn it.' He thumps his fist on the table.

'My mind's made up,' I say quietly.

'But you don't have to do this,' Manny yells.

'I do have to do this, Manny.' I place the gun on the table. 'But I don't want you to worry. You're going to be a real daddy soon. Not just a fill-in one for your brother. A real father.' I falter. 'And you're going to be so good at it.'

Manny fills the space between us. He draws me in with a fierce hug, then wraps his hands on either side of my face.

'You come back safe. This baby is goin' to need an uncle because *you're* goin' to be so good at it.' He releases me and leaves the room just as the two girls enter.

'How are the supplies?' Lariel says.

I shake off the emotions from Manny's words and focus on the task ahead. 'The supplies will be better if Elgee can come through with more nutrient packs.'

'If we're careful, it should only be a four-day walk from here.'

'*Only* four days. You make it sound easy,' says Kerina, teasing.

'It will be easier this time, Kerina. We're prepared for the trek. Last time we were running for our lives,' says Lariel.

'And this time?'

'This time, we're running toward our lives. Toward our destiny, and hopefully to our fathers, or did you forget?'

'Of course, I haven't forgotten.'

Lariel rubs her face. 'I'm sorry. I shouldn't have said that.'

'Do you really think they'll be there?' asks Kerina.

'If they are alive, Middtown is where we'll find them.'

A knock sounds at the front door. My body goes rigid, waiting. Manny calls out, 'It's just Elgee.'

'We're okay,' I say with a deep breath. 'Hopefully Elgee has the rest of our supplies.'

He enters the kitchen carrying a bag. 'I am da man!' He tips the contents on the table. Nutrient packs, blocks of shiny metal, and thermal blankets tumble out.

'What are the blocks for?' Lariel says.

'Magnesium blocks. They'll start a fire, no problem.' I pick one up and throw it to her.

She smells it and throws it in the air a couple of times, testing the weight. 'If you say so.'

'Don't worry. If yah get cold, I can always help keep yer warm.'

She throws the block at Elgee's head. His quick reflexes catch it and he drops it back in with the other supplies.

I whack him on the back of the head. 'Elgee, don't harass our travelling party before we've even left.'

He laughs. 'It's all good, mah friend, ain't it, Lariel?'

She pulls a knife from her back pocket and twirls it around. 'Yep. It's all good, *mah friend.*'

'Enough stuffing around,' I say, throwing them each a backpack. 'Let's split these supplies up. We need a good night's sleep because we won't get much tomorrow. As soon as it's dark tomorrow eve, we're leaving.'

I distribute the supplies between the group. 'You sure about this?' I stop in front of Kerina.

Her pale blue eyes stare back, defiant. 'Absolutely. You?'

'I've never been surer about anything.'

I shove some nutrient packs into her bag. Each bag holds one litre of nutrients. I continue to distribute the supplies between the four of us, conscious of the time. I need to get organised before we leave. There are other plans to be made tonight. Plans that don't involve my travelling companions.

Chapter 36

Kerina

I knock gently on the bedroom door.

'Come in,' says Constance.

I enter cautiously, recalling the noises I overheard one night. My cheeks warm even now at the embarrassment of Saxon knowing what I heard, then the talk Constance gave me.

'One day you will meet someone. A young man. He will make you smile. His touch will make your skin warm and your body ache.'

Sometimes when Saxon looks at me, my palms sweat and I find it difficult to remember the words I want to speak around him. I don't fear him, so why does my body react this way? Lately, my skin has tingled afterward in the place he touched. Is that what Constance means? I push such nonsense thoughts away.

'Good eve, Kerina,' says Constance, her stomach sitting high beneath the covers.

I hesitate in the doorway. 'I wanted to speak with you alone, before we leave tomorrow eve,' I begin.

Constance taps the space beside her. I settle on the bed, trying not to disturb her position too much.

'I wanted to thank you and Manny, but particularly you—'

'There's no need,' interrupts Constance.

'Please, let me finish. It's important I say this.'

Constance nods.

'You've been so kind to me, Constance. Taking me in, feeding me, helping me to try to retrieve my memories. I remember my own mother now, and you remind me of her in some ways. Not physically, but she was strong yet patient, kind but insistent. All the things you are. You're going to be a wonderful mother, Constance.'

'Aww, now you've made me weepy. My stupid hormones are going wild and make me cry at everything these days.' She holds out her arms.

I lean across and embrace the woman who has taken such a risk to care for me, even when the stakes were so high for her and her family.

'Kerina, you are worth the effort. You have to believe me when I say that.'

I shrug.

'You still don't know what's so special about you, do you?'

'I am Okodee?'

'Yes, that's true. But that's not what makes you so special.'

'Then what?'

'You are strong. You are determined. You are special because instead of shying away from what's in front of you, you face it head on. That is truly a wonderful and brave trait to have. It will hold you in good stead, now and forever. Don't ever lose it. Don't ever let anyone take it from you. And make sure to trust your instincts.'

'My father used to say that to me. To trust my instincts.'

'Then he is a smart man.'

'Do you really think we will find him?'

'I think a young lady who can survive the wastelands on her own can do anything.'

I grip her hand tight. 'Constance, if I never … If we don't …'

'Hush now. We will meet again, I'm sure of it.'

The door swings open and Manny enters. 'Sorry, didn't know yer had company.'

I stand up. 'I better make sure we are ready for tomorrow night.' I walk toward Manny. 'Thank you for all you've done, Manny. Words aren't enough, but they are all I have.' I point to Constance. 'Take good care of her.'

'I'll take good care of Constance, so long as you promise to take care of Saxon. Don't let him do anything stupid. Deal?' He holds out his hand.

I grin. 'Deal.' Although, my end of the deal might be harder to keep than his.

Outside, I make my way toward the bench seat overlooking the river. I need a moment alone to collect my thoughts. Is Constance, right? Am I really so strong?

'Are you ready to leave?' Lariel is silent in her approach.

'Yes, and no.'

'You can't stay here, if that's what you're thinking. You put them in danger by being here.'

'Don't you think I know that already?'

Lariel sits down beside me. 'We'll find our fathers, then search for another place I have heard about.'

'What is it?'

'It's a place where there will be others of our kind.'

'Okodee people?'

'That's what I'm told.'

'But what if there are people waiting for us at Middtown? What if they capture us again?'

The screams from my dreams that wake me in a cold sweat are real, and I can't face that again.

'If you want to see your father again, you have to trust me, Ker-ina. We are headed toward our destiny.'

The thought sends a shiver of anticipation through my body.

Chapter 37

Saxon

I travel quickly through the darkened streets. Most people are settled in for the eve at this time of night. I know this meeting I'm about to go to could put our plans in jeopardy, but it is worth it. Anastasia should help me, but after the last time at the records office she might have some suspicions about me. After all, it's me who owes her a debt for uncovering the truth, not the other way around. She's taking a much bigger risk than me sneaking out like this. If her father finds out, he will be furious. Then, once he knows why she snuck out, he could easily have me arrested. But I will be long gone before that can happen.

I hurry toward the rendezvous point, an abandoned playground in the middle of the community. It's safe during the daylight hours, but at night it can be a popular meeting point for mischief makers. It's a place I've spent many wasted hours as a youth. It's the place where I was first arrested and taken to chambers. I remember the fury on Manny's face when he collected me. The walk home was silent all the way, as was the week that followed.

'Saxon,' Anastasia hisses from behind a shelter. She steps out and waves me over.

My breath puffs out as I rush across to her. The temperature has dropped unseasonably for this time of year.

'You made it,' I say.

'Of course! Would you expect anything less of me?' She reaches for my hand.

I should have realised she would expect this. I lean toward her, playing along. Just as I am about to kiss her, she pushes a piece of paper between us.

'You don't need to do that. I got what you wanted.'

Her comment is like a punch to the sandbag. Hard, fast, and connecting.

'That's not why I kissed you,' I lie.

'It's okay, Saxon. I know you don't have those kinds of feelings for me. I just wanted to see how far you would go to get what you wanted.'

I swallow the bitter bile of remorse. 'Then you should know that I do what needs to be done.'

'And you should know that *friends* help out those they care about.'

Her words assault me. She is offering me friendship in exchange for trust.

Shame burns my cheeks. 'I'm not used to … relying on people.'

'You are in short supply of friends, Saxon, so you should try harder with the ones you have.'

'Did you know I was using you the other day at the records office?'

'Not immediately. I always have hope that you will come to your senses and discover how wonderful I am,' she teases.

'But I do know that,' I say earnestly. 'It's just … I can't feel the same way you do.'

She shrugs. 'It is what it is.'

'Anastasia, you have to know that I care for you, but only as a friend.'

'Then you should have come to me, as a friend.'

'Would you have helped?'

'Of course.' Her chin rises.

'I'm sorry, Anastasia, truly I am.'

She pushes her hair behind her ear. 'There is something you can do that will allow me to forgive you.'

'Anything, it's yours.'

Her eyes narrow. 'Tell me what you plan to do with all this knowledge.'

I shake my head. 'I can't do that.'

'You can and you will.'

She unfolds a piece of paper and passes it to me. I scan the page and am confronted with an unexpected offering.

'What is this? I asked for information on Rudolph's sister, Shianne.'

'You wanted confirmation she is Okodee, yes?'

'Yes, but what do you know of such things?'

'I told you, I know more than you think. I know Shianne was Okodee.' She steps toward me and whispers, 'And I know that map you hold will help your rambler find more of her kind at a place called Shirnaka.'

I look closely at the drawing and see a detailed sketching of a place I've never heard of. Of a place I never knew existed, yet Anastasia knew.

I kiss her on the cheek. 'You really are amazing.'

She smiles. 'There is one more thing.'

'What? You've already done so much.'

Anastasia caresses my cheek. 'Promise me you will stay safe and return to Nevertyre.'

'How did you know I was leaving?'

'Promise me, Saxon. That's all I ask.'

'I promise.'

With what lay ahead, I hope this won't be the first promise I break.

Chapter 38

Kerina

'Where did you get this?' Lariel snatches the map from Saxon. 'This is the place I spoke of last night, Kerina.'

'It doesn't matter where it came from, the point is we have it,' says Saxon.

'Whoa.' Elgee shakes his head. 'Do not tell me yer got this from where I think yer got it from.'

'Fine, I won't tell you.'

'For real? Yer got it from Anastasia?'

'What does Anastasia know about the Okodee?' asks Manny.

Saxon retracts the map from Lariel. 'Like I said, it doesn't matter. I trust her and that's the end of it.' He shoves it into his bag.

'It matters to me who you trust,' says Lariel. 'Who is this *Anastasia*?'

'Lariel!' I say. 'If Saxon says she can be trusted, then it is so.'

Manny clears his throat. 'So, you're really doin' this?'

'Yep. I need to see for myself where the *accident* happened.'

I flinch at his words. Knowing the fate of my parents, I can only imagine how Saxon is feeling with what he has discovered.

'You better be careful,' says Constance. 'This little one will need an uncle to help keep them out of mischief.' She rubs her stomach.

'I'll keep out of trouble and be back to meet them before you know it, I promise.'

He leans in for a hug as best as Constance can manage with her growing bump. He steps aside, allowing me to say my goodbyes.

A quick hug is all that's needed. I said what I had to last night.

Words still don't seem enough for the family who saved my life, but they will have to do. Especially when it's likely I'll never see them again. The thought makes me sad as I realise a truth. I envy this simple life and tightknit family. Could it be a life I might live one day?

Manny grabs Saxon by the shoulder and grips it before hugging him tight. 'Don't do nothin' stupid, yer hear?'

I nod at Manny as he embraces his brother, confirming our agreement from last night. I will try my best to ensure Saxon doesn't do anything stupid.

It's still dark as all four of us slip on a backpack and set off into the early morn. We need to put some distance between ourselves and the town before anyone notices Saxon and Elgee's absence.

'Mah brother's gonna cover for me. Tell people I'm sick. Ain't too hard to believe. People been gettin' sick a lot lately.'

I remember back to a time when I was a little girl.

'I don't want to drink it,' I say.

'You have to. We need to get your temperature down.'

My mother forces the spoon into my mouth. The foul-tasting liquid burns my throat. I want to spit it out, but that wouldn't stop my mother. She'd just get another batch and make me drink that. A cold material is placed against my forehead. It soothes my skin for a moment.

'How is she?'

My father watches on from the side. I can tell he doesn't want to get too close.

'Hot. Way too hot and it's been too long.'

'She can fight this,' he says.

'Yes, she can. But we can't.'

'How long should we walk for?' I ask nobody in particular.

'We should keep going as long as we can. If we rest every three to four hours that will be a good start,' says Saxon.

'Good for a stroll maybe,' says Lariel. 'Not good if somebody's looking for you.'

'You got a better idea?'

'We just walk as long as we can, then rest as we need. We can take turns at watching out for trouble. There's no point resting often because one decent stop should reset our energy levels. Plus, we have the nutrient packs to help us.'

'Makes sense,' says Elgee.

'Fine.' Saxon scowls, taking the lead.

I move toward the front, beside Saxon, while Lariel and Elgee follow behind. The wind blows their conversation away, so I hope it will do the same to ours.

'Is there something wrong, Saxon?' I ask.

'Nope.'

'If you have a problem, you best get it out now.'

He glances sidelong at me. 'What do you remember of your friend Lariel?'

'I remember enough to know we should listen to her.'

'Well, I've got more questions about her than answers. My instinct says I shouldn't trust her.'

Saxon once spoke about listening to his instincts. At that time, the words sounded ominous, like a warning I should heed. Now, his instinct could be timely and forewarned.

Chapter 39

Saxon

As a young boy, I travelled with my parents to Middtown on occasion. It was such a thrill to watch the landscape blur by from inside the solar-powered vehicle. Few people ever get to travel in such a style. But that drive was only a couple of hours. There was never a need to sleep out in the open wastelands like we have to on this trip.

I've slept outdoors under the night sky at home before. Once, when my parents were away working, Rudolph came to stay and showed Manny and me how to make a campfire. He let us stay up late, poking sticks into the flames. The orange light danced amongst the dark and mesmerised me as shadows danced on my brother's face.

Manny and I shared a rolled-up mattress with bedding. Rudolph called it a swag. I fought the sleep that threatened to close my eyes for as long as I could. Just so I could savour the freedom of being outdoors. It felt like another world, another time, where anything might be possible. I'm not much of a daydreamer, but under the stars, I gave myself permission to dream.

Tonight reminds me of that, except this time my body is weary from the walk. Elgee and Lariel share one heat blanket, while I share the other one with Kerina. The blankets are lightweight and thin, but designed to keep body heat enclosed. Temperatures are known to plummet in the wasteland once the sun dips.

I curl up in the bedding, acutely aware of Kerina's closeness as she lay beside me.

'Saxon, can I see that map?' Lariel asks.

I sigh. 'Can't it wait until the morn, after we've rested?'

'It won't take long,' she insists.

I growl and retrieve the map for her. 'Put it back when you're finished.'

I settle beneath the blanket, trying not to disturb Kerina, but she rolls over to face me.

'That was quite a walk today, are you okay?' I ask.

'I'm fine, stop worrying about me. Manny's soup has made me strong again.'

I smile. 'Manny enjoys cooking, just like our father did.'

She hesitates, as though weighing up what to say.

'Tell me about your father. Were you close?'

I lean up on one elbow. 'My father was a serious man. He worked hard and relaxed little. But when he did spend time with us, he made sure to give us his full attention.'

'Who looks more like him? You or Manny?'

'Manny has his features, especially his hair. Mine is more like my mother's. We both have his height and build, but I have his stubborn ways, so Rudolph says.'

Kerina is quiet for a while. I wonder if she is thinking of her own father. I find myself wanting to share more about my father. That's not something I would normally do, not even with Manny.

'Once, on a rare day off, my father took Manny and me to the cemetery.'

'That seems a strange to place to spend the day.'

'He said it was important for us to know our history. We walked around half the day, just reading the faded inscriptions on the gravestones. I think that's when Manny first became interested in the dead. He used to think burning bodies was unfair. I think being a mortician is his way of offering some respect to the departed. Rich or poor, dead is dead.'

My thoughts drift to the day of the only funeral I've been to. Both our parents had already been cremated at Middtown. Their remains were brought back to Nevertyre and delivered to our home. We held a service in our backyard later that week. Friends of our parents attended; Mumma Bear included. I didn't speak a word to anyone, not even Elgee. But he got it and never pushed me.

As everyone gathered around, Manny and I buried the sealed jar beneath the tree. We chose it because it had been our mother's favourite place to relax. She would lean against that tree and play with us, read to us, and just be.

Manny grew into an adult that day and my childhood ended. All at the same time.

'Does it bother you? That they were cremated before you got to say goodbye?'

I shake the ball of my necklace. 'A little, but I get to carry a part of them with me every day.'

Kerina reaches up to hold her own necklace. 'Do you think we'll make it safely to Middtown?'

I can barely make out her features in the dark, yet her fear shines through.

'I'm sure of it. This journey will not be like your last one. We have each other to lean on.'

She settles down into her bedding, the heat blanket already working to keep us warm.

'Kerina,' I whisper. 'We can only worry about the things we can control, but I promise, I'll help you find your father and others like you.'

Her breathing catches and I know she heard me. It's a promise I plan to keep. No matter what.

Chapter 40

Kerina

The walk is dusty and boring and there is little to look at along the way. Rubble buildings are scattered about, long since abandoned. They leave a reminder of the once dense population that lived between Nevertyre and Middtown. All long dead from the Burn and its aftermath. Trees stand straight and tall in parts, adding a contrast to the texture of the land. Spinifex grass has grown wild across the vast landscape.

The only sound as we walk along is the scuff of our footsteps as we try to keep a steady pace. Conversation is limited and we keep the rations strict, sipping water sparingly should our travel calculations be wrong.

'How much more, yer think?' asks Elgee.

'Two more days,' says Lariel.

'Are you sure we're headed da right way?'

'Of course, I'm sure,' she snaps.

'We should have pinched a solar-powered vehicle. Could have saved some time,' I joke.

Elgee kicks the dirt. 'Duh, why didn't we think of that?'

Saxon laughs. 'You've got a couple of contacts who could loan us a solar car, do you?'

'Maybe.'

'As if. You've never even been inside one,' scoffs Saxon.

'I have,' I say. 'They hum along and the scenes outside whizz past. The whole thing made me dizzy. I had to close my eyes because I felt like I wanted to vomit.'

Saxon pokes me. 'Not so tough without your punching bags then?'

'Don't be fooled,' I warn.

'Stop! What's that up ahead?' says Elgee, pointing in the distance toward a group of trees.

Two figures amble along in the distance. It is hard to determine if they are Agents or civilians. The only thing for sure is that we can't risk them seeing us.

'Quick, hide,' I hiss.

I scramble behind a rock, hoping my small frame is concealed. Saxon flattens himself on the ground and Elgee does the same. The long, tan grass should camouflage them. Lariel is already out of sight.

Voices carry through the space.

'Those damn Agents gonna haul my arse back in those chambers if I don't leave town.'

'We'd had enough of that place anyway. Been six months since we tried somewhere new.'

The voices get closer, complaining about where they've come from. It is clear they are not Agents, but that doesn't stop them from being trouble for us. If they look around, they might see us hiding in the sporadic vegetation.

Suddenly Lariel steps out from her hiding spot. 'Where are you from?' she demands.

So much for staying out of sight.

'Sheez lady, you near made my heart stop.'

'Where on this forsaken place did you come from?' his companion asks.

I step out from my spot to join Lariel. 'I believe she asked a question first.'

'We came from Middtown.' He looks between the two of us, weighing up the threat we might be to them. 'It's a day's walk that way.'

'A day? Are you sure that's all?' asks Lariel.

'Sure, I'm sure,' says the shorter one. 'But you don't wanna be stopping there.'

'Why is that?' I ask.

'Agents everywhere! Heard they been lookin' for someone.' He scrunches up his face to inspect the girls. 'Them Agents are usin' lagers to get information.'

'Anything else we should know?' I ask, undeterred by the knowledge of Agents.

'Come to think of it, there is. If you see two strangers on the road, you should probably stay hidden.' He pulls out a gun. 'Hand your stuff over. Nutrient packs, whatever you got.'

Saxon jumps up from his hiding spot and aims a gun at the man. 'I don't think so.'

'Damn! How many of you are hidin' round here?'

'Plenty more,' says Saxon, bluffing. 'Now be on your way. Leave your weapons and go.'

The shorter one shoves the taller one. 'Why you gotta try and be a hero all the time? Now we got no weapon and they sure as hell won't help us.'

The taller guy throws his gun on the ground and spits after it. 'I weren't gonna use it.'

I pick it up. 'You better go before my friend here changes his mind.'

The two men scurry off, muttering as they go.

'You ever shot a gun before?' asks Saxon.

I point the gun toward Saxon. I squint an eye, adjust the gun to the left and shoot. The bullet hits the tree directly in the centre, three hundred metres away.

'Guess so,' I answer.

'Damn girl, yer crazy!' says Elgee. 'Yer could have taken his head off.'

'Kerina's been shooting weapons longer than you've been sweet talking girls,' says Lariel.

I look at my friend, surprised by the knowledge. I don't

remember shooting weapons, but my hands, just like the self-defence, seemed to know what to do.

Saxon tucks his weapon away, his face serious. 'You heard them, let's go. We'll be there in a day.'

Chapter 41

Saxon

'**L**ook! That must be the place,' says Kerina.

In the distance, abandoned cars line the way into the community as crumpled buildings come into view.

'Well, whaddya know, those tinkers spoke the truth,' says Elgee.

As we move closer, we see the cars form a barrier between Middtown and the outside world. A fortress to deter any newcomers away from their town. Hundreds of twisted, rusted and burnt-out vehicles.

'Welcome to Middtown,' says Lariel. 'The divide between class is much more obvious here than what you boys are used to.'

'Wonder what kind of reception we'll get,' I say.

Elgee raises a brow to me. 'Us being the lower class?'

'I didn't say that,' Lariel intones. 'I just meant the class divide is not as obvious in Nevertyre. Wait until we get closer and you'll see what I mean.'

We pass the first group of townsfolk, who barely look at us. Perhaps the law is not as strict here for new arrivals. A group of ramblers might be common to this place. Or else we fit in better than expected. All of us are covered in dust from a couple of nights sleeping rough with nowhere to bathe. The men we pass are unshaven with beards bushy and long. The women have their hair pulled back, but wisps have broken free, giving them a dishevelled appearance.

We enter the central township without anyone accosting us. The dilapidated buildings on the outskirts give way to solid structures the closer we walk toward the centre. Solar panels sit on the rooftops. They are much more advanced than those used around Nevertyre. Instead of large aluminium frames surrounding the cells, each has been included within the tiled rooftop.

'No prizes for guessing who lives where,' I say. 'Sure seems like a lot of folk living in those shanties on the outskirts.'

'Mah kind of people,' says Elgee.

Lariel leads us forward with a sense of urgency. Her steps are long and fast as she walks with purpose.

'Slow down, Lariel. We don't want to bring any more attention to ourselves than necessary,' says Kerina.

Lariel stops to face us. 'We can't loiter around here. That *will* bring attention. The townsfolk out there don't come into the centre unless they have to.'

'So where are you leading us?' I ask, wary.

'I know an abandoned place up ahead. We can rest there, clean ourselves up, and devise a plan.' She scans the surroundings. 'Let's keep moving.'

A curtain moves back into place from an upstairs window. Hopefully, it's just a curious resident and nothing more. I follow the others as an uneasy feeling creeps in.

The crowds get thicker. People are dressed in bright Witon clothes. Their skin is clean with hair washed and styled. Nothing like the residents we saw on the way in.

'Do you see what I mean about class now?' asks Lariel. 'There is such an obvious divide here compared to Nevertyre, with very little common groupings.'

'I don't like this,' I mutter. 'Elgee, stay close.'

'What for? Are you gettin' one of yer feelings?'

'I don't know, but something is just … off.'

Lariel turns left at a corner up ahead. The street is deserted. There's nothing to suggest anybody has passed through here for a long time. Even the doorways are free of warble plants.

'Where are you taking us?' I ask, tired of Lariel's vagueness.

She slows down, scanning the buildings around her.

'What are you looking for?' Kerina asks.

Lariel ignores our questions and leads us into the alcove area. Buildings surround the solitary entry point.

'Is this the place?' asks Kerina.

Lariel turns to face Kerina. Her face is pale and holds a haunted expression. 'Please forgive me.'

'What are you talking about?' Kerina asks, looking around.

'I didn't have a choice.'

I grab Lariel by the elbow and swirl her to face me. 'What have you done?'

'I'm sorry,' she whispers.

A dozen Agents appear, guns and stunner lasers drawn.

'It's a trap!' I yell.

There's nowhere to run. We are boxed in, with the exit too far behind us. The Agents will use their weapons against us without hesitating and we won't stand a chance. Lariel knew exactly where she was taking us. This ambush was planned well.

Chapter 42

Kerina

I glare at my so-called friend. 'What did you do?'

'I had to,' says Lariel. 'I'm sorry.'

I don't understand what is happening. Lariel has doublecrossed us? Me?

Shots sound out, causing me to duck.

'Hold your fire,' yells Lariel. 'Nobody is meant to get hurt.'

'You set this up?' I grab her and thrash her about. 'How could you?'

Agents run toward us with weapons raised. Each wears the grey uniform. The red trim looks so out of place in this decrepit, abandoned space. They come toward us from all directions. Each was easily hidden within the crumbling structures around us. This must be why Lariel insisted on coming to this place, so she could herd us into this dead end.

'Run!' shouts Elgee.

We return the way we came, leaving Lariel behind. We are out in the open and there's nowhere to hide. It's a perfect rendezvous point to capture us. More shots sound and something tears into my arm. I scream as the force knocks me over. My skin burns as it rips open.

'Kerina!' Saxon stops to help me.

Elgee grabs him. 'Come on!'

Saxon shrugs him off. 'Keep going. We can't all get caught.'

Elgee hesitates.

'Go! We'll catch up.' Saxon lifts me up as my blood drips onto him.

'Don't stop for me, keep going,' I say.

'You're coming with me.'

He pulls me up and I cringe as he lifts my wounded arm.

He spins me around and wraps my good arm around his neck. I lean into him and we try to run away from the encroaching Agents. We stumble along until, suddenly, Saxon is knocked to the ground from behind.

'Saxon!' I scream.

He tries to fight off the Agent, but others overpower him. He swings and connects with one just as another steps in and grabs him. The Agents pin his arms behind his back. Saxon jostles and thrashes about.

'Leave him, it's me you want,' I say.

'Don't, Kerina,' he yells. 'Get out of here!' A gun connects with the back of his head and he slumps to the ground, lifeless.

'Saxon!'

The burning in my arm makes it heavy and sluggish to move.

I fall forward, landing on my knees. 'Saxon?' He doesn't move.

Lariel rushes toward the group. 'Get off them. Nobody was meant to get hurt.' She kneels beside me. 'You're shot.'

'Don't touch me,' I say, shoving her away.

She cowers from me as though I had slapped her. I wish I had. How could she betray me like this? She called us sisters.

An Agent pushes Lariel aside, while two others drag Saxon off. His head hangs forward, lolling about as his legs drag behind.

'Get your hands off him,' I scream at the Agents.

They take no notice of me and continue to drag Saxon away. The remaining Agents turn their attention to me. I search around, but can't see Elgee anywhere. Hopefully that means he escaped. Two Agents lift me off the ground. They grip my arm, pressing against the wound.

Rage builds and the self-defence lessons come back to me as I lash out at them. I fight them off with a strength I didn't know was within me. One Agent tries to grab me, but I block him easily. My punch connects with his nose and I feel some twisted satisfaction when I hear it crack. The Agent drops to the ground, blood streaming through his fingers. I kick another Agent in the stomach as hard as I can. He is sent sprawling across the ground. These Agents have underestimated me, just as I underestimated myself. But no more. I can fight for my survival and I will fight for it, no matter the cost.

They keep coming and I keep fighting. Kicking, punching, blocking. *Crack!* Something connects with my ear. A ringing sound echoes before another thump connects with my cheek. My sight blurs before the last blow knocks me off my feet. Noises are foggy and shoes seem to pound all around me. I hear a screaming, but it's not me. I take one last look at my traitorous friend, then my vision goes dark.

Chapter 43

Saxon

It's hard to tell how long they've had me in this room. It's bright white, a contrast to how my face must look. The only furniture is the table in front of me, the chair I sit on, and another one opposite me. The decor is quite different to the dull confines of the chambers in Nevertyre.

A lone Agent stands guard near the door, but he takes no notice of me. The white wall in front of him holds his attention, rather than the prisoner before him. There are no restraints on me, yet I feel weighted down in this restricted space. Perhaps that is their intention.

'How long do I have to stay here?'

The guard looks straight ahead, ignoring the question.

I pinch the bridge of my nose and sigh. I stretch out my neck, tipping it from side to side. It seems hours since I saw Kerina get shot. How bad was the wound? Did she escape? Hopefully she and Elgee got away. If they did, then this incarceration will be worth it.

The door squeaks open and an Agent enters. I try to hide my surprise. If the Agent recognises me from the market in Nevertyre, he shows no signs of it. Instead, he takes his time sitting in the chair opposite. He makes a show of placing some documents in front of me, but not directly for me to see.

'What were you doing in the laneway?' he eventually asks.

'Lost my way,' I say, crossing my arms.

'And your friends, they all lost their sense of direction as well?'

'Must have.'

'Yet, you were the only one to get caught.'

I look up sharply. 'What did you say?'

The Agent checks his paperwork. 'Our arrest record shows only one arrest. A white male who wouldn't give his name.'

'It's a bit hard to speak when you're being beaten unconscious.' I reach for the lump on the side of my head. It's tender to touch and my head pounds when I move.

The Agent grits his teeth. 'The men have been spoken to about such … unnecessary force.'

I try to piece the information together. What game is this Agent playing? Kerina was shot and most likely captured. Unless she managed to get away. Perhaps my fight was enough of a diversion for her to escape with Elgee. Or, more likely, this man is lying.

'Why was I arrested? I haven't done anything wrong.'

The Agent reads through the paperwork in front of him.

'You showed suspicious behaviour. We don't need any more reason than that.'

'If walking along the street is suspicious behaviour, then you must have to arrest many people.'

The Agent turns to the guard. 'You may leave. This man is no threat.'

'But sir?'

'That's not a suggestion, it's an order.'

The guard looks at me for the first time. Confusion crosses his face as he hesitates, deciding whether to follow the command or not.

'Leave us. Now!'

'Yes, sir.'

The Agent and I now size one another up. Something shifts in the Agent's composure and I'm sure he remembers me.

'You will not be held to charge this time. You are a rambler new to this community who plans to move on, yes?'

'I'm not a rambler. I have my own home to return to.'

'And yet you have travelled far from it.'

He knows where I am from. He remembers me. I lean closer, unsure why the Agent doesn't disclose more. Perhaps there are listening devices hidden in the room.

The Agent smiles. 'Your mind must be racing, yet it is quite simple. You have something I want. Something that was promised to me but I never received it.'

'I have nothing that interests you. Stop this game and speak clearly.'

The Agent lowers his gaze to the table. His finger traces an invisible line on the table. A straight line followed by three horizontal lines. Top, middle, bottom. He repeats it again and again. The Okodee mark.

'Do we understand each other now?' asks the Agent.

I lean back in the chair and glare at the man across from me. His message is clear. He wants Kerina, and he expects me to hand her over. There's just one problem. I don't have her, and neither does this man. So, the question remains, who has her?

Chapter 44

Kerina

A sliver of light creeps through the doorway. I arch my neck upward, stretching it out. A small window sits high above, carved into the wall. My head pounds from the thump I received. I try to sit up, but the movement makes me dizzy.

'Owww,' I groan.

Slowly, I inch my way into an upright position. The effort makes my ribs ache. I don't recall being punched, but who knows what happened after I passed out. The only thing I remember as I slumped to the ground was Lariel watching on, doing nothing to help me.

I force myself to stand and look through the opening in the door. The effort leaves me breathless.

'Don't bother, you can't see anything.'

I shrink back from the voice in the dark. 'Lariel?'

My eyes adjust to the darkness. I scan the space to check for any other surprises.

'It's only you and me.'

'Where's Saxon?'

'I don't know. I'm so sorry, Kerina, you have to forgive me.'

'You set us up. You delivered me to them on purpose.'

Lariel nods.

'Did you know all along? Is that why you came to find me?'

Lariel tries to calm me, but I slam her against the wall.

'You lied, and for what? Look where we are!'

I circle the small space, pacing out my rage.

'I know, I'm so stupid for believing them. When they captured me after our escape, they offered me a deal. My father for you.'

'And you agreed? You believed they would allow that? After everything you know of them?'

Lariel sobs. 'I was desperate. Do you remember what I was like? I was nearly dead when they caught me. They fed me and took care of me. I was too weak to think properly and so grateful to be treated well instead of beaten.'

'You said *your* father. What about mine?'

Lariel shakes her head. 'It was always just my father who survived. They only needed one survivor to set an example.'

I stagger away from my traitorous friend at her revelation. All along, both my parents had been murdered and she never told me. I slump against the wall. Looking at Lariel, I can barely recognise her as the same friend Saxon pinned down in my room. I had been so relieved she was alive and safe. The deception makes me choke.

'You knew my father was dead and you used that knowledge against me. You planned to hand me over all along,' I say, devoid of emotion.

Lariel covers her eyes. 'They told me if I didn't find you and bring you to them, they would kill my father.'

'How do you know he is even alive?'

She looks up now with eyes full of hope. 'Proof of life. They showed him to me. He is alive!'

I slide down the wall, my head hanging between my hands as I digest this news. I would never trade a friend's life like that. No matter how great the reward. *But didn't I do just that when Lariel was taken on the road?*

'You're certain it was your father? Not a man made to look like him?'

'It was him. They gave me their word he wouldn't be harmed so long as I brought you back to them.'

Kerina laughs. 'If they are so good at keeping their word, then why are you in here with me?'

'I don't know.'

'It's because their word means nothing,' I say. 'And you have just given them a good reason to kill your father, not to mention the two of us in the process.'

Lariel sobs. 'I'm sorry, Kerina! I was desperate to hear news about him. To know that he survived after we were taken.'

'Your stupidity has got us right back where we started. Worse! Now Saxon has been captured as well. He saved my life and if they hurt him, Lariel, I will never forgive you. That I can promise you.'

I turn away from Lariel. Saxon's instincts were right about her, and I assured him they were wrong. What have I done?

Chapter 45

Saxon

I cross the road from the chambers. It took less than ten minutes for me to be officially released. The Agent watched on the whole time. His presence was a reminder that my freedom might be a temporary thing if I can't deliver the promised goods. There was something else about the Agent that gave me a feeling of familiarity. It might have been a mannerism or gesture, but I can't quite place what it was.

A sharp whistle floats my way. A call and respond sound from my youth. I know Elgee is around here somewhere. I whistle back and wait for him to reply. It comes instantly. I follow the sound to find Elgee hidden behind a crumbled wall, watching me through the space. He emerges and hands me my backpack.

'Man, am I glad to see you,' he says.

We try to keep a normal pace as we walk away from the chambers. We scout around for ajar doors that might indicate an abandoned building. It doesn't take long to find one. We move inside and check we are truly alone.

'All clear, mah friend. Ain't nobody but us round here.'

I thump my bag on the ground and embrace my friend.

'I'm so glad you're safe, Elgee.'

'Ahh, you know me. Always manage to wrangle my way out of trouble.'

I laugh at the truth. Nothing ever sticks to Elgee. No accusation, no evidence, no hard feelings. He is well known for his sweet taking ways at the market.

'Where's Kerina? Are they letting her go?'

I shrug. 'It was a trap. I knew Lariel couldn't be trusted!'

'I did not see that comin'', says Elgee, shaking his head.

I clench my fists. 'I wanna kill her. How could she do that?' I punch an empty plant holder and it smashes to the ground. Warbles scatter along the ground.

'The question is, what are we gonna do now?' says Elgee.

I lean against the wall. 'I don't know, just let me think for a minute.'

The people who took Kerina used Agents. They must be powerful people to have Agents working for them. Agents were searching for ramblers in Nevertyre, asking questions. One particular Agent has shown up in both locations who knows about Kerina, yet didn't know she had been taken.

'There is one person who might be able to help. It's a long shot, but we have little choice.'

If I'm right about this Agent, then we might have just found an ally. If I'm wrong, then I might never get home to meet Manny's baby.

'What are our supplies like?' I rummage through the bag.

The weapons are still there with spare bullets. Some nutrient packs remain, but not enough for us to last very long.

Elgee checks his pack. 'We'll need to stock up. 'Specially if we're gonna cut through this town in a hurry.'

'Elgee, you're my best friend and you know me well. So, when I ask this next favour, well, you just gotta listen and do as I say.'

'What kind of plan you comin' up with?' asks Elgee.

'It's one I hope works, but there's a catch. You can't come with me.'

Elgee shakes his head. 'Nah way, I'm comin'.'

'I need you to be my back-up, Elgee. If I'm wrong about this person, I might need you to come rescue me.'

I meant it to lighten the mood, but I was also being serious. If I'm wrong about the Agent, then I won't be any help to Kerina. I will be arrested and it will take a lot more than luck to be released.

'I can't just stand around waitin'. What else can I do?'

'You're good with people. See what information you can find out about the people who might have taken Kerina. Find out the whispers around town, the talk on the streets. Start with the towns-folk on the fringes of town. They're usually the best sources.'

'All right, that I can do. Might even scrounge up more supplies.'

I check the time. 'Let's meet back here in eight hours. Wait another two. If I don't come back, then you head back to Nevertyre.'

'What? No way am I leavin' you here.'

'Elgee—'

'No way I'm doin' that so shut up about it.'

We fist tap and hug before I leave my best friend behind. People will confide in Elgee. If anyone can get the information we need, it's him. Back home in Nevertyre, people share secrets with him all the time. I'm confident Elgee will get information and supplies for us. Now all I need to do is get arrested, again.

Chapter 46

Kerina

The light above the doorway doesn't change, so it is hard to know what time of day it is. Time seems to have paused in this prison space.

The night air is warm as we sit outside our home.

'Kerina, if anything should happen to us, you must be ready to stand strong on your own.'

Kerina knew the stakes. It had been drilled into her from a young age. She was different. She was valuable. She was Okodee.

'I understand, Father, but don't speak such things. Nothing will happen to you or Mother. We are safe here.'

As the memory plays out, I can't help but wonder when I will feel safe again.

Suddenly, the door swings open to our cell and light floods the room. A man fills the space. He steps closer as Lariel and I both scramble to our feet, ready to defend ourselves.

'Why are we here?' I ask. 'Where are you taking us?'

Screams from a previous place of captivity return to the forefront of my mind. Hopefully, it's anywhere but there. I adjust my stance, fists clenched, and wait for him to speak.

The guard ignores the questions; instead, he points to me and curls his finger toward him. I shake my head.

'If you resist, I will hurt your friend.' He smirks, daring me.

Lariel might have betrayed me, but she was once my best friend. I won't let him hurt her because of me.

'Please don't leave me,' says Lariel, grabbing my arm. 'I can't stay here alone.'

Her voice starts to rise and the man's fist clenches in anticipation.

I shake Lariel by the shoulder. 'Stop it, don't panic, Lariel. That's what they want, what he wants.'

The man steps toward us.

'I. Won't. Leave. You. Behind.'

The words are offered as comfort, even when she deserves no such thing after her actions.

I turn toward the guard. 'Back up and let's go.'

He moves aside and I shove past him. I show no fear because I am not afraid. I feel strong because I'm angry. These people took me from my family and murdered my parents, all because I am Okodee. Something I know little about or even understand properly. I want answers to who wants me captured. Who did Lariel make a deal with? Who do they work for?

The man directs me down a narrow corridor. There are doors built into the walls, but there is no dividing feature to show where the rooms end. The wall forms one long corridor with fluorescent lighting overhead to light the way. There are no windows, which suggest we are underground somewhere. Thankfully, no screams filter through the walls.

The guard follows behind as I walk along the space. He pokes me in the back, urging me forward. The gesture makes me nervous.

'Stop,' he orders, checking behind us.

Satisfied we are alone and not being followed, he presses his thumb against a black screen outside the door. A blue light scans his fingerprint and the door swishes open. He shoves me inside the space. I scowl at him before surveying the room. It's empty except for a table and two chairs.

'Sit.' The guard retreats and the door closes, leaving me alone.

I ignore his command and face the door, ready for whoever enters. I will have a better chance of defence standing than sitting.

I don't have to wait long. Within minutes the door opens again and a white-haired man enters. I can't hide the surprise.

'Sit down and listen. We have very little time,' says Rudolph. 'I cannot get you out, but be ready for an Agent who says my name.'

'Who is he? Why is he helping?' Panic rises within me. Rudolph's discussion by the river with the Agent is still fresh in my mind. 'Why should I trust you?'

'I don't have time for your questions, but I promise they will be answered later. Now remember, wait for the Agent that says my name. He can be trusted and will help get you where you need to go.'

'Where's that?'

'Shirnaka.' He stands to leave, but hesitates. 'Tell Saxon … the stories are all true.'

Then he's gone, like an apparition disappearing before my eyes.

Chapter 47

Saxon

The Agent I spoke with must have seniority in this place. Therefore, my arrest needs to be serious enough that I will be interviewed by him, yet not so bad he can't release me without arousing suspicion. The Agent knew who I was but didn't let on. He thinks I will lead him to Kerina, which means he didn't give the order for the ambush. Someone more powerful did and kept that Agent out of the loop. But why? Especially when the Agent obviously knows about the Okodee people. I have little choice but to approach him. This man still has enough power and sway to find out more than I can.

Thirty minutes later, I find himself lining up behind a handful of other people at the museum. They have daily tours to show people what the world was once like. They are lessons that must be learnt if humans are to survive as a species in the future. The Burn destroyed much of the country and its people. Few survived, and many that did died from hunger or disease afterward.

As I follow the group around, I devise a plan. I know not all the information is out on display because they do something similar in Nevertyre's museum. It is changed every couple of months. Usually more of the same information, just in different examples. As I listen to the guide drone on, I keep my eyes peeled for something I can use.

After twenty minutes in one area, I am rewarded for my patience. A doorway to the right is signed: DO NOT ENTER.

'… so that gives you an idea of how people once lived. Next, we will learn more about the cause of the Burn and how it nearly wiped us out. Let's go!' The guide leads the group around the corner. This is my best opportunity. I try the handle, but it's locked. The three other people in the group and the guide have already walked off. If I trip the alarm, it will take only seconds for the tour guide to return and security will arrive shortly after. With that in mind, I search for a sharp, thin object. Any penetration to the lock without the keypad being activated will sound the alarm. I remember my pocket knife. I check the hallway is empty, then shove the point in the lock.

'ARARARARARAR.' The alarm pierces through my ears. As predicted, within seconds, the tour guide runs around the corner.

'What did you do?' the guide screams over the alarm. Spit flies from his mouth. 'This has never happened before.'

'I was looking for the toilet,' I lie.

'This is not good,' mutters the guide, panicked. He runs to the door and stares at the keypad. He punches in some numbers and the screeching noise stops.

An eerie silence falls over us, but it doesn't last long. Heavy footsteps run around the corner and two guards appear, stunners drawn.

'Get your hands behind your head,' yells one.

'On the ground,' yells the other.

I don't resist as I'm shoved to the ground. The guide also drops to his knees, his hands locked behind his head. In other circumstances, the reaction would have made me laugh.

'I don't think this is necessary,' the guide tries to intervene. 'He was looking for the toilet.'

'Through a door clearly marked "do not enter"?' says one guard.

'Can't read,' I say. 'Just tried to open it and the alarm went off.'

The two guards eye me with suspicion. They whisper between themselves before making a decision. They drag me up to a standing position. I am taller than both of them and could probably fight them off if I needed to, but that's not in my plans.

'We're taking you to the chambers. You're under arrest.'
I hide my smile.

Chapter 48

Kerina

I am left on my own in the room for a long time after Rudolph's visit. The bright white walls make my eyes ache. I lean my head against the table and close my eyes. My body remains ever alert. Eventually the guard comes to fetch me. He tosses me a nutrient pack, which I slurp down greedily.

'Let's go.'

I follow behind. 'Where are we going?'

The only response is a snort. I don't know what to make of this guard. Does he work for Rudolph or is he a danger? I follow without further questions. I know he will not give me any answers. We pass nobody on the way to the room and soon arrive back where we started. He unlocks the door and moves aside. I enter the room and the door slams closed behind me. My eyes quickly adjust to the darkened room.

Lying on the ground in a crumpled heap is Lariel.

'Lariel!' I rush toward her. 'What's wrong?'

She looks up, surprised. 'You didn't leave me.'

'Of course not, but what's wrong? Are you hurt?'

Lariel groans. 'I'm not hurt, just broken. Don't you see? It's all been for nothing.' Her eyes are puffed red from crying.

I push the hair from her face. 'What's been for nothing?'

'Us! We have no power. Okodee … are expendable.'

'You're giving up?'

'It doesn't matter, because we'll be dealt with soon.' Lariel adjusts herself so she is sitting up. 'Look at your arm, Kerina.'

I look but see nothing of interest. 'What about it?'

'You were shot. Look at the wound.'

I remove the material Lariel must have wrapped around it while I was unconscious. My skin has already started to heal. 'But how can that be?'

'Think about it, Kerina. How many times have you been sick in your whole life?'

'I had a fever once. My mother was worried it wouldn't go down.'

'That fever killed half the people that lived around us. Nobody who got it recovered. They all died, except you.'

'That doesn't explain my arm.'

'How long did it take for you to recover once Saxon found you?'

'They fed me—'

'How long?'

'Okay! I get it, not long.'

'Don't you see? You and I are not like others. We have strong healing abilities. We are capable of surviving on little. We are Okodee. That is why we were hidden by our parents. So that nobody knows our abilities or can take advantage of them. But it's pointless.' She slumps forward, head in her hands.

I let this revelation sink in, but I am still confused. 'If we're the same, then why do they want me so much?'

Lariel shrugs. 'All I know is you are more valuable than me. I don't know why, and I don't know what that means for you. I do know that I heard a female voice speak the last time. She asked specifically if you had been captured yet.'

'Did you recognise the voice?'

Lariel nods. 'It was the Primo Dictor of Middtown's wife.'

'How do you know such a thing?'

'They called her "Governess".'

Chapter 49

Saxon

I settle back into the white room I found myself in earlier. At least this time I have some control over the situation. I grip my hands together, hoping this plan will work. The alternative is unthinkable. I can't leave Kerina to be locked up again. Besides, I made her a promise and that is one thing I always keep.

The door opens and the familiar Agent enters.

'Your company was so pleasant I decided to come back for more,' I say.

The Agent sits opposite me. 'I'm told you would not give a name upon arrest.'

'I'll give my name when it's warranted. It wasn't.'

'You don't think breaking into a contained area makes the request warranted?'

I shake my head. 'I wasn't breaking in, just lost.'

The Agent raises an eyebrow. 'Again?'

'I'm really bad with direction.'

The Agent releases a deep breath. A serious look clouds his face. There are signs of strain around his eyes, weariness.

'I'm not sure I will be able to overlook this … indiscretion.'

I lean forward. 'Then you'll have to find a way. Especially if you expect to get what you want.'

The Agent leans back in his chair, arms crossed. His focus never leaves me, but I know he is weighing up the possibilities.

'Stop this game and speak clearly,' says the Agent, repeating my words back to me.

I move my finger to the centre of the table and draw a shape. The Agent watches on. My finger traces an invisible line on the table. A straight line followed by three horizontal lines. Top, middle, bottom. There is no mistaking the reference to the Okodee symbol from yesterday. The Agent stands up and removes a rectangular device from his pocket. He walks around the room waving it about. There are not many places for concealing anything.

Satisfied, he puts it away and returns to the table. 'We can speak freely now, Saxon.'

'So, you do know me.'

'Of course. I know many things about you and your friends.'

'Yet you don't know one of them was taken by thug Agents.'

The Agent's jaw twitches but he doesn't respond. If the Agent knew Kerina had been taken, he wouldn't be wasting his time with me now. That tells me many things, including that this man can be trusted because we both want the same thing. However, this Agent's motivation remains unclear. Hopefully, I will determine the reason soon enough.

'It seems you don't have as much control over your men as you thought.'

The Agent's fists clench, yet he manages to control his anger. 'Kerina?'

I contain my surprise at the Agent's knowledge. 'Yes. And I need your help to get her back.'

'Before I agree to help you, I need to know something.'

'What?' I ask, guarded.

'Does Kerina have any idea of her, shall we say, background?'

'Kerina can answer that for you when we find her.'

'I just hope we're not too late.'

I push the chair back, leaning over the table. 'What the hell does that mean?'

'It means someone with a lot of authority ordered her abduction. Someone with that much power must have plenty of means at their disposal.'

'Always a dangerous combination,' I say. 'But I'm sure you're a man with resources too.' I extend my hand. 'So, will you help?'

'Yes,' says the Agent, gripping my hand. 'Let's go.'

Chapter 50

Kerina

'What else do you know?' I demand, pacing our confined room.

'We heal quicker than others. Sickness eludes us most of the time. Our bodies can withstand more than most. Anyone else who had been found by Manny and Saxon would most likely be dead. They would not have recovered like you, nor would it have been as quick.'

'Constance gave me special remedies. She added them to the soup to help with the healing. Plus, they shared their nutrient packs.'

'Yes, but your recovery was remarkable. I heard Manny and Constance talking about it not long after I arrived. Constance knew about me from your memories. She wondered why someone who was described as near death could look as healthy as I did and make it to you on my own. Especially after the way they found you.'

I stop pacing and stand still in the small area. My parents' concern comes back to me.

'How is she?'

My father watches on from the side. I can tell he doesn't want to get too close. Fear lurks behind his eyes as he stares at me.

'She's too hot and it's been too long,' says my mother. She rinses out the cloth and applies the cool, soothing material to her forehead.

'She can fight this,' he says.

'Yes, she can. But we can't.'

'My parents knew of this … ability?'

'Of course. That was one of the things that made them believe such things could be possible. That the whispers of Okodee were true. That is why they went to such lengths to protect us and prepare us.'

'Why us though? What makes us this way?'

'You saw the shanties when we arrived. You saw the people who live there. They survive on the nutrient cocktail given to them. The drink was created to make food unnecessary, but not all nutrient packs are created equal.'

I had never thought much about the nutrient packs. They are just bought and consumed to fuel the body. 'What are you saying? Some nutrient packs have less sustenance?'

'Yes, and no.'

'I don't understand, Lariel.'

'In the beginning, after the Burn, and after the fires had raged and destroyed everything, very little would grow. Few animals or plants survived it. Scientists, paid by the government, created a chemical concoction for humans to survive. Something that could sustain them without solid food being necessary.'

'Yes. And millions died from starvation until then. It was a good thing! But what else are they putting in the nutrient packs now, Lariel?'

She shrugs. 'I don't know. But I do know they are being tampered with.'

'How do you know all this?'

'I know I've lost your trust and I'm sorry for that. But please believe me when I tell you these things. It doesn't matter how I know. What matters is that Okodee are different. Our parents tried to keep us safe, but that didn't work. The only way is to be with our own kind.'

'How many are there?'

Lariel shrugs. 'Hundreds? Thousands? Maybe more.'

'So where are they then?'

Lariel sighs. 'That is the most important question. And Saxon has the answer.'

I remember the map Saxon showed us before we left. It is the same place Rudolph told me about. Shirnaka.

Chapter 51

Saxon

I run toward the shanty buildings to find Elgee. The Agent told me to meet where I was first arrested in two hours. The Agent would have what was needed by then. As I get closer, I notice the townsfolk walk about unhurried. Nobody is in a rush like me. I slow my pace to avoid unnecessary attention. As I search the area, gaunt faces look up at me. Lethargic children sit in the streets or lie on their parents' laps. Where are their nutrient packs? The community in Nevertyre isn't like this. There is a poorer sector, but the people aren't malnourished like this.

It doesn't take long to spot Elgee speaking with a group of people. His dark, dreadlocked hair is out of place with the shaved, tattooed heads around him. I try to get his attention. A small nod from Elgee confirms he has seen me. I wait near the corner, knowing he will be garnering whatever bits of information he can. Elgee is a showman at times, always talking, joking, and networking with those around him. He has the ability to put people at ease almost instantly, and for that they trust him.

Something tugs on my sleeve. A young boy, no taller than my waist, looks up.

'Do you want to see a trick?' The boy smiles a toothless grin.

I look toward my friend, who is still in discussions with his new acquaintances.

'Sure, kid, show me your trick.'

'A token for my effort?'

I remove one from my pocket and hold it out for him to see.

'When you've shown me, I'll decide if it's worth a token.'

The boy nods, happy with the arrangement. First, he produces three cups. He squats down and places each one on the ground. Then he slips a plastic disc beneath the middle cup.

He taps on the top, pointing it out. 'Watch this one.'

He shuffles the cups around. I watch, focused only on the cup I have been told to watch. The boy stops the movement, continues, then stops again. He repeats the actions.

'Which one has the disc?' he asks, with a grin.

I tap the middle one.

'Are you certain?'

I nod, confident in my choice. The boy pauses, then removes the cup. An empty space is revealed.

'Where is it?' I ask, surprised.

The boy removes the cup on the left and the cup on the right. Both are empty.

'You've lost it?' I say.

The boy laughs. 'Give me your hand.'

I do as he asks. The boy turns it palm upward, clicks his finger, and the disc falls from his other hand onto mine.

I laugh and pass the disc back. The boy accepts it and tucks it into his pocket.

'My payment?'

'Well earned.' I dig into my pocket and pass the token to the boy.

He quickly secures it from prying eyes.

'Where did you learn such a trick?'

'Sometimes what we see is not always what we are looking at.'

The boy takes a bow and retreats backward. I turn to look for Elgee before realising the significance of the boy's comment. Rudolph has said the same words to me many times over the years.

'Hey, who told you that?' I call after the boy.

But he has disappeared, just like his magic trick.

Chapter 52

Kerina

Without warning, the door flings open. An Agent stands before the two of us.

'Kerina, let's go.'

'Who are you?'

'Hurry, we have only minutes. Rudolph sent me.'

I don't need to be told twice. 'Let's go, Lariel.'

'Are you sure about her?' he asks.

I glare at him. 'If I'm leaving, then so is she.'

Lariel scrambles to stand. 'You won't regret this, Kerina, I promise.'

'Move it! We haven't got long,' says the Agent.

I push against the Agent. 'If you double-cross us, I will kill you the first chance I get.'

The Agent salutes me. 'Understood.'

We follow him as he leads us down a hallway. It is the opposite way to the direction I went before. The Agent used Rudolph's name so I should trust him. But can I trust Rudolph?

'It's not far,' says the Agent. 'There is a back entrance they must have used to bring you in. I'm sorry, I didn't know.'

They come to a doorway with a keypad.

'Hey!' A voice travels down the hallway toward them. 'Stop!'

The Agent keys in a code, and the lights flash red. 'Damn it.'

'Hurry up,' I say.

'Stop or I'll shoot,' yells the voice.

Beep, beep, beep, beep. The light flashes green and the door unlocks. The Agent pushes it open and ushers them through. The guard gets closer and the Agent raises his gun to shoot. It stops the guard's pursuit.

'Agent Tambler?'

'Lie down. Push your weapon this way.'

'Agent Tambler, what are you doing?'

'I don't want to hurt you, but I will. Now push your weapon this way.'

The man does as he is asked. Tambler collects the gun and attaches some restraints. They tighten the guard's arms and legs together.

'When they ask, you don't know who did this to you. That is the only truth that will keep you alive. Anything else and you will not survive long, nor will your family. Are we clear?'

The guard nods.

'*Are we clear?*'

'Yes!'

The Agent pauses, undecided.

'Hurry up,' I say.

My voice seems to snap him out of his indecision. Tambler runs toward us and slams the door behind him.

'It looks like my cover is blown,' he says grimly.

'Your cover? Who are you?' I ask.

The Agent takes a bow. 'I am an undercover operative. A double Agent, if you like.'

My eyes narrow. 'I've worked that much out, but who are you really?'

The Agent stands tall. His broad shoulders are pushed back with pride. He removes the peaked cap to reveal short blond hair.

'I'm Tambler. Ryen Tambler. I believe you know my father, Rudolph.'

Chapter 53

Saxon

The cover of darkness does little to hide us. The moonlight is bright tonight. The solar-powered vehicle is so quiet it's hard to believe the engine is running. The Agent was right about where to find it and how to get it out of the compound. It was simple. Elgee just needed the right code to punch in.

I have been staring at the wall since we got here. I can't make out the opening, but this is where the Agent said to wait. It feels like we've been waiting for hours, but it can't really be that long. Suddenly, three figures burst through a concealed doorway.

'Thought it was only two of 'em.'

I turn to see the extra figure running toward the vehicle. The Agent jumps into the driver's seat as Elgee opens the back door.

'What the hell is she doing here?' I say.

The Agent presses the accelerator. 'Ask Kerina, it was her choice.'

'I wasn't going to leave her there,' says Kerina.

'She should be left to rot there,' I say, glaring at Lariel.

'I'm sorry for what I did, but I was desperate,' she pleads.

The car races down the street away from the prison.

'You could have got us all killed. You got Kerina shot,' I continue.

Lariel is lucky a seat divides us or I might not be able to control my rage.

'I'm fine, Saxon,' says Kerina. 'Look.' She pulls up the torn sleeve to show me her arm. It's already healing.

'But that's impossible! I saw you get shot.'

'Ahh, the beauty of Okodee,' says the Agent, laughing.

He swerves around the corner, driving toward the exit road out of town.

'What do you know of it, Ryen?' asks Kerina.

'I know enough,' he says.

'Ryen?' scoffs Saxon. 'Is that your name? Agent Ryen.'

'Agent Tambler, but you can call me Ryen. I believe my Agent days are now behind me.'

I turn to Kerina. 'Are you okay? Did they hurt you?'

'I'm fine.' She opens her mouth as if to say more, but hesitates.

'Kerina?'

Her eyes skip toward Ryen. 'Really, I'm fine.'

'Uh oh. Road block straight ahead,' says Ryen. 'Damn, they were quick!'

'No problem,' says Elgee. 'I found some friends in Middtown who don't like authority round here. They've been lookin' for a reason to kick up some stink. You get us through and they'll stop anybody followin' us.'

'You made friends here already?' says Ryen, sceptical.

'Mmm hmm. I'm a likeable guy. I make friends wherever I go.'

'You're sure?' asks Ryen.

'Don't ever second guess Elgee. If he says it, then it's true,' I say.

Ryen increases his speed. 'All right, then. Seat belts pulled tight.'

He maintains a straight line for the roadblock. The headlights show two vehicles parked either side of the road. Agents form a straight line in between. There's only a narrow opening to fit through.

'Ever hear of a game called bowling?' asks Ryen.

I shake my head.

'Seems you might get to see one in action.' Ryen increases speed. His eyes focus on the blockade in front. 'It's where you knock the pins out of the way.' The Agents straight ahead don't budge. 'Hold on. We might get a strike!'

Chapter 54

Kerina

'We're going to hit them,' I scream.

Ryen doesn't slow, but the guards must understand the need to move or die. They each dive in different directions. The car clips one guard who thumps on to the roof of the car and bounces off the back.

'Oh man, yer skittled him!' says Elgee.

Ryen bursts through the barricade.

I look through the back window. The guards scramble for the cars parked on the side. The drivers accelerate and head straight for us.

'They're coming after us,' I say.

Ryen drives past the people in the shanty village. Some throw their arms up to cheer and wave, others pump their fists in the air. All clearly demonstrating whose side they are on.

'Come on now, come through with da goods,' says Elgee, watching out the window.

I spot a group nearby who nod, slowly but deliberately.

'Oh yes! Thank the stars and sun they came through,' says Elgee. 'Just head straight.'

Dust whirls up and around, making it hard to see out the windows. The two cars giving chase are suddenly slowing down. They roll to a standstill.

'What did your friends do?' I ask.

'Just let the air out of the tyres. No destruction and no proof to lead back to 'em.'

'How far can we go with this thing?' asks Saxon.

'As long as the sun shines and the power lasts, as far as we want,' says Ryen.

After a while, I break the silence. 'You never answered me, Ryen. What do you know about the Okodee people?'

'My father would tell me stories when I was growing up. I didn't see him that often so I always looked forward to his stories.'

'What about your mother?' I ask.

'She believes.' He laughs. 'Oh yes, she certainly believes.'

'Your dad didn't live with you?' asks Saxon.

Ryen's body tenses. 'No.'

I wait to see if Ryen will reveal who his father is, but he doesn't. I feel guilty for not sharing my knowledge with Saxon.

'My father worked away,' says Ryen. 'He was once a great scientist. Respected by many people, particularly those in his field. When he met my mother, he was already involved in something that required his full commitment.'

I listen to Ryen speak and can't help but wonder if his story is being told for my benefit only. Perhaps there is something more to it that I need to be listening for.

'My father is a driven man. He has pursued his passion for many years. Although it's more like an obsession. He first worked for those who would turn against him; now he works for those who seek the truth. My mother is also a truth seeker, a sympathiser, but she has her own reasons for doing so.'

'So how did you end up working as an Agent?' asks Saxon.

'It was more a case of good timing. You could say the position fell into my lap.'

I wait for him to elaborate, but he doesn't.

'It was an opportunity to support our cause and learn more. The intelligence I've gained has been invaluable. We have knowledge of the main players and the means to which they will go to get what they want.'

'What do they want?' asks Saxon.

Ryen looks in the rear-view mirror and his eyes lock on me.

'Okodee people. And nothing will stop them.'

Chapter 55

Saxon

The solar-powered car continues to travel until late in the night when the power levels drop.

'We can stop here. If they've sent anyone after us, they will not get this far now,' says Ryen.

'Will they send people?' asks Elgee.

Ryen shrugs. 'No doubt they'll be setting up things to ensure our capture. That's why we need to be smart and get the girls to a safe place.'

'Shirnaka?' says Kerina.

'We will all be safe there until my father gets word to me about the next move.'

'Hold on. Are you sayin' we can't go home?' says Elgee.

'Not for the time being.'

'What about our families?' I say.

Ryen pokes the fire from the magnesium blocks that burn strong. 'They will be fine.'

'But they'll be taken in for questioning. Constance is pregnant! Stress isn't good for her.'

'They just need to stick to the story.'

'How the hell are they supposed to know the story?'

Ryen stands. 'I know you don't want to trust me, Saxon, but you have to.'

I get up close to Ryen's face. 'I don't have to do anything for you.'

Ryen shoves me. 'Back off.'

'Why? What are you gonna do?'

'Hey!' Kerina jumps up. 'We need to work together if we are going to make it. Saxon, you have to stop being suspicious, and Ryen, you need to stop speaking in riddles. If we are to trust each other, we need to be honest with one another.'

She glares at us both until Ryen steps back. I shove past him and storm off. My instincts are always right, and this time they tell me Ryen can't be trusted.

'Saxon, wait.'

Kerina's footsteps are light. I stop, waiting for her to catch up.

'I'm sorry for losing it back there, but there's just something about that guy …'

She stands with hands on hips. 'What? Explain it to me.'

Her long, dark hair shines in the light. It's so different to when Manny and I first found her.

'Don't you trust me?' she asks.

Something about her captured my attention when I first saw her, just like it has ever since.

'I saw Ryen back in Nevertyre as an Agent. He threatened Rudolph! Then he shows up after my arrest, pretending not to know me.'

'He had to so his cover wasn't blown.'

'Perhaps, but how did he know about you in the first place?'

She shrugs, but I'm not convinced. She avoids my gaze, as though hiding something.

'Kerina.' I reach for her hand.

She looks up, surprised by the gesture.

'When I first saw you, I told Manny you were a fighter. The more I learn about you, the more I know I'm right. There are so many unanswered questions about this guy Ryen, and yet you seem to trust him so easily. Why?'

She hesitates. 'He has not proven himself otherwise, so I must trust him. He seems to know the most about me and … my situation.'

'And me? Do you trust me?'

She shivers before answering. 'Yes. It's you I trust the most.'

'Then I will trust you.'

Chapter 56

Kerina

I am strapped to a metal table. I have been left securely on my own. The cotton nightshirt does little to ward off the cold, sterile air. I try to look around the room. It looks similar to a doctor's room on the rare occasion I have visited one. A woman enters the room and her golden hair curls around her face. She smiles at me.

'My goodness,' she laughs. 'You really do look so normal. It's quite remarkable.'

She pulls out a syringe and flicks the end. 'This might hurt, but I only need a few samples. Be a good girl and be brave.'

I try to resist, but it's no use. The restraints are too tight. It stings as the needle enters my skin. The dark red liquid is drawn up quickly. Four more vials are taken. As each one is drawn, a nauseous feeling washes over me. Content with her samples, the woman puts them aside. Next, she picks up a scalpel.

I wake, startled. Sweat drips off my forehead and I shove the thermal blanket off. I gasp for air, desperate to draw in as much oxygen as I can. The night sky is still dark, so I can't have slept for long.

Saxon stirs. 'Are you okay?'

I rub my belly, trying to settle the sick feeling. 'I didn't mean to wake you. I was just … hot.'

'Did you have another dream?'

I hesitate before nodding. 'It was so real. My skin still stings from the needle.'

Saxon leans up on his elbow. 'What needle?'

'A woman came and took vials of my blood. But do you want to hear the weirdest bit?'

Saxon moves closer. 'After everything that's happened since I met you, I'm not sure what weird is anymore.'

I smile, knowing he is trying to put me at ease. 'The woman laughed and commented on how *normal* I look. As though I were an abnormality.'

'Do you think it was a dream or a memory?'

I run my finger along the vein in my arm where the woman withdrew my blood. 'I don't know. I can't tell most of the time.'

Saxon reaches across and gently caresses my arm. His fingers are cool against my skin. I try to stop my body from shaking, even though I'm not cold.

'I'm not an abnormality, am I, Saxon?'

I search his green eyes, wanting only the truth from him. I know he will give me that. Saxon's lips are set in a tight line. He swallows before speaking.

'You are as normal as I am. If that makes us both strange, then so be it. Okay?' He caresses my arm, so soft but reassuring.

I let the words sink in. 'Okay.'

In that moment, I feel as whole as any other human. The same as Saxon or Constance or Manny. My DNA might say differently, but for now I hold on to his truth. I'm not a mistake or a freak. I'm just Kerina.

The cool air wraps around me and any heat from the blanket is now lost. I shiver again, but this time it is from the cold. I'm just a normal human being who heals fast and is marked different to most. I lie back down and face Saxon.

I reach for his hand. 'Thank you.'

We lie that way for a long time. I draw strength from him, knowing he doesn't think I'm an abnormality. I might even begin to believe it as well, if I try hard enough.

Chapter 57

Saxon

'How much further?' I ask.

'You're not very patient, are you?' says Ryen.

I roll my eyes. 'Do you even know the answer?'

'Of course, I have been here many times.'

'Is it true there are others like us?' asks Lariel.

'Yes, many. Although at this place it can be hard to work out Okodee from the others.'

'What do you mean?' I ask, alert.

Ryen grins. 'You'll see.'

'What's all those li'l towers?' asks Elgee. 'Looks like stacks o' pebbles.'

'They are. They're littered all about here. It's a good way to see if things have been disturbed by outsiders.'

'What do you mean? Like a trap?' Elgee strains to see more.

'Have you noticed the landscape we've been passing?'

I look out my window and see a cave high atop a hill. A perfect viewpoint. There are no buildings around, though.

'This place you're taking us to—Shirnaka—it's not above ground, is it?'

'Good for you, Saxon,' says Ryen. 'I wondered who would work it out first.'

'You mean the people all live underground?' says Kerina.

'Don't worry, nobody is locked in. Everyone is free to come and go as they like. Most stay because everyone is safe and hidden. Both sympathisers and Okodee live together—it makes no difference at Shirnaka.'

Ryen drives toward a small mountain. He stops the vehicle a couple of hundred metres away.

'The people who live here get nervous easily,' he explains. 'They don't like outsiders much.'

'That seems to be happenin' a lot lately,' says Elgee.

Ryen exits the car. 'You should all stay here, except Kerina. I'll need you to come with me.'

I get out of the car. 'If she's going, so am I.'

Ryen sighs. 'Fine.'

He walks toward the mountain with his hands in the air. Anyone watching him will know he means no threat. Suddenly two camouflaged figures emerge to the left.

'It's Tambler. Ryen Tambler. I bring friends.'

The shorter figure walks closer, dressed in sandy-coloured material. A hood covers the face completely. What they lack in height, they make up for in confidence. A weapon is positioned on me, making me nervous as I am unarmed. The figure removes the hood to reveal a woman. Her face is weathered, but the resemblance is too similar.

'Hello, Mother,' says Ryen.

'Mission accomplished, I see.' She smiles widely and draws her son in for a hug.

Something tugs in me and I push it away. After my mother died, I avoided any kind of affection. The memory of my own mother's hugs was too raw.

Ryen untangles himself from his mother's embrace and waves the others out of the car. The weapons are no longer raised, so any threat seems to have passed as the others join us.

'So, you went for one and came back with four?'

'It got complicated. There was nothing else I could do.'

'Hmmm. Your father will not be pleased.'

'He's here?' Ryen looks around.

'He is, and he's looking forward to a report from you. Bring your friends. I'll have someone hide the vehicle.'

She turns and we have no choice but to follow her.

Chapter 58

Kerina

Inside the underground labyrinth, there seems to be no order to the laneway of passages and rooms that have been built within it. People are gathered near the front entrance, watching the newly arrived visitors with interest. I follow behind Ryen. Some parts of the cave are so low that even I have to duck. I turn back to see how Saxon and Elgee are coping. Both are nearly doubled over.

Voices travel down the hallway, and soon our group emerges into a common area. It's a surprisingly large space filled with people. The first thing I notice are the marks around their necks. People once wore these inked drawings on their skins with pride. Some covered a small part of their body, others entire parts of skin.

The tattoos mark their neck like a necklace surrounding the décolletage.

'So that's what you meant by hard to tell?' I say.

The chatter stops one by one as the inhabitants of Shirnaka notice the guests. All eyes turn toward us, staring, waiting. I reach for my own necklace, wishing I had hidden it. It seems out of place to wear here.

An old man walks toward us with a grin spread from ear to ear.

'Rudolph?' cries Saxon. 'What are you doing here?'

I watch as confusion sweeps across Saxon's face. Perhaps I should have told him the truth about Ryen. Rudolph envelops Saxon with his hug and pounds him on the back with affection.

'So good to see you. You had me worried there for a moment

when you took off like that. Worried me more when I learnt they had arrested you!'

'What are you doing here, Rudolph?' Saxon grips the old man at the top of the arms, as if he might disappear if he lets go.

'There's plenty of time to explain. Ahh, here he is.' Rudolph reaches for Ryen. 'Outstanding job, well done.'

Ryen grips the old man's hand. There is pride on both men's faces from those four words.

'Saxon, I see you've already met my son,' says Rudolph.

Saxon appears to choke on the words. 'You can't be serious!'

Ryen has the decency to look away at the revelation.

'I've never lied to you,' says Rudolph.

'Well, you sure as hell haven't told me the truth either.'

'Come. There's plenty of time to talk later, but first you need to rest. Get cleaned up and then get some nutrients into you.'

Saxon looks back at me. I nod and follow behind him. As we pass through the crowd, they step apart to make room, not particularly bothered by this new group. Perhaps they are used to newcomers, or maybe they are just welcoming of their own kind.

A young boy tugs on my hand. Tight curled hair springs from his scalp. 'Are you the chosen one to help us?'

The boy's mother ushers him away before I can ask him what he means. He must be mistaken. I'm no leader. I can barely make sense of my own situation, let alone help others. A low hum spreads through the crowd. Some high murmurings join in and before long a melody plays out for all to enjoy. No words, just musical harmony by humming.

Rudolph turns back to face me. 'That is the rhythm of the future. That's what they believe you to be.'

'Me? How can I be that person?'

'There's no mistake, Kerina. I know the facts of who you are.'

'Who am I?'

'The Okodee leader. Now and into the future.'

Chapter 59

I roll over in the hard bed and reflect on the eve before. The community of Shirnaka were hospitable but distant. There were lots of weary faces and furtive glances, and few made any attempt to speak with us. The only one readily accepted into the fold was Ryen. His status in Shirnaka must be significant. Men and women approached him to speak, some for lengthy conversation, others seeking just a moment of his time. Most just shook his hand and congratulated him on his safe return.

There was some unexpected celebration with the meal, though. A sweet liquid treat, rarely drank, except on special occasions. Rudolph declared the group's arrival to be a momentous event worth celebrating. Young and old enjoyed the dark, rich drink. I had tasted it twice before. The last time was at Manny and Constance's commitment ceremony. The time before was my parents' funeral. Rudolph provided the drink both times.

I had no chance to speak with Rudolph before he retired for the eve. The old man was welcoming, but guarded. Something has shifted in our relationship. I once had complete trust in my father's best friend, but now, something grates from within. It's obvious that Rudolph is held in high regard at Shirnaka. As well as speaking with Ryen, many sought out Rudolph to speak with. Time and time again I observed the old man with head hunched, deep in conversation with another.

If he wasn't speaking with people, then his affection lay with Ryen's mother, Larinda. Another mystery. I have not known

Rudolph to ever have a love interest. Rudolph's never spoken of romantic gestures or tales of a broken heart, yet here in Shirnaka, it is no secret he loves her dearly.

I dress quickly and neaten the space in the room. Elgee snores loudly with one leg hanging from the bed. Like me, his height makes it difficult to sleep in small spaces, but even that can't stop Elgee from his slumber. I creep out of the room and make my way along the narrow alcove.

'Saxon! Good morn to you. I was just coming to find you.'

I shake Rudolph's offered hand. 'We have much to discuss, old man.'

I follow him through the narrow corridors of the underground cave structure. I haven't been this way yet. Rudolph directs me to a room.

'Sit down,' he directs, before seating himself behind a makeshift desk.

I sit opposite with legs wide and hands gripped. 'I'm not sure where to start with my questions.'

'Why don't I begin?' Without waiting, Rudolph continues. 'First, you must understand that my life in Shirnaka has been hard to keep a secret from you. Many times over the years, I have wanted to tell you boys, but there was no need. In fact, to do so might have attracted danger for you both.

'Your parents knew my sister Shianne. They also knew of my vendetta against those who took her. I never gave them details and they never asked. Shayne, your father, often warned me against my crusade. But I took no notice and told him little, until the night he came to me with information about a newborn baby, marked with Okodee. That's when your parents first came to understand the dangers of being associated with Okodee and the lengths those in power will go to hide their existence.'

I let this new information sink in. I've always known Rudolph to be secretive, so it shouldn't surprise me, but I can't help feeling betrayed.

'You could have confided in us, Rudolph.'

'It was best this way.'

I lean forward. 'I have a question for you then. Will you answer it truthfully?'

'Anything. I will not keep secrets from you from now on.'

'What happened to your sister?'

The old man's face crumples with despair. 'That is the one question I have no answer for and have searched for all these years.'

Chapter 60

Kerina

I wake early and wander the quiet corridors of the underground dwelling. They are mostly deserted for this time of day. I need some fresh air, so I return the way we entered yesterday. I manage to locate the doorway, hoping to step outside again, if only for a short time.

'What are you doing?'

I turn in fright at the harsh voice. 'I just wanted some fresh air.'

The voice belongs to a lady. One eye is shut, the other is wide and staring. The skin surrounding the closed eye reminds me of melted candle wax.

'It was burnt off,' she says.

'I didn't mean to stare.'

The working eye runs its gaze up and down my body, assessing me. Taking in everything about me. I stand straight and try not to be intimidated.

The woman steps closer. 'Rudolph called you the Okodee leader. You look like a confused young girl to me.' She turns and walks away, leaving me uncomfortable and disheartened, as though I have failed before I've even begun.

I push the door open. No alarms ring out and no security guard rush toward me. I simply step outside and feel the warmth of the early morning sun on my skin. I check the door, making sure I can get back into the cave before letting it close behind me. I sit on the ground, legs curled up with my chin resting on my knees. I stay that way for a while, taking in the wide, barren land before me. I listen to Rudolph's words from last night. *'Okodee leader. Now and into the future.'*

Surely the old man is mistaken. Why would he think such a thing? But as much as I want to refute it, pieces of the puzzle fall into place. My parents' deaths, Lariel and I being taken, my considerable value compared to hers. I am still confused by my dreams and returned memories. I doubt I will ever know for sure the fact from the fiction. I need to speak with Rudolph to learn more.

I hurry back inside and ask for directions to where I might find him. A kind, elderly gentleman points me in the direction of Rudolph's private chambers.

'Come in,' Rudolph responds to my knock.

I enter the room tentatively. 'I'm sorry to disturb you—'

'Nonsense, come in! I just finished speaking with Saxon a while ago. It must be the morning for explanations. I imagine you have many questions for me?'

His tone is understanding, concerned. I look around his chambers, my body tense.

'I see you managed to hang on to that locket,' he says, looking over the top of his glasses.

I grip it protectively.

'A local jeweller here in Shirnaka created it. Have you found its secret message?'

I nod. 'But I don't understand its meaning.'

'Time lost, time true. Now is the time to do. Are you sure it makes no sense to you?'

I consider the words, knowing he understands them perfectly. After his announcement last night, they make more sense, although I don't have the courage to agree with them yet.

'You think I'm the Okodee leader. You think it's the right time for me to step up and lead.'

'I am certain. Any longer and we might miss our chance.'

'But what if I don't want to? What if my destiny is not what you say?'

'Kerina, we can't delay it any longer. You need to bring the communities together and help educate those who have been told lies. But most importantly, you have to stop those who mean the Okodee people harm.'

I wish Rudolph would stop calling me a leader. I don't feel like one.

'You are the rightful leader, Kerina, you'll see. But only you can choose your destiny.'

Chapter 61

Saxon

I wander the corridors aimlessly. My head swarms with all the new information. One thing is certain, Rudolph is not the man I thought he was. The man has a whole other life that I knew nothing about. Rudolph claims Manny doesn't know about any of this, but is that the truth? Manny kept our parents' death a secret at Rudolph's command. What else has my brother stayed silent about?

I come to the end of the corridor, where a ladder leads upward. I climb the ladder for several metres, unsure where it will take me. It's difficult to climb, with little room to bend my legs or arms. As I near the top, I work out I have just climbed a ventilation shaft, a simple and old-fashioned way to let fresh air into the underground dwellings.

I poke my head out the top and the crisp, fresh air hits my face. The effort from climbing has left me breathless. The land stretches out around me as I take in the view. The stacks of pebbles are scattered about like a dot-to-dot puzzle from this aerial position. Across the horizon, the last rays of the sun set. Faint shades of pink spread across the sky, mixed with swirls of purple. My thoughts drift to Kerina, and I find myself wishing she were here to watch the phenomenon. How many sunsets did she miss in captivity?

After a while, I make my way back down the ladder. My feet barely fit on the rungs. Going down is even more difficult than going up. Finally, my feet hit the solid ground. I look up and the distance makes me dizzy. I turn to walk back to my room and collide with a solid figure.

'Saxon! What are you doing here?' Ryen looks up the shaft.

'Just checking out the view.'

We both stand awkwardly.

'Why didn't you tell me Rudolph was your father?'

Ryen shrugs. 'It was nice not sharing something with you for once.'

'What are you talking about?'

'My whole life I've known about you and Manny. I've heard so many stories about the two of you through Rudolph.' He laughs. 'You'd be surprised what I know.'

'So, you know more about me than I know about you, so what?'

'It's not that. Don't you see? I've always had to share you with him, and I *hated* it. Do you have any idea what it must feel like to a little boy who just wants to see his dad? All the while knowing it's impossible.'

'Of course, I know exactly what it feels like, Ryen. My father is *dead,* so it really is impossible. What I don't understand is why Rudolph kept you a secret.'

'He was protecting you.'

'From what?'

'From the same fate of your parents.'

I grip Ryen by the throat. 'Don't speak about my mother and father like you know anything about them.'

Ryen wrestles against my hand. 'But I do know. I'm probably the only one who knows the whole truth.' His face grows redder.

I shove him against the wall. 'If you're lying to me, I'll break your neck.'

'You don't trust me, I get it. But I will not lie to you, I promise.'

I release my grip and step back. Ryen rubs at his neck and

the colour returns to normal. He steps toward me, but I hold my ground.

'You went to Middtown to get answers about your parents' murder, didn't you?'

I nod. 'They were trustworthy, both handpicked by the Primo Dictor to work for him. They were law-abiding and had a high standing in our community. So why were they killed? It makes no sense.'

'Imagine this. Your father was the head chef for the Primo Dictor's most important functions. Shayne would have overheard many conversations. After a while he starts putting things together. Meanwhile, your mother has access to all parts of the house when caring for the children. Marlene starts snooping for your father and discovers something.'

A picture forms in my mind as I try to put the pieces together.

'My parents found out something important that got them both killed.'

Ryen nods. 'Now you're putting the pieces together. Unfortunately, there is even more to this twisted story.'

My mind spins from what Ryen has told me. My parents uncovered something huge. A secret that got them murdered. What was it?

Chapter 62

Kerina

I lie on the bed, alone in the room I share with Lariel. I want to gather my thoughts before I venture out to meet anyone else. Lariel on the other hand couldn't wait to go and speak with everyone. She is confident these people will help reunite her with her father. I don't have such a possibility. I remove the ruby locket. There is no other feature on it besides the red stone. I hold it close to her eye and read the magnified message. *'Time lost, time true. Now is the time to do.'*

Could Rudolph be right? Am I meant to be a leader? There is so much more I need to know first, and I'm not going to learn it sitting around here.

I cross the room and follow the hallway toward the common room. Inside, I search for a familiar face. Lariel is immersed in conversation with an older lady. The woman turns toward me, one eye melted closed, one open. It makes sense Lariel would speak with a woman who suffered the same fate as her father.

Elgee has also fit in well. He stands across the other side of the room, laughing and joking with a small group around him. I sweep the room once more, but Saxon is nowhere to be found.

'So, you're the one Ryen has been searching for?'

An older girl stands before me. Her neck has red flowers creeping up the edge and around her throat. Her dark eyes are piercing.

'I'm Kerina. And you are?'

'Vera.'

'You don't seem happy about Ryen finding me.'

A long-painted nail twirls in circles near my face. 'I don't believe you're the wow factor we need.'

'Are you always so friendly?' I swat Vera's hand away.

'I'm in a particularly good mood today.' Vera kicks out a chair. 'You wanna sit down?'

I don't, but I sink down anyway, resting one foot on the seat.

'Have you grown up here?' I ask Vera.

'More or less.' Her response is evasive and we both know it.

I look around. 'How many people live here?'

'A few hundred. Most have heard about us and found their way here. Some were born here. Others, like you, have been rescued and brought here.'

Elgee wanders across to join us.

Vera's long nail reappears and twirls toward him. 'This one has to be a sympathiser.'

'What's that mean?'

'It means you're not Okodee, but you're on our side.'

'Lady, I was just goin' on a road trip and now I'm here.'

'So which side are you on?'

'Is this a test?' His eyes narrow.

'He's on our side,' I say. 'Give him a break.'

'I'm not going to tiptoe around something that might make others uncomfortable.'

'I ain't uncomfortable,' says Elgee, leaning toward Vera.

'Good, because we're sick of hiding. It's not our fault we were born with *additional abilities.*'

'If there are so many of you, how come nobody knows nuthin' about you more than whispers?' asks Elgee.

'People fear the unknown. They don't want to believe in anything out of the ordinary, so they trust those in authority who tell them what to believe.'

'There is authority everywhere, even here,' I say. 'It can't be avoided.'

'No, but it can be bought. And that's where the problem *out there* lies.'

Chapter 63

'What's with all the secrecy?' I ask, following Ryen. 'I thought everyone here was on the same side.'

'We are, but we're still human. There is a lot of temptation for someone to share our knowledge with the outside world.'

'You think somebody is feeding outsiders info?'

'I have my suspicions. Obviously, we stay here as much as we can, but there are times when a convoy is sent out to gather intel on the situation.'

'What exactly is the situation?'

'You really have no idea, do you?'

'You keep speaking in riddles, so no.'

Ryen unlocks the door to another room and ushers me inside. Shelves run along one wall. He pulls out a tray and withdraws a folder, then passes it across. I open the folder and pull out the sheets inside. *TAMBLER, Ryen* heads each sheet. Ryen steps back, allowing me some space to read the information. It's his family tree. Ryen's name sits at the top. His parents' names sit below: Rudolph and Larinda. Other names flow from each parent. Rudolph lists his sister. Shianne and Ryen both have the Okodee symbol beside their names.

I look up. 'Is this true?'

Ryen nods.

'But how could you be an Agent knowing what they might do to you?'

'I had a role to play and I played it well. Nobody suspected a thing. It was actually very easy to do. It's all just smoke and mirrors anyway. If you show confidence, Saxon, nobody will second guess you.'

'But what about your mark? How do you keep it hidden?'

Ryen turns around and removes his shirt. His entire back is decorated in intricate detail.

The centrepiece is a mandala shape with vines creeping up to his neck, concealing his mark.

'It was all or nothing so nobody would suspect anything.'

'That's quite the cover-up,' I say.

'Tattoos were once commonplace, so nobody really cares.'

I sit down at the table and look at the folder again.

'We've begun to develop a theory. These records have helped us find a pattern for why some people are Okodee and some aren't.'

'What's the theory?'

'We already know that government scientists were conducting tests. These tests started a long time ago. The data has been used to help understand perceptions of those born Okodee.'

'And what are those perceptions?'

Ryen laughs. 'Most people think the story is a myth. A fairy tale if you like. Humans with abilities that nobody else has.'

'You keep saying abilities, but what exactly do you mean?' I interrupt.

'You saw how quickly Kerina recovered after you found her.'

'We gave her extra nutrient packs, but yeah, it was quick.'

'You've seen how quickly she healed when she was shot.'

Saxon nods, unable to refute the evidence.

'There are other abilities as well. Little food and water to survive harsh conditions. Tests have been conducted on those who choose to volunteer.'

'Did you volunteer?'

Ryen grins. 'Of course, several times.'

I imagine what those tests entailed, and I can't help but have a grudging admiration for Ryen.

'It's the records that allow us to keep track of the abilities, Saxon. They even allow us to make connections between relatives.'

'But how? How did these changes evolve?'

'After the Burn, humans got sick. They were starving and dying by the thousands. The government employed scientists to look for a way to make humans stronger and more adaptable to the new world. They had created vaccines in the past to ward off disease. Why not vaccines to increase abilities?'

'Okodee,' I whisper, finally understanding.

Chapter 64

Kerina

'We found five more. Didn't even know what was so special about them until we picked them up.'

'You're sure?'

'Yeah, we checked for marks. Some were faint, but they were there. We'll know for sure tomorrow. One got stabbed trying to run away.'

'Damn it! They're not supposed to be damaged before they get here.'

'They'll be fixed up before the buyers arrive.'

'They better. It's getting harder to find buyers. People are starting to talk more. They're even getting sympathisers.'

'We'll just keep searching. Up the rewards for those we know support our efforts and enjoy some extra financial rewards on the side. You worry too much.'

'I'm right to worry. You should do more of it instead of drinking your payments away.'

I sit up and wipe the sweat dripping from my forehead. It's stuffy in the room with no window to open for fresh air. It might take me some time to get used to living below the ground.

A quiet snore rumbles from Lariel, oblivious to my bad dream. I tiptoe toward the door, careful not to disturb her. Once in the passage, I walk in the direction of the common area. The room is deserted at this early hour. I continue walking to see where it takes me. Hopefully, I will find my way back in the dark. There are so many bunkers and narrow pathways down here.

A figure emerges ahead. They are tall like Saxon, but I don't call out. Instead, I follow them. I keep my tread light and walk faster. The figure carries a torch with them. It illuminates their face as they turn the corner. Ryen.

'About time.' A female voice cuts through the silence.

'Patience, Vera. You should learn some.'

I slow down and keep hidden in the dark.

'I've been patient for months! While you've been off playing Agent, I've been stuck here. I was just about to rip somebody's eyelids off when you finally came back.'

'I'm here now, but you still have to be patient a little longer.'

'Why? What's the plan now?'

'It hasn't changed, although Saxon is an addition I had not expected.'

'Underestimated, you mean. I've seen the way he looks at Kerina. He'll not let her go quietly, especially at your command.'

'He will and he must if we are to succeed.'

'Succeed at what?' I step around the corner.

Ryen shines the light in my face before lowering it.

Vera glares at me, hands on hip. 'Speaking of underestimating.'

I lock eyes with Ryen. My instinct had told me to trust him, but now I'm not so sure.

'I asked you a question. Succeed at what, Ryen?'

He scratches his head and sighs.

'She might as well know,' says Vera.

'We need to succeed at two things. Exposing the runners and integrating Okodee people into the community.'

'The runners?'

'They are the ones who hold the power to enflame people's fears. They are the ones who most likely took you …' he glances at Vera, 'and many others for payment.'

I look grim. 'Slave runners.'

Chapter 65

Saxon

'Elgee? Are you awake?'

A groan from the other bed emerges. 'I was havin' the most bea-u-tiful dream. What yer gotta wake me up for?'

I laugh. 'Which girl did it involve?'

'I ain't sharing nothin' till yer tell me where *you* disappeared to last night.'

'Did you miss me?'

'Nope. But I did notice another little lady whose head kept swivelling left and right each time somebody walked into the room.'

I sit up straight. 'Kerina?'

Elgee laughs. 'Oooh, you got it bad for dat one.'

'No, I don't, it's just—'

'Don't start tellin' me lies. I ain't ever seen you so fixed on someone before.'

I throw the pillow at Elgee.

'Oomph,' he groans, blocking the throw.

'Elgee, can Okodee even be with, I mean, are they supposed to … is there a rule?'

Elgee throws the pillow back at me. 'They ain't from another planet, yer tinker. There's no rules who you can and can't fall in love with.'

'I ain't in love with her,' I mumble.

Elgee swings his long legs out of bed. 'Whatever, let's get back to where you disappeared to last night.'

I stand up and scratch my head. 'Ryen showed me their record room. It lists all the people they think are Okodee and why.'

'Like a family tree?'

'Yeah, sort of. He, ahh … he also said he knows why my parents were killed.'

'That's pretty serious. Did he tell yer why?'

I shake my head. 'He says I'll work it out in my own time.'

'Dat's crazy. Why can't he just tell yer?'

I shrug. 'I know I set off to find answers, but the closer I get and the more I learn, well, I'm not sure I'm ready for the truth.'

Elgee walks toward me and offers his hand. 'Come on. Let's go hang with the residents of Shirnaka. See if we can't learn something else dat might be useful.'

A small gathering has formed in the middle of the common room, surrounding the couches.

Elgee pushes me forward and the people in the front separate, making room for us. Rudolph lies motionless on the couch. His face is sunken on one side and his skin is grey.

I rush toward him. 'What happened?'

'Think it might be a stroke,' says Vera.

Ryen holds his father's hand. Rudolph grunts and growls until I move forward, reaching for his hand. Ryen and I lean on either side of the old man.

'Not long … for this world … now,' he grunts.

'You hang in there, Rudolph. You're strong,' I say.

Rudolph growls. 'Trust Ryen … like you do me.'

I look at Rudolph's son, still unable to believe I never knew he existed.

'Kerina … is the key. You boys protect her … she's the one we need.'

Ryen stares at Rudolph with determination clear on his face, a burning defiance. 'I'll protect her, Father, I promise you that.' He looks to me expectantly.

I nod my head. 'We'll both look after her, Rudolph.'

The old man clutches both our hands together. His final act to unify the two of us.

Chapter 66

Kerina

I walk into the common space to find people embracing and muffled sobs. I look around, trying to work out what's happened. Two faces stand out to me: Saxon and Ryen. Between them lies Rudolph, his face at a strange angle, unmoving. Ryen's mother pushes past me into the common area.

'Where is he?' she screams.

'Mother!' Ryen walks toward her.

Larinda pushes him aside and dives toward the figure on the couch. Wails of grief fill every area of the room. Ryen stands behind her, his hand resting on her back, supporting her. Saxon watches on, fists clenched. Emotions fight for control across his face. I move toward him and gently lead him away from the scene of sorrow.

I find a quiet alcove and turn to face Saxon.

'I can't believe it,' he says. 'He was like a father to me and now he's gone.'

Grief overwhelms him, and he crumples into himself. I support him as best I can while he weeps for the strange old man. The revelations of the last few days must have been hard for Saxon, especially learning that Rudolph led a life that included having a son. I try to comfort him by holding him tightly.

Eventually, his emotions subside and he releases his grip, but not his hold. His distraught eyes search mine. His kiss is quick and I wonder for a moment if I imagined it.

'I'm sorry. I shouldn't have done that,' he says.

My chest rises and falls as nerves flutter through my body. 'Life is short. If today has taught us anything, it is that.'

'You never know what's around the corner,' says Saxon.

Slowly he inches his mouth closer to mine. I move toward him, granting permission. Our lips meet. The touch is so light yet the pressure is more intense than anything I have felt before. Emotions rush through me as Saxon wraps his arms around and draws me closer. I melt against him. His mouth urges my lips apart, again and again. Then for some reason he stops. His breath ragged.

I entwine my fingers in his hair. 'That was … new. For me.'

'That was … perfect. For me.'

He draws me in toward him and hugs me tight.

'I'm sorry about your friend,' I murmur in his ear. 'Rudolph was a kind and compassionate man.'

'He was both those things and more. I admired him so much.'

Saxon releases me and steps back to create some space. 'I loved his stories and even though it turns out I *didn't* know everything about him, he was always there for Manny and me, especially when it counted.'

'He must have had his reasons for keeping you in the dark about things.'

'Hopefully Ryen will shed more light on that. Rudolph said it was to protect us, but I'm not sure.'

'You still don't like Ryen, do you?'

Saxon crosses his arms. 'You seem to like him, and Rudolph was his father so he must be trustworthy but … I don't know. There's just something about him that grates on me.'

I smile. 'I think you have more in common than you care to admit.'

'What's that?'

'Jealousy.'

'That's stupid,' says Saxon.

'Both of you are jealous of the other for sharing Rudolph in different ways. You both have memories of him, but they are for different reasons. It's not stupid, Saxon, it's understandable. Perhaps one day you can share those memories together.'

Chapter 67

Saxon

The memorial for Rudolph is short but sentimental. Such an elusive figure, it turns out, but a man of great knowledge and power. I walk to where everyone is gathered in the common room.

'It seems you'll take up Rudolph's position as the new leader here,' I say to Ryen.

'Yes, but my mother will take care of things when we leave.'

'We? Where are we going?'

'We can discuss it at the meeting. Follow me.' Ryen leads us through an intricate maze of passageways before directing us into a room. I roll the door closed behind us.

'Thank you all for coming,' he begins.

'Let's cut the formalities and get on with it,' says Vera.

'What yer want with all of us?' says Elgee. 'We're caught up in this world of yours now.'

'Rudolph made sure your families were safe before he left Nevertyre,' says Ryen.

'Yeah, but it seems we can't go home yet, so what we doin' here wif you?'

'It's simple. We need Kerina. She is the key to everything.'

'I told you that you were the one they wanted,' says Lariel. 'You are the most valuable.'

'But why? I don't understand what's so important about me.'

'Years ago, genetic tests were conducted to create a stronger mankind. We had to become a more resistant human race. Samples were taken from many people. Most were willing, but not all.

The government created a vaccine of sorts to inject into newborn babies. It was found these babies resisted sickness, healed quicker, and required less nutrients and water. As they grew, they could last days and even weeks on very little. But what the government didn't think about was the greed humans can succumb to. A black market was created and Okodee born are valuable to this market. They are being captured and sold off. The birthmark makes them easy to distinguish. They can work tirelessly, even with punishment, because they heal so well. It seems adolescence is the optimal age for when the vaccine works best. It is also when their physical strength peaks.'

'Wait a minute. You're saying there's a slave trade with Okodee people?' I say.

'That's exactly what he's saying, and the government hasn't done a thing to stop it,' says Vera.

'But if the vaccine works so well, why don't they make more and give it to everyone?' asks Lariel.

'A fire destroyed the vaccine and all records of its creation, along with the team of creators. The government tried to cover up the fire by saying the trials had failed. They were embarrassed because decades of work had been destroyed with no way to recover the information,' says Ryen. 'They stopped administering the vaccines after that, except that didn't work either.'

'What do you mean that didn't work? It's a vaccine,' says Kerina. 'It wears off.'

'It seems the vaccine worked so well that those injected with it could produce offspring with the same characteristics,' says Ryen. 'It's evolution at its greatest. Mankind fighting back against Mother Nature, who fought back against mankind. It's actually quite brilliant.'

'You sounded just like Rudolph then,' I say quietly.

'He was the one who started putting the pieces together. He was a scientist for the government and studied their trials. He knew that there was talk surrounding the fire and whispers of a cover-up. He realised the possibility one day when the previous Primo Dictor's nanny came to him with a problem. The newborn granddaughter was marked. Of course, the Primo Dictor vaccinated his own son to prove it was safe. This vaccine was passed down genetically from father to daughter. It made Rudolph understand the potential of producing offspring with already modified DNA.

'The son was not yet Primo Dictor, but he would be one day. He became terrified for his child. He wasn't to know his father would only rule for a few more years. He did know what might be in store for his daughter and the government should anyone find out. The vaccine had stopped being administered twenty years before. His father's government had already created an elaborate web of lies to cover up the fire and inability to reproduce the vaccine. But rumours were spreading about the Okodee and the possibility of their evolution. So, he gave the baby to the nanny to find a home for her. Somewhere to keep her safe until he decided how to proceed.'

'The nanny knew of such a family?' says Lariel.

'The nanny knew Rudolph could find one,' says Ryen.

'And the nanny was trustworthy?' I ask.

'Of course! Rudolph trusted her completely. She was, after all, his best friend's wife.'

Chapter 68

Kerina

Three things happen simultaneously. Saxon understands why his parents were killed. Ryen readies himself for an attack from Saxon. And my head feels like it might explode with the sound of a thousand drums thumping in my mind. I grip the side and scream from the pressure. My ears, my eyes, my head. A screaming from afar, yet so close. Me. People moving in slow motion. Strange colours. As though I am underwater. My vision blurs, noise around me fades, and my legs collapse.

'Hello, Kerina,' says the nice lady.

'She's getting so big,' says my mother.

'Yes, almost as big as my son, Saxon. He is a similar age.'

I look up into the green eyes of this woman.

'I brought this for you.' The lady hands me a silver locket. 'You must wear it always.'

The two women exchange a look.

'It's from Rudolph,' the lady mumbles.

'Can I keep it, Mother?' I ask.

My mother kneels on the ground, making her the same height as me. 'Of course! It's a very special gift.'

The nice lady bends down and hangs the heart around my neck. 'You must wear it always and keep it safe. Guard it with your life.'

I look down at the ruby stone sitting in the middle of the locket. 'It's beautiful,' I say.

'Just like you.' She taps me on the nose.

I awaken and snatch for my necklace. The cold surface makes

me sigh with relief.

'How do you feel?' Lariel asks.

I find myself back in the bedroom.

'How long was I out?'

'You fainted. Elgee caught you and carried you back here.'

'It's been a few hours,' says Ryen, moving into my view.

'My head was pounding. It felt like it was being hammered from the inside.'

'It's okay. Keep resting,' says Lariel.

Saxon leans against the wall, not looking at me. I force myself to sit up.

'You knew!' I accuse Ryen. 'All along you knew and you didn't say anything.'

'You had to put it together by yourself. It was the only way you would believe.'

I stand up. My headache is gone and my mind is clear. My mission is obvious.

'I am the granddaughter, aren't I? My father is the current Primo Dictor.'

Ryen doesn't move a muscle.

'Rudolph arranged it, and Saxon's mother took me to my new parents. Sympathisers.'

This time he nods.

I grip the locket between my fingers. 'When my head felt like it was going to explode, memories flooded back. I remembered your mother, Saxon. You have her eyes.'

His head turns toward me sharply.

'She brought me this gift. She put this locket on me and told me to guard it with my life. There is a message on the inside. It didn't make sense when I first read it, but it does now.'

'What does it say?' asks Lariel.

'*Time lost, time true. Now is the time to do.*'

'And are you ready, Kerina?' asks Ryen. 'Ready to do? To lead?'

I turn to Saxon for support, but find only contempt in his eyes.

He pushes off the wall. 'My parents' deaths were PED, Public Enemy Directive. Only someone with great power could order such a thing. Someone that could create a plausible cover-up. It didn't make sense before, but now it does. My parents were killed … because of you.' He storms out of the room.

Chapter 69

Saxon

The underground space is crushing me, I can barely breathe. The walls shrink inward and I can't get enough air into my lungs. I push past anyone in the way.

'Watch it,' they shout after me.

I take no notice of them as I stomp along the passageway. After a while I find myself at the base of the ladder. I know the narrow opening above will lead me outside and that's exactly where I need to be, outside and alone. I lift one foot after the other and make my way up the rungs. I heave and puff my way to the top. By the time I burst through the opening, I can contain myself no longer. I roar to the open, empty landscape. I release rage, hurt, frustration, and disappointment into the invisible air. I continue screaming until my throat becomes raw. I collapse, angry and broken about my murdered parents.

Now I have answers about their death, but no evidence to prove who murdered them. Anastasia said it was a Public Enemy Directive. That can only mean one thing. The grandfather found out that the baby survived. He must have wanted to ensure my parents remained silent. Or perhaps Kerina's father was covering his tracks? Making sure there were no witnesses to Kerina's existence.

I pull myself through the hole completely and curl myself up on the flat landing. My mind jumps back and forth. Kerina is alive because of my parents. My parents are dead because of Kerina.

Footsteps echo up the narrow ventilation shaft. Someone has

followed me, and I don't need to guess who. Ryen pokes his head through the hole.

'If you don't mind, I'd rather be alone,' I say through gritted teeth.

'I do mind, because you acted like a tinker back there.'

Ryen pulls himself through the hole. He tries to give me some space, but there is not much room. Instead, I stand and move away, as far as the ledge will allow me.

'It's not Kerina's fault,' Ryen says quietly.

'I know that.' I kick at the surface. 'I just need some time.'

'We don't have the luxury of time. I need your whole mind focused on what is ahead.'

I sigh, knowing what he says is true. If we are to act, then it needs to be now. People are already chasing Kerina, and now Ryen's cover has been blown they will be after him as well.

'Ryen, when you were younger and Rudolph came to stay here, how did you feel?'

'Exhilarated!' His face softens. 'It was exciting to have him around. He would give me his undivided attention. Sometimes he would stay for days, sometimes it would be weeks. I hated when it was time for him to go. Months could pass between his visits.'

I sit down beside Ryen. 'I had that same feeling with my father. He worked long hours, so when I had his attention, I savoured it for the long droughts in between.'

'It was addictive,' says Ryen.

'Yes. The difference between us is that I only had that for eight years. The drought has been long and I am thirsty for something I will never have again.'

'I understand.' Ryen pats my back. 'But you only have tonight to get it together.'

He disappears down the hole, leaving me to my own thoughts.

I know my reaction was unreasonable. Only two days ago, I was crushing Kerina with my lips, and yet earlier I wanted to squeeze her neck with my hands. It's this anger that scares me the most.

Anger is what got me into many scrapes and fights growing up. I work hard to keep it under control and I can't lose my way here.

I lean back and watch the colours dance across the sky as the sun sets once again. The cold has already started to creep in. Soon the desert temperature will plummet, but for now I'll sit and remember my parents. Hopefully, the memories will help remind me of the goodness in people. That's why my mother would have helped with the baby. She had a kind heart and would never turn anyone away. She could never have known there would be such devastating consequences.

Chapter 70

Kerina

I pace the room as the revelations from earlier spin around inside my mind. I haven't seen Saxon since he stormed out last night. Ryen assures me he just needs some space and that he will come around soon, but I'm not so sure.

'My parents were killed … because of you.'

The guilt boils up and makes me want to vomit.

I can't even begin to grasp the fact that I am the heir to Middtown. My biological father is the Primo Dictor. He took over when his father died several years ago. My father is responsible for ruling the communities and leading the Dictors who govern in his absence. They must do as he directs. That is now my birthright.

There is a knock on the door. 'Come in.'

Vera stands awkwardly in the doorway. 'I'm not good with girl talk.'

'Did Ryen send you to keep an eye on me?'

'No!' Vera crosses her arms. 'Nobody tells me what to do.'

'Has that always been the way?' I sense a change in tension, but don't let it go. 'You were captured once, weren't you?'

Faster than I think is possible, Vera is on top of me. She has me pinned to the bed with a knife at my throat.

'Don't *ever* presume to know anything about me.'

I push back against Vera's forearm. 'Why? Scared somebody might start to care about you?'

The blade pushes against my neck as Vera seems to battle with the demons inside her head. Her rose tattoo creeps around her neck and licks the edge of her chin.

Suddenly Vera grins. 'You might just be worth all this effort after all.'

She climbs off me and offers her hand, pulling me from the bed. We stand eye to eye.

'I was taken and enslaved and they worked me until I collapsed every day. Then they beat the crap out of me for fun when they had too much to drink. I promised myself revenge and escape as soon as I had the chance.'

'Did you get your revenge?'

Vera runs the knife down my cheek and along my neck. 'I'm standing here, aren't I?' She winks and clips her knife away. She lies on the bed, making herself comfortable.

'You don't have to stay with me,' I say. 'I don't need a babysitter.'

'I know that, and just so you know, I'm not staying because I like you.'

I sit on the edge of the bed. 'That's good, because I don't like you much either.'

Vera laughs. 'Then this should work out fine.'

I nod, accepting Vera's twisted offer of friendship.

'So how do you feel knowing your daddy is the Primo Dictor?'

'It makes sense now, all the lessons and secrecy growing up. My father, that is, the man who raised me, taught me things like self-defence and how to shoot.'

'It's nice that he cared. My father taught me to how to fight as well. He beat his wife and kids every chance he got. Fighting's all I know,' says Vera.

I'm sure Vera doesn't share this information for sympathy, so I don't offer any.

'It was the Dictor of Middtown's wife.' Lariel's overheard conversation resurfaces.

'It can't be true.' I jump to my feet. 'I think I know who has been sending people to capture me.'

'Who?'

'The Governess. My biological mother.'

Chapter 71

Saxon

'W e're meeting in ten minutes,' says Vera. 'Don't be late.'
I roll my eyes. 'She's even bossier than Constance.'
'I like a girl with spirit,' says Elgee.
I punch him in the arm. 'You like *any* girl.'
'Speaking of girls … have yer spoken to Kerina?'
I shake my head. 'Doubt she'll want to speak to me after what I said.'
'Trust me, mah friend, she'll understand.'
'Perhaps. Come on, let's go, or Vera will be back to round us up.'
Elgee follows me down the corridor to the meeting place. We squeeze into the small room. Elgee's legs take up most of the room on one bench. Lariel sits squashed beside him while Kerina stands opposite, avoiding my gaze. I try to concentrate on what Vera is saying.
'Kerina knows who ordered the people to capture and imprison her. She knows exactly who is trying to hunt her down.'
'Who?' says Ryen.
'You won't believe it. It's so simple and so damn obvious!' says Vera, shaking her head.
'Yer gonna keep us in suspense or tell us?' asks Elgee.
This time Kerina looks right at me.
'It's my mother. My *biological* mother.'
Silence surrounds the group for a moment before everyone talks at once. Kerina breaks her gaze from me.
'Quiet!' says Ryen.

The chatter stops abruptly.

'You're sure about this, Kerina?'

She nods. 'Lariel, do you remember the conversation you overhead?' Kerina asks. 'When you were last captured?'

Lariel gasps. 'The Dictor's wife, of course!'

'Do you want to share?' asks Ryen.

'The last time I was captured, when Kerina made it to Nevertyre, I heard a woman asking if the other one, meaning Kerina, had been captured.'

'You're sure it was the Primo Dictor's wife?'

'There's no doubt, unless there's more than one governess in Middtown.'

'She's making certain Kerina doesn't claim her right to govern,' says Vera. 'She wants her daughter dead.'

'But if she wanted me dead, I would be,' says Kerina.

I shake my head. 'You're right. She has the means and the power to kill. No, she must want something else.'

'But what else could she want from me?'

I pinch the bridge of my nose. 'Whatever she wants, it can't be good.'

'Then it's settled. We leave tonight,' says Ryen. 'The sooner we get back to Middtown, the better we can manage this.'

'Are you crazy? What do we want to go back there for?' I say.

'So, I can meet my biological father,' Kerina says simply.

I shake my head with fists clenched. 'I don't think that's a good idea. Not until we have a solid plan.'

Kerina returns a steely look. 'He helped me once. He'll do it again.'

Chapter 72

Kerina

We file out of the room and move in separate directions to pack. Ryen said to meet in the common room in two hours.

'I'll meet you there, I just want to see somebody,' says Lariel, veering off down a passageway.

I make my way along the narrow corridor, my mind a jumble of thoughts.

Somebody grabs my elbow. 'Can I speak with you in private?'

'Saxon, I don't think that's necessary.'

'Please, it's important.'

I shake his grip off. 'Fine. Follow me.'

I lead him back to my room. He hovers in the doorway.

'You better close that if you want privacy,' I say, standing opposite him.

He shuts it gently and turns back to face me. 'I'm sorry. I should never have said those things to you. I don't blame you for my parents' death.'

I cross my arms. 'Especially now you know who to blame?'

'Yeah, I mean no!'

I sigh. 'Don't worry about it, Saxon. Just forget it happened.'

'Kerina!' He steps toward me. 'I never meant to hurt you. I lashed out from the shock. It's no excuse, but I *do not* blame you, I promise. I care too much about you.'

I tug on my necklace. His eyes are pleading and his emotions raw, but I can't tell him what he wants to hear.

'It doesn't matter anyway,' I whisper, moving away.

'What do you mean?'

'It means I accept your apology, but I can't let feelings get in the way. None of it matters now because I need to focus on what's ahead.'

'Why? What do you plan on doing?'

'What I was born to do. Govern Middtown.'

Saxon raises his eyebrow. 'You want to be the next Primo Dictor?'

I stand straighter, taller. 'Saxon, I *will* be the next Primo Dictor. It's my birthright and the best thing for the Okodee people.'

'What about what's best for you?' He closes the space between us and tucks some hair behind my ear. His thumb lingers on my jawbone and strokes my cheek gently.

I fight every impulse in my body and refuse to respond to his caress. 'It. Doesn't. Matter.'

Saxon fights the emotions that seep across his face until a neutral expression settles. I waver slightly before removing his hand from my cheek. I step backward, away from him.

'Rudolph said I was the one meant to lead the Okodee. This is the best way to do it. If I'm in a position of power, I can educate opinions and rule fairly, but most importantly, I can hunt down those who break the law.'

His jaw is clenched and he nods curtly. 'I understand.' He turns and leaves me alone in the room.

I stagger back on to the bed and wrap my arms tight around my middle. I cannot afford to be swayed by my feelings for him, no matter how strong they are. If everything is true, I have a long battle ahead that will require all my attention. My father might have saved my life once, but he still owes me a lifetime of debt to make up for all I've been through. The first way to make up for it is to let me help govern.

There's only one true obstacle in my way. One dangerous enemy. My mother.

Chapter 73

Saxon

I shake the bag viciously and shove my clothes inside, along with the other few things I brought with me.

'What did that bag ever do to yer?' asks Elgee.

I ignore my friend and dump the bag on the ground.

'You talked with Kerina?'

I don't answer; instead I neaten up the room and make the bed.

'Saxon?'

'*What*?'

'Easy, mah friend.'

I kick the bed in frustration and sink down on it. 'Damn it! I'm sorry, Elgee. I ain't mad at you. I shouldn't be such a tinker.'

'You two have a lover's quarrel?'

I grunt. 'No quarrel … and no lovers, that's for sure.'

'What are yer talking about?'

'Kerina made it pretty clear that my feelings weren't … reciprocated.'

'Mmm hmm. Well, the girl has a lot on her mind. Maybe some time might help.'

I stand up. 'I appreciate what you're doing, Elgee, but time won't help. Unless it was going *back* in time.'

Elgee picks up my bag and passes it to me. He grips my shoulder. 'Come on then. Let's go see if we're ready to turn Middtown upside down.'

We meet the others in the common room. I shiver as I enter, making sure to move away from the couch where Rudolph died. I sit at the table near Vera.

'You two ready?' she asks.

'Sure am, little lady,' says Elgee.

'I'm only gonna say this once,' says Vera, settling her legs on the table. 'If you give me a smart mouth, I'll give you a split lip, understand?'

Elgee holds his hands up. 'No problem. Just messin' around.'

'Just so we're clear, you two are extra baggage we don't need. Ryen should never have brought you back here.'

I cross my arms. 'Do you seriously think that you, Ryen, and Kerina are just going to drive into Middtown, knock on the door, and ask to speak with the Primo Dictor? And hope his wife doesn't answer?'

'That's exactly what we're going to do,' says Kerina.

I spin around. She's pulled her hair back. Her chin is lifted high, daring me to challenge her. She's so different from when Manny and I first found her, but still the same—cautious but defiant. So much has changed, for both of us.

'But Vera's wrong. We do need the two of you.' She stares at me. 'If you'll help?'

The stuffy air thickens and my pulse quickens. This is the moment. I can choose to continue with this crazy plan. Or I can hitch a ride to Middtown and make my way back to Nevertyre with Elgee. It would be easier to go back to Manny and Constance, except I made Rudolph a promise. And I never break a promise. Kerina waits for my answer. Her chest rises and falls with quick breaths, the only sign of nerves.

'We'll be coming to Middtown and we'll stay with you the whole way. At least until I know for certain you're safe.'

Kerina swallows. 'You don't have to do that out of a sense of obligation.'

'I'm not. I'm doing it because even though it might not matter to you, it matters to me.'

She is the first to look away.

Chapter 74

Kerina

People gather around as the group gets ready to leave. Elgee shakes hands with some people, and Lariel hugs the woman with one eye before joining me.

'Who was that woman?'

'A sympathiser with friends in Middtown. She has contacts who might be able to help find my father.'

Lariel's eyes are full of hope and optimism, fuelled by the thought of seeing her dad again.

'Lariel, you know your father could be …'

'He's not dead, Kerina, I'm sure of it.'

I nod, not wishing to push the issue. I'm the last one to give advice on false hope and hollow truths. After all, isn't that what this mission is? We are pinning all our hopes on one man who gave his daughter away as soon as she was born.

Larinda enters the room. She walks with a confident stride. Not rushed, but determined in her direction. She continued to love Rudolph over the years, even when he was barely around. Vera told her the old man was their glue. He kept Shirnaka together, and if he wasn't there the people deferred to Larinda. They trust her and she'll lead them well.

'You be safe,' says Larinda, gripping her son by the shoulders.

'I promise,' Ryen replies, wrapping his arms around her.

The embrace is quick but full of meaning, both still grieving.

'Let's go,' says Vera.

We slip our packs on and wave goodbye. A low hum spreads

through the crowd. Some higher murmurings join in and before long a melody plays out for all to enjoy, just like when we arrived. No words, just musical harmony through humming and sounds. Rudolph called it the rhythm of the future. It's a pity he won't be here to see what that future is like.

We leave the underground fortress the same way we came in. Ryen leads us out. He pauses at the doorway, hesitant to walk through. It's as though an invisible barrier stops him. He seems to gather his thoughts, then walks outside into the open. Vera follows without any hesitation and doesn't look back.

The car is squishy with the extra person, but nobody complains. I suspect Elgee enjoys being in the back with the girls. I made sure I wasn't seated beside Saxon. I couldn't stand to be that close to him and still try to keep my distance.

Ryen turns around to face everyone. 'This is the last chance for anyone who wants to back out. Not one of you is being forced to come on this mission.'

Nobody volunteers to stay behind.

'Good, let's go then.' He turns the key and the engine begins first try.

We drive away from the sanctity of Shirnaka and a tremor of anticipation runs through me. Orange dust streams along the side of the car covering the window, making any view impossible. I've travelled so far, yet my journey seems to be just beginning.

'My mother told me that before Rudolph died, he shared something with her,' says Ryen.

I look between Ryen and Saxon sitting in the front seats. Both knew Rudolph as a father figure, and both have been left behind to see out his wishes.

'She said he knew without a doubt the Okodee people and their families would be accepted into the community. That now was the perfect time to rise.'

'How did he know this?' asks Saxon.

'It didn't matter how he knew things! He just knew such things, and he was always right.' Ryen looks in the rear-view mirror, locking eyes with me.

I smile, recognising the truth in the dead man's words.

Chapter 75

Saxon

The first day is uneventful and long. We drive until nightfall. It's agreed that we will take shifts keeping watch. There's enough of us to take it in turns for an hour before getting some sleep. Then at the first break of daylight we can continue, charging the car as we go.

Vera takes the first shift. The rest of us split up the thermal blankets to share and get some rest.

'Yer not really me type, but you'll do,' says Elgee, lying down next to me.

I elbow him in the ribs. 'If you spoon me, you're a dead tinker.'

Elgee chuckles and then instantly falls asleep. He's always been able to do that, nothing stops him. I try to switch off, but it's hard. Especially knowing that last time it was Kerina sleeping next to me. This time she is as far away from me as possible, lying next to Lariel. I try not to remember how close she was when we whispered to one another. I try not to remember her holding my hand beneath the stars. Eventually, I drift off with that very image in my mind.

'Your turn.'

I wake to Lariel shaking me. I sit up fast and the blood rushes to my head, making me dizzy. Everyone in camp is still asleep. Lariel is already settling beneath the thermal blanket next to Kerina. My cheeks warm from the dream I was having. I shake my head. I've got to stop thinking about her. She made it very clear what she wants to happen. Nothing. I tuck the blanket around Elgee and move to sit in front of the car. Lariel has left a weapon leaning against it. I pull my jacket tight and grip the gun.

I gaze into the darkness and imagine the time before the Burn. The landscape was once full of houses and shops, and buildings that seemed to reach the sky. The population was out of control and communities, or cities as they were known, were crowded with people. The Burn spread quickly. The landscape was a tinderbox, waiting to be lit. The fire whirls that started from the intense heat and wind conditions spread all over the land. Explosions caused smaller fires to spread. With wind speeds of over two hundred kilometres an hour, there was little that could be done to stop the tornado-like furnaces. The Burn was selective in its destruction. Some places received hardly any damage while others were annihilated. The chaos was unimaginable. The human cost, immeasurable.

Suddenly, I notice a light on the horizon. It's too small to be the sun. I concentrate on the glow. It grows bigger and brighter. After a while, I realise it's two lights, car headlights.

'Wake up! Everyone, get up.'

The travelling party jumps to life.

'There's another vehicle coming our way,' I say.

Everyone packs their things and each takes a position. Kerina, Vera, and I move behind the car, while the other three remain at the front.

'Let's hope it stays dark long enough for them not to see us,' says Ryen.

'Otherwise, let's be ready for them. You all remember the plan?' Vera loads her weapon.

'Kerina, you stay hidden, no matter what,' says Ryen.

She scowls at him.

'Saxon and Vera, you stay on either side of Kerina. Keep her protected.'

Vera climbs across Kerina, leaving her lying next to me.

'Elgee and Lariel, you're both with me.' Ryen sits inside the vehicle.

The car gets closer. Hopefully, they don't see us, they keep driving, and the trip remains uneventful. That's when I see the first rays of dawn break through the horizon.

'It's not going to stay dark for much longer,' I say.

Kerina settles her gun. 'Then let's be ready.'

Chapter 76

Kerina

I lie between my bodyguards, unhappy about having to stay hidden, but ready to fight if I need to.

'Don't do anything stupid,' hisses Vera, as though reading my mind.

The car gets closer. For a moment it looks like it will pass by, then the driver hits the brakes. Tyres skid against the dirt and dust flies up like a windstorm. It reverses before doing a half circle. The headlights are bright and point toward us. Someone gets out of the car. Their face is in shadow and I can't see how many others are in the car.

Ryen emerges from our car wearing his Agent uniform. 'Good morn, my friend. Identify yourself. I'm Senior Agent Tambler.'

Ryen's uniform adds authenticity to his authority.

'I'm Agent Burrows,' says the man.

Ryen steps toward the man. 'Are you travelling alone, Agent Burrows?'

The man hesitates, then turns toward his car. He nods his head to somebody inside. The passenger door opens and another Agent steps out.

'I'm Agent Kain.'

'I have two other Agents with me. Off duty, though.'

Elgee and Lariel emerge from the car, but don't follow Ryen. I know they have weapons beneath their clothes. They will be aimed toward the Agents.

'From where do you come?' asks Ryen.

The two Agents walk toward him slowly.

'We are out doing patrols from Nevertyre.'

I feel Saxon tense at the mention of his home community.

'Nevertyre? You're a long way from home.'

'Yes, sir. We've been at Middtown for the past couple of weeks. They had some trouble there a short while ago.'

'There's always some of kind of trouble,' jokes Ryen. 'Not like Nevertyre, hey?'

Burrows smiles. 'Middtown does seem to overreact at times.'

Ryen throws his head back and laughs. 'Very true, my friend, very true. So which trouble do you refer to this time?'

I hold my breath, knowing what he will say next.

'There was an incident, some prisoners escaped, injured an Agent on their way out.'

'Ahh, yes, I heard about that. We're on our way back to Middtown now.'

'Tell your Agents to be cautious then. Trouble has been brewing,' says Burrows.

'Damn sympathisers,' says Kain.

'Agent Kain! Keep your tongue in check,' says Burrows, glaring at his partner.

Kain scowls but steps back, removing himself from further conversation.

'The Primo Dictor can't keep everyone happy. Just so long as we're on his list, hey?' Ryen lightens the mood.

'Yes, sir.'

'Well, we best be on our way. Travel safely.'

The men shake hands and return to their vehicles.

'Elgee, pretend you're going to the toilet,' whispers Ryen. 'It will stop their suspicions as to why we aren't leaving now the sun is shining.'

Elgee wanders off to the side and does as Ryen directed.

'You other three stay down until it's clear,' he hisses. 'We got lucky.'

'Even luckier now that we know your cover is still in place,' I say.

'Perhaps,' says Ryen. 'Or maybe a trap awaits me.'

Chapter 77

Saxon

'I think we need to split up,' I say the next night. 'It will be less obvious if we enter in two groups.'

'Elgee made some friends last time,' says Kerina. 'Maybe they'll be willing to help again?'

'Oh, they'll be helpful again, no problem.'

'How about I enter with the car and see what I can find out?' says Ryen.

'No!' says Vera. 'What if they know you're a double Agent and arrest you?'

'I'm the best chance we have of getting Kerina near the Primo Dictor.'

'How are you going to explain where you've been the last couple of weeks?' says Vera.

'I'll tell them I was kidnapped or something. It doesn't matter what. I'll make sure they believe me.'

'I think Ryen is right,' I say. 'Lariel and Vera can stick with Kerina. Elgee and I can seek out sympathisers from the community and Ryen can get intel.'

'It won't work. They'll never believe you, Ryen. Not unless you can prove you're trustworthy,' says Lariel. 'And I know just how you can do that.'

Kerina shakes her head. 'Absolutely not, Lariel. No way!'

'Take me with you, Ryen. Tell them you managed to overpower me and capture me, but Kerina got away,' says Lariel.

'No! Ryen, no. There has to be another way,' pleads Kerina. 'You can't hand Lariel in. She can't be imprisoned again.'

'It's a good plan,' Vera says. 'It will ensure Ryen's cover isn't blown and give him access to things we can't get to.'

'Shut up, Vera,' says Kerina. 'Saxon, tell them there's another way. You and Elgee can talk to the community and get help that way.'

I pinch the bridge of my nose. 'I never thought I would say this, but I agree with Lariel. This is a good plan.'

I watch the emotions cross Kerina's face. Fear, anger, doubt. Guilt eats at me, but I know if Ryen takes Lariel in, the authorities will have no reason to doubt his story.

'If something happens to Lariel, I will never forgive you.' Kerina stares at me. 'Any of you.' She turns and stomps off.

'I'll go,' I say.

Vera blocks my path. 'She's not going to listen to you.'

'She did make that pretty clear, I suppose.'

'She won't listen to you because she cares too much, you big fool.' Vera jabs me in the chest, then follows after Kerina.

'Told yer,' says Elgee.

'Get some sleep,' I say. 'It's going be a big day tomorrow.'

I retrieve my bag with the thermal blanket and curl up near a tree. I'm on third watch so my sleep will be broken halfway through. Elgee joins me after a while. I try to lie still and keep my breathing even.

'I know yer awake,' says Elgee.

I don't answer. I'm in no mood for chitchat.

'Fine, but just so yer know, it was a good call. Think what you want about Lariel, she's got guts givin' herself up like that. Kerina will come round. Just give her some time.'

Within minutes, Elgee's low snore floats past me, asleep already. I roll flat on my back, watching the stars above. The sky is clear and I imagine lines connecting them to create pictures. That was another thing Rudolph taught me—to make pictures from the sky. I keep staring at the night sky, waiting for a sleep that won't come.

Chapter 78

Kerina

I don't talk to anyone during the next day's drive to Middtown. Deep down I know the plan is the best chance we have, but to hand Lariel over to the authorities seems unforgivable.

'I know what you're thinking, but I'll be fine,' says Lariel. 'I've made it through tough scrapes before. This will just be short term anyway, until we get what we need.'

'What if we don't?'

'Then I'll get her out,' says Ryen. 'Lariel won't be imprisoned any longer than she has to be, Kerina, I promise.'

His demeanour is determined, but the promise leaves me feeling hollow. Once again, I am giving up my friend's freedom for my own.

We arrive on the outskirts of Middtown. Far enough away that anyone watching won't notice us, but close enough that the walk isn't far.

I hug my old friend tightly. 'I will get you out. I promise you that.'

'Just do what you have to.'

Ryen throws Lariel some cuffs. 'Better get in the back and put these on.'

The goodbyes are quick and before long the car is just a speck in the distance. We start walking toward civilisation. Soon the shanties come into view. There seem to be fewer people standing around than the last time we arrived.

Saxon stops the group. 'Vera, you stay with Kerina and see what you can find out. We need to know about the Primo Dictor. What are his moves? When does he leave his house? Is he guarded at all times? We need to come up with a link to get Kerina near him.'

'Who made you the boss?' says Vera.

'Got a better idea?' says Saxon, his jaw clenched.

She shrugs. 'What are you and Elgee going to do?'

Saxon smirks. 'What Elgee does best. We're gonna draw out people's secrets.'

We make our way into the crowd of people and then split into two groups.

'Be careful,' I say.

The boys have already left, but the shift in Saxon's head suggests he heard me. I turn and Vera follows.

'See that bench seat over there?' I say. 'I'm going to sit there while you wander around the crowd.'

Vera grabs my sleeve. 'I don't think we should split up.'

'It will be fine. We have to watch people without staring. See who makes eye contact for that moment too long.'

'What if they do?'

'Then that's the person we need to speak with because they see everything and know everything that's going on around here.'

I make my way over to the bench seat, head down, eyes darting around the area. I pluck off a lone flower. The centre is yellow with white petals. These daisies once ran wild through grass if left unweeded. Slowly, I pluck each petal off. My head is angled toward the flower, but my attention is all around me. I strain to listen to conversations.

Occasionally I look up, waiting to see if anyone has noticed me. I lock eyes momentarily with an older woman. I take care to keep my roving eye moving. I count to ten and check again. Sure enough, the same woman is watching me. Her head is bent like mine as she rummages through a sack, but her eyes are flitting about, just like mine.

I stand to stretch, then amble toward the woman without

looking at her. As I get closer, I look for Vera. It's not too hard to find my new friend. She is standing right behind the woman.

Chapter 79

'Do you think Ryen can find out what we need?'

'Yep, but I'll tell you somethin' for nothin'. These people will know more than all the intel those Agents can get.'

I follow Elgee down a narrow pathway. It leads to where I met the boy with the magic trick. He had spoken the same words Rudolph used to tell me. '*Sometimes what we see is not always what we are looking at.*'

I didn't understand how the boy could know them at the time, but it makes sense now. Rudolph must have passed through here many times. He would have mixed with the community and gained knowledge that way.

'Raider, mah friend!' Elgee holds his hand out.

'Elgee?'

'In the flesh!'

'Wow, I did not expect to see you round here again.'

'Are we good here?'

'Yeah, all good. No trouble today.'

'But you had some after we left?'

'Nothing we couldn't handle.' Raider turns toward me.

The man's head is shaved and covered in pictures. There are tattoos on every space. 'Thanks for your help last time,' I say. 'It meant a great deal to us.'

'We're always happy to mess with the Agents.'

I offer my hand to shake his. 'We must be on the same side then.'

Raider grips my hand. 'Let's walk. It's good to keep movin'. It's not always Agents listening in.'

I look around, sizing up the crowd nearby. Nobody takes much notice of us.

'Did you miss me? Is that why you came back?'

'Sure, that's one reason.'

Raider laughs. 'Oh yeah? What's the other reason?'

'We want a meeting with the Primo Dictor,' Elgee says seriously.

Raider looks up sharply. He veers us away from the throngs of people, toward the less crowded streets. He walks between the two of us, his back almost broader than both of ours put together.

'Why do you want to meet with the Primo Dictor?'

'We have something valuable of his,' I say.

Raider stops abruptly and knocks on a door two times. He repeats the gesture three times. The door opens and a young boy appears.

'It's all good, Benjy. Why don't you heat some water for hot drinks?'

'Is dat your son?'

Raider nods. 'It's just me and him after his mother died. Benjy doesn't talk much, but his mind is sharp as a nail.'

I take in the room. A long table with chairs surrounding it takes up most of the space.

'Go ahead, sit down,' says Raider, his easy smile gone.

I feel my pocket, but it's empty.

'Looking for something?' asks Raider, holding my gun. He pushes it across the table. 'Gotta watch yourself in Middtown. Kids here can pickpocket before they can speak.'

'We don't want trouble,' I say. 'But we won't shy away from it either.'

Raider slouches in the chair. 'That's good to know, because we *do* want trouble. Your help would be very appreciated. Think of it as balancing the scales for our help last time.'

'What sort of help do you want?' I ask, cautious.

'Help to kill the Primo Dictor.'

Chapter 80

Kerina

I walk toward the woman. She is half bent over, but still blatantly staring at me.

'Do you know me?' I ask.

The woman shakes her head.

'Then why do you keep looking at me?'

'I could ask you the same thing, but I already know the answer.'

'What's that?'

'You think I might be the kind of person you can ask questions of.'

'Are you?' says Vera, stepping in front of the woman.

The woman reaches down for her sack and pushes it against Vera. 'I might be if you can carry that for me. My back plays up a bit these days, not enough nutrients for my weary bones.'

Vera carries the sack and follows behind me and our new acquaintance.

'Do you have a name?' asks Vera.

'I do,' says the woman.

We turn down a laneway where the crowds have thinned.

'I'm Vera and this is … Kailey.'

'If you say so.' The woman stops at a door and knocks twice, then repeats the gesture three times. The door opens. 'Go in,' she says. 'Don't be shy.'

I enter first. 'Saxon? Elgee? What are you doing here?'

They swirl around to stare at us. 'How did you two get here?' says Saxon.

'We met this woman and she asked us to follow her.'

'You're such a show-off, Raider. You had to beat me,' says the woman.

'Of course! You taught me well, Mother.'

'Well, now that we're all here, let's get started,' says the woman.

All signs of a bad back are gone as she stands straight and tall.

'Raider, are you settin' us up?' asks Elgee.

Raider grins. 'I told you to watch yourself around here. Nothing is as it seems.'

'Ain't that the truth,' says the woman. 'Hi boys, I'm Lace.'

'Why didn't you tell *us* your name?' asks Vera.

'Because these boys are much prettier than you two.' She winks at them and sits at the head of the table.

When Vera and I join, the table becomes full.

'Raider had a feeling about you.' She points to Elgee. 'Then when we *assisted* your escape, I said to him, they'll be back. Didn't I say that, Raider?'

He sighs. 'Yes, old woman, you sure did.'

She slaps him on the back of head. 'Enough with the old. Anyway, I said they'll be back and when they come back, they'll owe us and they'll help us.'

'What sort of help are you looking for?' asks Vera.

Saxon and Elgee grumble and lean back in their chairs.

'You told them already?' says Lace.

'Just before you barged in.'

'Told them what?' I ask.

Saxon and Elgee look down at the table.

'What did he tell them?' I demand.

'We want your help … to kill the Primo Dictor.'

I shake my head. 'You're out of your mind.'

'Oh no, my mind is clear,' says Lace. 'It's time for his offspring to take over.'

'He doesn't have any,' says Vera, moving slightly toward me.

'There's one nobody knows about,' Lace says with a smirk. 'The one who was born Okodee.'

Chapter 81

Saxon

Vera shoots me a fleeting glance before settling on Lace. Kerina's attention bounces between Raider and his mother. Nobody says a word as Lace's plan sinks in.

'What do you know of Okodee, old woman?' demands Vera.

Lace pushes her chair out and stands up. 'I'll show you something.'

She walks over to a cabinet in the corner. She unlocks the drawer, removes a box, and sits it in the middle of the table for everyone to see. The group hunches forward, eager to see the contents. She removes the lid. My nerves stretch a little further as I try to make out what I'm looking at.

Vera reaches for the bag of liquid. 'Is that what I think it is?'

Lace pulls the box out of her reach.

'If you think that is the last sample of Okodee vaccine, then you would be correct.'

'Why do you have it?' asks Vera.

'My sister worked for the government as a scientist. She helped formulate the vaccine. She even helped administer it until the project was destroyed. She managed to smuggle this out just before the fire.'

'You didn't answer my question,' says Vera.

'I have it … because my sister gave it to me the night she was murdered.'

I close my eyes, knowing the answer to my next question. 'How did she die?'

'A building collapsed on her, just like your parents, Saxon.'

My head spins. 'You knew Rudolph, didn't you?'

Lace smiles. 'Now you're putting it together.' She closes the lid and returns the box to the drawer.

'Rudolph's dead,' I say. 'He had a stroke.'

'I'm sorry to hear that. He was a good man.' She leans against the cabinet with her back to them. 'Rudolph tracked me down a few months after the accident. He worked with Aurora, my sister. He knew what was going on. He knew if he didn't act fast that he would be next. Somebody was covering their tracks and wiping out lots of evidence. Every person who was killed that night was lured there under false pretences. By somebody with enough power that they wouldn't question the need to attend. Sound like anybody you know?'

'It does, but not the person you're thinking,' says Kerina.

Lace slams her hand on the cabinet. 'It was the Primo Dictor. He must have ordered it. He's the only one with that much power.'

'You're wrong,' says Kerina. 'Another has just as much power, if not more. It might seem like it was ordered by the Primo Dictor, but I guarantee you, it wasn't.'

'Then who, smart girl, who?'

'The Primo Dictor's wife. My biological mother.'

I groan as Kerina reveals her identity.

Lace gasps. 'You? You're the one they called Kerina?'

'I am, and the Primo Dictor can't be killed. He's our only chance. It was he who gave me up and let me live.'

'You think you owe him?' asks Raider.

'No, he owes me. He has to make amends for not acting sooner when it was in his power. He'll allow me to help govern and I'll create communities that are accepting of everyone.'

Lace stares. 'Those are big statements for a young lady.'

'I don't make them lightly.'

Lace snorts. 'Well, you're gonna need more help than you've got. Lucky for you, I have an army.'

Chapter 82

Kerina

Lace invites us to spend the night. Raider has a connection who can get a message to Ryen. Then we just have to wait until he makes contact to see if he's found out anything.

'Do you think Lariel is okay?' I ask Vera.

'Can't you see I'm trying to get my beauty sleep?'

'Why? Do you want to impress Elgee?'

Vera sits up. 'What?'

'I've seen the sneaky looks and hushed conversations you have with him.'

'You're imagining things, I promise you. Besides, you're one to talk.'

'I don't know what you mean,' I say, snuggling down further below the blanket. 'I think it is you who is imagining things.'

It's Vera's turn to snort. 'Are you telling me the painfully obvious avoidance of Saxon is just my imagination? The fleeting looks when you think nobody is watching is just my imagination?'

'Enough! I can't be distracted by Saxon, no matter what I feel, so just leave it alone.'

'You started it,' says Vera. She thumps her pillow and lies back down.

'You didn't answer my first question.'

Silence settles between us before Vera answers. 'I'm certain Lariel is fine. Ryen will make sure of it. He is very resourceful when he needs to be.'

Vera's words hold little comfort to me. I allowed Ryen to hand

Lariel over to the authorities. That sort of guilt is hard to squash.

'We need to act fast,' I say. 'A delay might prove costly to the plan.'

'We need a solid plan first because rushed actions might prove costly. Now shut up and get some sleep.' Vera rolls away from me, ending any further conversation.

I run through the plan so far. Lace is going to round up her army—a group of sympathisers with numbers that grows larger by the day. From what Lace told us, the Primo Dictor is not governing fairly to his community. I have my own thoughts about who is calling the shots. Is my biological mother that powerful? Does she govern through her husband?

The next morning, I awake to find myself alone. I wander out to the kitchen. Saxon sits at the table making notes on a piece of paper.

He looks up. 'Good morn.'

'Where is everyone?'

'Lace was gone by dawn to spread the word of a meeting tonight. Raider left with her to get word to Ryen.'

I sit down at the table opposite Saxon. 'What about Elgee and Vera?'

'They've gone to find supplies.'

I strain to see what Saxon is doing. 'I didn't know you could sketch so well.'

The image has such a strong likeness to me, the details so accurate. Only someone who has stared closely at the subject could draw them so well. The thought unnerves me.

'It's not my best work. It's rushed. Lace wanted me to come up with a picture of you that could be spread throughout the community.'

'Why?'

'So people can start putting a face to the new leader.'

'But I'm not the new leader, well, not yet.'

'She thinks this will get the momentum happening. With enough support and when the truth comes out about who you are, it should help the cause.'

'What do you think?'

Saxon leans his head on his hand. 'I think Lace's intentions are good. But we still need to get past your mother first. From her recent actions, she won't hesitate to kill you herself if she finds out our plans to overthrow her and her husband.'

Chapter 83

Saxon

Elgee and I make our way through the community. The streets are full of people and lanterns are strung between the buildings.

'What's the occasion?' I ask a young girl.

Her round brown eyes stare at me in disbelief. 'It's the annual ball.'

'Do you have a ticket?'

The girl laughs. 'No silly. Only friends of the Primo Dictor get invited. They've already started to arrive.'

I scratch my chin. 'Hmm, maybe I should become friends with him, what do you think?'

The girl claps her hands. 'Yes, you should! I'm going to marry a Dictor one day. Then I can get invited and our whole family can go.'

'Of course! Why didn't I think of that?' I reach into my pocket and retrieve a token for the girl. 'Here, buy yourself a treat instead.'

The girl snatches it. 'Thank you!'

I turn to Elgee and grip him by the shoulders. 'That's it. That's our way in.'

Elgee raises an eyebrow. 'What am I missin'?'

'Did you hear the girl? The Dictors *and their families* all get invited to that ball.'

Elgee shakes his head. 'I know what yer thinkin', but that ain't how we get access.'

'We can trust Anastasia. She *will* help us.'

Elgee shakes his head. 'So many people are already involved. You sure you wanna include her?'

I urge him to keep walking. Less chance of anybody listening in on our conversation that way.

'We have to include Anastasia. She can deliver Kerina to her biological father without any interference. We just need to get a message to her somehow.'

'How do you plan on doin' that?'

I search the street. There's a festive feeling in the air and people are keen to celebrate. Members of the community might not be invited to the ball, but they plan to have just as much fun.

I sit down on a bench seat out the front of a shop. 'It's easy, my friend. We just need to wait until she drives past. I'll make sure she sees me and she'll do the rest.'

Elgee shakes his head and joins me. 'That's so crazy it might just work.'

We stay sitting on the bench seat for the remainder of the afternoon. A few cars pass, but none carry the Dictor of Nevertyre and his family. Just as I'm about to give up, a black car drives past. The back window is wound down enough for me to see two wide blue eyes peeking out from the gap. I stand and nod toward the shops. The car keeps driving. For a moment I think I might have missed my chance, then suddenly the car stops twenty metres up the road. Elgee and I walk inside the shop and wait near the front window. After a moment, Anastasia passes by the front and enters. I grip her arm and pull her toward me.

'Saxon!' She throws her arms around me. 'I've been so worried. You've been gone for weeks. Are you okay?'

I disentangle myself from Anastasia. 'I'm fine. Are Manny and Constance okay?'

'They're safe and well. I can't talk long or my father will send our driver to get me.'

'You once told me I could trust you. Well, I need a favour and you're the only one to do it. Can I trust you?'

'Of course! What do you need?'

'I need you to get Kerina—'

'The rambler?'

'Yes, I need you to get Kerina to meet privately with the Primo Dictor.'

'Why would you want that?'

I hesitate—how much should I tell her? But if I am going to trust Anastasia, she needs to know everything.

'Kerina must speak with the Primo Dictor because he is her father.'

Chapter 84

Kerina

'Sit still,' says Vera, poking and prodding my head. 'I'm almost finished.'

'Where did you learn to do hair anyway?' I ask.

'I didn't always have a shaved head,' says Vera. 'Finished! Now stand up and let me see.'

I stand up and my gown bunches out. Vera has created long curls that cascade around my neck. You can hardly tell where the hair is pinned back. It looks like the hair naturally falls that way.

Knock, knock.

'Come in,' I say.

Saxon enters the room. His jaw falls slack before he composes himself. I smooth the lemon-coloured gown. Delicate bows have been handsewn with diamanté in the middle of each, making it sparkle as I move.

'She should pass with flying colours, don't you think, Saxon?' says Vera, smirking.

He swallows. 'You look … beautiful.'

My cheeks warm at his compliment. I can't let Saxon's words distract me, but they are nice to hear all the same.

'There will be no question that you belong there tonight,' he says quietly.

For a moment, I wish he was my date and we were going together.

Vera interrupts the daydream. 'You're confident Anastasia can be counted on?'

'Vera, stop asking me that,' says Saxon. 'I trust her.'

Vera holds up her hands. 'Fine. I don't trust anyone, so it's on you if this doesn't work.'

Elgee enters the room. 'Wow, check you out! Think we gonna have a problem though.'

'What? Why?' I say.

'Think yer gonna attract too much attention looking so good.'

I've never dressed in such fine clothes. Surely the other guests will know that I am an imposter straight away. I sneak one more look at Saxon, who stares back, unwavering.

'Is it time to go?' I ask.

'Yep. Lace said to put this on.' Elgee hands me an oversized coat. 'Should cover dat gown so you don't stand out until we get there.'

I shrug into the jacket. It is five sizes too big, but covers most of my dress.

'You definitely won't stand out in that walking down the street,' says Vera, laughing.

'Shut up,' I say. 'It's the best we can do.' My nerves are stretched tight and I'm in no mood for Vera's smart mouth.

'Everyone knows the plan,' says Vera. 'Ryen will introduce you as his date to anyone who asks. Ryen is on duty and must be seen as interacting with the visiting Dictors. You will need to make polite conversation, Kerina. Then follow Anastasia's lead. Ryen will be keeping an eye on you to make sure it is safe. If he gives any indication of trouble, you must get out of there, understood?'

'We've been over it, Vera. I know the plan.'

'Hey!' Vera grabs me by the wrist. 'This isn't just about you and meeting your father. This is about so much more than that.'

'I know what's at stake,' I say, shrugging her off. 'You don't have to remind me. Now let's go so I can get on with it.'

I stomp out of the room. I don't need a pep talk about how high the stakes are. I know the risk with this first encounter. I could be wrong about my father. He might have cared enough to protect me once, but that was a long time ago. He's made no effort since then.

Did he realise that by letting me live, he risked me turning up in his life again? Was that his intention? There are so many questions, but I'm not sure how many answers I will get tonight.

Chapter 85

Saxon

The path is dark, just pale moonlight illuminates our way along the street. Vera keeps her distance from behind, making sure we aren't followed. Elgee is up ahead, checking there's no trap waiting for us. I walk silently with Kerina. This is the most awkward I've felt with her. Perhaps it's because she looks so damn pretty all dressed up tonight. She looks like the Primo Dictor's daughter should. I'm reminded of the role she was born into. We might never have met if she hadn't been abandoned at birth. She should be greeting guests right now in the foyer as they arrive. She could be standing alongside her parents and maybe even siblings.

'Hey, I just thought of something. The Primo Dictor and his wife never had any more children after you,' I say.

'One Okodee born was probably enough,' Kerina jokes.

'The charts Ryen showed me suggested the second generation didn't need the vaccine. The gene mutated so well it could come through, regardless.'

'If that's true then perhaps my fath— the Primo Dictor wouldn't risk more offspring born with the gene.'

I shake my head. 'I don't think it's guaranteed to evolve. Unless your mother was also a carrier.'

'The thing I don't understand is how she found out after so many years. He must have told her I didn't survive the birth, so what changed?'

'They don't have any other children. That means you are the sole dependant, which means there's no question you're destined to govern. It is your birthright. She wants to make sure that never happens.'

We continue walking until the lights get brighter near the Primo Dictor's compound. A dark figure stands on the corner. Ryen turns to face us. He raises a hand and hurries toward us.

'Are you ready, Kerina?'

'Of course. Is Lariel being treated well?'

He nods. 'I have her in isolation. Agents give those people a wide berth, knowing they are there for violent or unpredictable behaviour. It's not ideal, but it's the best way to keep her safe.'

Kerina shrugs off the jacket and hands it to me.

'Wow!' says Ryen. 'You are breathtaking.'

'It's just a dress,' says Kerina, brushing off the compliment.

I scowl at Ryen. 'You better keep an eye on her tonight.'

'I will. Your girlfriend Anastasia better be counted on.'

'She's not my girlfriend.'

Kerina watches me.

'Anastasia is a good *friend* whose word is reliable.'

'If you say so,' says Ryen, offering Kerina his arm. 'If you're meant to be my date, then we're going to have to make it look real. That means getting a little closer.'

I step back with gritted teeth. Ryen grins, goading me on purpose, I'm sure.

Kerina loops her arms through his. 'We're not going to have to dance, are we?'

'Probably.' Ryen leans in. 'But I will hold you tight and lead the way, so don't worry.' He winks at me, loving the position he has me in.

I scrunch up the jacket and resist the urge to punch him in the face.

'Let's go then.' Kerina walks along the street on Ryen's arm.

I watch on, wishing that it was my arm she held on to, hoping she turns back one last time. She doesn't. I turn to leave and walk straight into Raider.

His face is serious. 'We've got a problem.'

Chapter 86

Kerina

The closer we get to the compound, the brighter the lights. Some guests arrive by car, Others, like ourselves, enter by foot.

Ryen hands over the invitation. It is a magic ticket giving us unlimited access. The Agents on duty know him, so they take little notice of the invitation. Instead, their curiosity is piqued by his date. I keep my arm linked with Ryen's as we walk up the curved footpath. Two musicians are set up at the base of the stairs. Strains of their instruments float through the night air to reach her ears.

'What are they playing?' I ask, enthralled.

'The violin? You've not heard one before?'

I shake my head. 'I've never been to something like this.'

'Well, hopefully you will get used to it.'

We stroll past the violin players and I pause to listen. The musicians bow their head in appreciation.

'We best keep going. Don't want people to think you've never enjoyed such music.'

'It might blow my cover?'

Ryen laughs and urges me forward. At the foyer, the line stalls as guests enter. They are each greeted by the hosts before passing through to the ballroom. I clench my fists. In moments, I will come face to face with my biological parents. Will they recognise me and call security? Will they fall to their knees and beg forgiveness?

The line moves forward, and in an instant I am standing opposite my biological mother and father.

'Governor. Governess,' says Ryen. 'May I present Christina Routh.'

He doesn't falter at the made-up name. I reach for my father's hand.

The Primo Dictor takes it and shakes it warmly. 'Welcome, Christina. May you enjoy the evening.'

'Thank you, Governor. I am honoured to be here.' I move along and reach for my mother's hand. 'Governess, I am privileged just being in your presence.'

Her grip is firm. 'It is our privilege to meet you.'

Once the formal greeting with us is over, they move their attentions along to the next guests. I follow Ryen toward the ballroom, trying to stop the tremor in my hands.

'I can't believe I just met my parents,' I whisper.

'Well, I couldn't see any resemblance,' says Ryen, gripping my trembling hands. 'You did well. Just keep it together and wait for an opportunity.'

'Do you think we'll get our chance?'

'Of course you will!' says a blond-haired girl, appearing from nowhere. 'I don't commit unless I know I can carry through with it.'

Ryen grips her hand. 'You must be Anastasia. It's a pleasure to have you on board. Saxon neglected to brag about your beauty.'

Anastasia flips her hand about. 'I highly doubt Saxon notices such things.'

'Then he's a blind fool,' says Ryen.

'Such a charmer.' Anastasia reaches for my arm. 'Kerina? Come, we shall walk aimlessly until the first dance begins.'

'Perfect. It will allow me to speak to those I must flatter.' Ryen leaves us alone.

'Flattery can work wonders, but never trust one whose words flow like silk from his mouth,' Anastasia says conspiratorially to me.

'Ryen is trustworthy.'

Anastasia smiles. 'I've no doubt he is trustworthy when it comes to his missions. But for matters of the heart, I imagine he is practised in the art of flattery.'

'You're probably right.'

'Nevertheless, he is quite handsome,' says Anastasia. 'I believe he will owe me a dance later. But first, let's integrate you.'

Chapter 87

Raider and I wait for Elgee to join us. Vera paces the path, impatient. Finally, Elgee appears from within the shadows.

'She's in,' he says.

'That's not good, because we've got a new problem,' says Raider.

'What kind of problem?' says Vera. 'I thought you had everything under control.'

Raider sighs. 'It was under control. But I just got word about something else that's been going down.'

'To do with Kerina?' I ask.

Raider shakes his head. 'Not initially. Some sympathisers we know have been undercover following a lead of traders. Trying to find out where the supply and demand is coming from. They had a face-to-face meet with the traders, who were bragging about how they're gonna catch the biggest trade yet. They showed our friends an image of the person they're looking for. They said word has spread that she'll be the most valuable catch. That a client is willing to pay a fortune for the unharmed delivery.'

I back away. 'Don't say it, Raider, don't you say it.'

'The image was of Kerina.'

'Damn it!'

My fists clench and I spin around, looking for something to punch. I knew I should have gone with her; instead, I sent her off to the devil herself. I might have just sealed her capture.

'Are you saying the Governess knows what Kerina looks like?' asks Vera.

'That's exactly what I'm saying.'

'We have to warn them.' She turns to run toward the compound.

Elgee grabs her wrist. 'How do you think we're gonna get in there?'

'She's caged in there. The Governess just has to give one order, then Kerina is captured and it's all over.'

Elgee shakes his head. 'I thought you were a fighter, girl? You givin' up already?'

'I don't quit,' she yells in his face.

'Good! Because I got an idea.'

Raider crosses his arms. 'I smell a bust coming on.'

Elgee grins. 'It's a bust all right, but we're bustin' in, not out.'

'What are you talking about, Elgee?' I ask. 'We need to get a message to Ryen.'

'Are you gonna stroll up to the gates and ask an Agent to give it to him?' He taps Saxon on the side of the head. 'Think, yer tinker. They got security all over the place. Agents from all different communities come with the Dictors.'

'I see where you're going,' says Raider. 'We need to blend in as security, not guests.'

Elgee nods. 'You get yer friend to swipe some uniforms and we're in, baby. Straight through the front gate, no questions asked.'

'That just might work,' I say. 'Can you get the uniforms?'

'I'm on it,' says Raider. 'Vera and Elgee, go tell Lace what's going on and get some weapons for us. We'll meet back here ASAP.'

They disappear into the darkness with footsteps so light I can't even hear them. Raider and I go the opposite way, toward the chambers.

'This better work,' I say. 'If something happens to Kerina ...'

'It'll work. She can take care of herself until we get to her,' says Raider. 'Besides, she's got that double Agent Ryen with her.'

I run with Raider, adrenaline pumping through my body. Ryen better do his job well and protect her, or I'll kill him.

Chapter 88

Anastasia points out people, explaining who each one is. Then, she adds her own bit of juicy gossip about them.

'… that one is rumoured to have quite the liking for a woman he's *not* married to.'

'How do you know so much about these people?' I ask.

'I told Saxon I'm nothing like my father and I meant it. I listen and learn and I will not stick my head in the sand when it comes time to govern.'

'You will govern?'

'Of course! I won't be the Dictor for a while, but I will assist in advice and guidance initially. I am the firstborn, so even though I have brothers, it will be my prerogative to decide if I want to be Dictor or not. And I choose yes.'

'I hadn't thought the same rules would apply in the communities. Wasn't your father elected?'

'Yes, but only because nobody else wanted the job from within the former Dictor's ranks. He was not the easiest man to work for and lacked loyalty from his employees. My father was already working alongside the Dictor and was the most obvious successor.'

There is some bustling and the room becomes crowded.

'It's time for the formal speech and then the dances will begin,' whispers Anastasia.

I watch the Governor and Governess make their way through the crowd. Agents flank them, but from an unobtrusive distance.

The Governor takes his position on the stage. A hush falls over the crowd. I use the time to take in everything about him. His hair is dark with specks of grey that frame his face. Glasses sit on the end of his nose, causing him to look down at the crowd. He pushes them up, but they fall straight back to their original position.

'It is with our pleasure that my wife and I welcome you all here tonight,' he begins.

I take little notice of his words. Instead, I take in his mannerisms, searching for anything I might possess. As soon as I think this, I am overwhelmed by guilt for the parents who raised me as their own, only to be murdered for their efforts. I'm so focused on the Governor that I almost miss the nudge to my ribs. Anastasia leans toward me.

'I might be imagining things, but the Governess seems to keep staring at you.'

I look up to find what Anastasia says is true. The Governess stares directly at me. Her eyes don't linger for long as she scans the crowd, but her gaze always falls back on me. The Governess can't possibly know who I am, can she? Applause breaks out and I clap my hands along with the crowd. People begin moving and chatter fills the space again.

'I need to speak with the Primo Dictor now,' I say.

Anastasia slowly moves through the crowd, nodding at those she knows. 'In a moment, the Governor will retreat to replace his glasses.'

'How do you know this?' I ask.

'I told you, I watch and learn and I know he's put on the wrong glasses. Now follow me.'

I look over to see the Primo Dictor making his way through the crowd in a similar direction to us. The Agents follow him, but he waves them off and walks toward a door.

'Governor!' Anastasia calls out.

He halts and turns toward the voice. 'Anastasia?' He smiles. 'What's got you yelling?'

'I wanted to introduce you to—'

'Christina Routh. We met earlier,' I say.

His forehead wrinkles before good manners take over his memory loss. 'Yes, of course.'

'Oh no! My father is calling me, I'll be right back,' says Anastasia.

'Well, it was lovely to meet you, Christina, but if you don't mind, you will have to excuse me. I just need to attend to something.' He turns to leave.

'Oh, but I do mind … Father.'

Chapter 89

Saxon

'Mah collar is too tight,' complains Elgee.

'Just act like this is another boring security detail that you've done a hundred times,' says Raider.

We walk toward the checkpoint. The Agents inside ignore us until one eventually comes over to the window. 'Yes?'

'Just changing shifts. The Dictor likes to keep his security fresh,' says Raider.

'Which Dictor?'

'Nevertyre,' I say.

'How do you get a gig there? I heard that place is one of the easiest to work. Everybody wants to get assigned there.'

'Is that right?' I step forward to check the other Agents aren't listening and lean in. 'If you give me your name and work details, I could put in a good word for you.'

'Seriously? You'd do that?'

I shrug. 'Sure. Heard there are a few spots coming up soon. Why should we be the only Agents to have it so good? We gotta look out for each other.'

The Agent scrambles around to find something to write his details on. He shoves a piece of paper at me.

'I'd owe you big time. Thanks a lot.'

'No problem. So, are we right to go in?'

The Agent ushers them through the checkpoint. 'Yeah, yeah, sure. Have a good night. Don't work too hard!'

The Agent laughs at his own joke as we pass by. I try not to run into the compound. The music grows louder as we get closer. We enter through the front door like everyone else. Other Agents are easy to spot, but they all keep their distance from their assignments.

'Let's split in two. We can cover more ground and find Kerina faster,' says Vera. 'Elgee, you go with Raider.'

We disband in different directions. My head swirls around the room.

'Try to be inconspicuous,' hisses Vera.

I walk the perimeter of the dance floor and find Anastasia talking to an Agent—Ryen.

I cross the floor and tap him on the shoulder. 'We have a situation.'

Anastasia raises an eyebrow. 'Saxon? How did you get in here?'

'Where's Kerina?'

'I did what you asked. I left her over by the doorway talking to the Primo Dictor.'

I follow her gaze and see the empty space in the doorway. Ryen shakes Anastasia's hand, a polite gesture to finish the conversation for anyone interested in their encounter. He walks past me.

'Follow behind me. Don't make a scene. Remember, there are people watching everybody's actions.'

'That's the problem. Somebody *is* watching Kerina's moves and she could be in trouble.'

Ryen nods as he passes by people, not committing to conversation, but not ignoring them either. Then one lady steps in front and blocks our path.

'Governess! How lovely to see you on the dance floor,' says Ryen.

'If only my husband were here to dance with me,' she says.

Ryen offers her his arm. 'I have some moves if you are brave enough to test them out.'

'Of course.' She smiles, but her eyes watch me.

'Governess.' I nod to her before leaving the floor, trying to keep the panic at bay.

Chapter 90

Kerina

The Primo Dictor leads me to a private room.

'I don't know what kind of joke this is, but if its money you want, I won't pay.'

'You think I want you to buy me off?'

'Why else would you make such preposterous claims.'

'You and I both know my claims are true. I am your daughter.'

'Impossible!'

'I'm the one you gave up to Marlane Vespa. I'm the one you told your wife died during childbirth.'

He draws his hand to his mouth. 'It can't be true. Is it really you, Kerina?'

'How did you know my name?'

'It's the one I gave you.'

A range of emotions cross the Dictor's face as he wrestles with the revelation.

He reaches out as if to touch me, then stops himself. 'It's not safe for you here.'

'You're the Primo Dictor, how can it not be safe? Unless you mean me harm.'

'No! I did all I could to protect you.'

'By giving me up? And not fighting for me?'

He cringes at my words. 'I thought if your life was away from prying eyes it would be easier.'

'Easier for who? You can't begin to imagine the events your actions have caused.'

'Does my wife know you're alive?'

'Your *wife* has been trying to capture me!'

He shakes his head. 'No, she wouldn't harm you, I'm sure of it.'

There's a knock at the door.

'Governor, are you in there?'

'It's my personal Agent,' he whispers. 'Yes! I'll just be a couple more minutes.'

'Yes, sir, but it's the Governess. She's looking for you.'

'Tell her I'm coming and to have her dancing shoes ready.'

'Yes, sir.'

The Dictor turns to me, grief etched on his face. 'Every day I have thought of you, wondered about you and how your life turned out.'

'But never searched for me?'

'I couldn't …' His voice breaks. 'Even in the darkest moments when I wanted to. I knew when I made that regrettable decision, it could never be undone.'

'What about now? Would you want me in your life now?'

'Yes!'

His vehemence surprises me.

'Even knowing your wife wants me dead?'

'I can't believe she would. I'd … have to speak with her.'

'Gerrard, are you in there?'

'Here's your chance, Governor.' I hold a finger to my lips, then hide behind the desk.

The door creaks open. 'Gerrard, our guests are asking for you. What's the matter? You don't look well.'

'Lillyanne, I have a confession. Please close the door.'

It clicks into place. There is some shuffling of footsteps.

'What is it, Gerrard?'

'This is hard for me to say, but first you have to know how sorry I am to have lied to you all these years. But I have good news! Our daughter Kerina … is …'

'Alive? Yes, I know.'

I'm sure they can hear me breathe as I listen to my biological parents speak.

'Did you honestly think I would never find out, Gerrard?'

'But how did you know?'

'You're such a fool. I've been tracking her for months, years really. And it's finally paid off. She's here tonight. Actually, you already met her when she arrived with that Agent Tambler.'

Chapter 91

Saxon

I stand near the edge of the dance floor, waiting for Ryen. My eyes sweep the room the whole time, hoping to spot Kerina. Ryen finally makes his way over to me.

'Are you right, twinkle-toes? We've got more important things than dancing to worry about.'

'Are you saying I should have refused the Governess a dance? That wouldn't have been suspicious at all. Nobody says no to the Governess.'

'I'm aware of that.'

'What are you doing here, Saxon?'

'The Governess knows *exactly* what Kerina looks like.'

Ryen's face pales. 'We need to check the private rooms.' He struggles to keep his emotions in check. 'It's the only place they could be.'

'Let's go.'

Ryen grabs my wrist. 'It's not that simple. The Primo Dictor's personal Agent will be close, especially if he does his job right. He won't make it easy to check the rooms.'

'Then you better come up with a story fast.'

'Any luck?' says Raider, appearing beside us with Vera.

I shake my head. 'Watch that space.' I point to the exit Anastasia indicated earlier.

'I was watching it,' he says. 'I just saw the Governess go through.'

'Damn it!' I say, fists clenching. 'I guarantee it's not for a toilet break.'

'Stay here,' orders Ryen. 'If we're not back in thirty minutes, leave via the front gate. You too, Vera.'

'No chance, Ryen, I'm coming.'

'Vera! Can you just do what I ask for once?'

'Fine, but I'm not leaving without Kerina.'

Ryen and I move quickly down the hallway. He knows his way around, so I follow him. We try the door handles along the way. Some doors open, but are clear when we check. Some doors are locked, but give no response when we call out. We turn a corner and collide with an Agent.

'Stop! Who gave you clearance to be back here?'

'I could be asking you the same question,' says Ryen.

The Agent notices the stripes on Ryen.

'Sorry, sir. Didn't realise.' He salutes. 'Just following orders.'

'Whose orders?'

'The Primo Dictor's personal Agent.'

'Where is he?'

The Agent bounces on the balls of his feet. 'He uh, had to umm, take a dump.'

'Are you telling me the Primo Dictor's personal Agent has left his subject unattended?' says Ryen, getting in the Agent's face.

He swallows. 'Not exactly. I'm here watching for him.'

'You can leave. I'll deal with him when he returns.'

The Agent hesitates. 'He said not to leave until he got back.'

'And I'm ordering you to leave. Which of us do you think you should listen to?'

The Agent bounces a couple more times, then flees.

'That should stop further questions.'

Smash!

Something breaks behind the closed door. I try the handle, but it's locked.

'Hello? Is somebody in there?'

Crash!

Chapter 92

Kerina

'Calm down, Gerrard. There's no need to break things,' says the Governess.

'Who are you?' says the Primo Doctor. 'Do you hate me so much?'

'I'd have to care about you to hate you, and I don't care. I haven't for many years.'

Bang, bang, bang. 'Is everything all right in there?'

I recognise Saxon's voice.

'Where is she?' demands the Governess.

'Why? What do you want with her?'

'What should have been done when she was born. What you were too weak to do.'

Knock, knock, knock. 'This is Agent Tambler. Open the door.'

'Show some mercy, Lillyanne. She's your daughter. *Our* daughter.'

'No! She's an abomination. She's Okodee and it's your fault.' She laughs. 'Your father told me on his deathbed. He told me everything. Don't you see? We've been trying to clean up your mess ever since you confessed to him about the girl. He asked me to tie up the loose ends. I weeded out the names of most of the people involved in the cover-up, along with some sympathisers.'

Crunch!

I peek around the desk. Ryen is standing in the doorway, or what's left of it.

'This is a private conversation, Agent Tambler,' says the Governess.

'I apologise, but I heard something break and there was no response to my calls. It's my duty to investigate.'

The Governess waves him off. 'Just Gerrard being clumsy. He knocked a couple of vases off the table. No need to break the door down.'

I make eye contact with Ryen, then retreat behind the desk.

'Hey you, strange Agent. Come here.'

'Yes, Governess?' says Saxon.

'Is there something in here you're looking for?'

'Just signs of trouble so we can do our job.'

Silence echoes throughout the room. I have no doubt she knows Saxon is an imposter. Time stretches out. I hold my breath while my heart pounds.

'There is no trouble here tonight, but I thank you for your vigilance,' says the Primo Dictor. 'Come, Lillyanne, our guests will fear we have abandoned them.'

I remain still as their footsteps leave the room.

'Oh, Agent Tambler?' says the Governess, pausing. 'You really should conduct more thorough checks on all Agents in future. It's amazing how many people have things to hide.'

'Noted, Governess, thank you.'

The footsteps trail down the hallway, but I still dare not move.

Ryen pokes his head over the desk. 'That was too damn close.'

'No argument from me. Let's get out of here,' I say.

Saxon appears beside me 'Are you okay?'

'Yes, I'm fine.'

'Kerina, you need to leave the back way. There's no way you can walk out the front door,' says Ryen.

'Did he hurt you?' Concern laces Saxon's eyes as he searches my face.

He still cares about me, even after I told him whatever is between us doesn't matter.

I shake my head. 'He didn't hurt me, but I know that *she* wants to.'

My biological grandfather ordered my parents to have me killed. He devised the accident that killed Saxon's parents. My mother set it all in motion and only has one more person to go. Me.

Chapter 93

Saxon

'What are we going to do? If the Governess doesn't see both of us back out there, you'll fall under suspicion,' I say.

'And we still need to get Lariel out,' says Kerina.

'Saxon, I need you to go back out there—'

'I'm not leaving Kerina here alone.'

'Just listen! Go out there, make sure the Governess is distracted and not searching for Kerina. Send Vera back here while I wait with Kerina.

'I can get out on my own,' says Kerina.

Ryen ignores her. 'Send Vera back. Then make sure the Governess sees you once more. After that, grab Elgee and get the hell out of there.'

I stretch my neck from side to side. I wrestle with leaving Kerina behind, but know this is the best option.

'I'll be fine, Saxon. I'm a fighter, remember?'

I nod, hesitate once more, and leave. I hurry back the way we came. The hallway is clear. I step back into the main room to find Elgee and Vera waiting nearby. I search the room for the Governess. She's easy to find. The dance floor is clear and only she and the Primo Dictor are dancing. Both are all smiles and seem to be having fun. A good act from both of them. I walk slowly so as not to attract attention.

'Vera, check the Governess is not watching, then make your way down the hallway. Ryen will be waiting with Kerina. You need to get her out of here.'

'Understood.' She checks the passageway is clear and disappears through the doorway.

I search the room once again until I see the familiar face I'm searching for. I stroll over to Anastasia, careful to check her parents aren't nearby and might recognise me. I can tell she saw my approach, but she doesn't turn to acknowledge me.

'I need one more favour,' I whisper.

'Always with the favours,' she replies. 'Luckily, that's what friends are for.'

The music stops and the crowd applauds. The Primo Dictor and his wife make their way back to the chairs at the front. I grab Anastasia's hand and guide her closer to the seats.

'I need you to get the attention of the Governess so she is distracted. It will be easy, just follow my lead.'

I take a deep bow in front of Anastasia. She giggles loudly and covers her mouth in an exaggerated manner. I bend down and kiss her hand. As I do, I see the Governess lean forward to watch. I stay bent and retreat backward from Anastasia. She laughs again and sends a flirtatious kiss my way. I pretend to catch it and grin widely. I turn without urgency and make my way through the crowd. Elgee waits near the doorway.

We are at the bottom of the stairs when a deep voice calls out. 'Agent, stop!'

We both pause.

'Not you, you're dismissed.' An Agent appears, along with the one Ryen sent away earlier. He waves Elgee off.

'You,' he pokes me. 'I want your Agent identification.'

I shrug. 'I didn't think I'd need it tonight.'

'Well, you do. You have ten seconds to produce it or you're under arrest.'

'I don't think so.' I walk away. Elgee turns back, but I shake my head.

Oomph! I am knocked to the ground.

'You don't have it because you're a fraud,' the Agent hisses in my ear. 'Don't bother denying it. We know exactly who you are. A sniggering little sympathiser.'

Chapter 94

Kerina

We arrive back at Raider's house. Our escape was perfect, almost too easy. Elgee sits at the table, his head held up by his hands.

'Where's Saxon?' I say.

'He got arrested.'

'*What?*'

'That's okay, Ryen can get him out,' says Vera.

Elgee shakes his head. 'Don't think he's going where Ryen can get to him.'

I pace the floor. 'She ordered it, didn't she?'

'I reckon so. It all seemed a bit coincidental for my likin'.'

I slam the table. 'She's done this to get to me. That's why it was so easy to sneak out of there.'

'Let's just wait and see what Ryen knows,' says Raider. 'Maybe it ain't what we think.'

'Did you speak with the Primo Dictor?' asks Lace.

'Yes.'

'Well, don't hold back. What did he say? Is he an ally?'

'I'm not sure. I think he wants to be, but his wife has much more power than any of us imagined. She's known about me for a very long time and he had no idea that she knew. But I think the revelations tonight will soon tell what kind of Dictor he is.'

'You mean what kind of father,' says Lace, her voice tinged with sadness.

'We need to get you another meeting with him,' says Vera.

'How? She knows about me. The two of them will be watching each other. Both waiting to make their move.'

'I think she's already made her move,' says Vera. 'We need to prepare a counterattack. Be ready for any possibility.'

'Vera, I think you and I need to take a walk,' says Lace. 'Talk tactics, that sort of thing. Raider, you're with us.'

They leave through the back door while I wait uselessly in the room.

Elgee moves in front of me. 'He's gonna be okay.'

I look up at Saxon's best friend. 'This is all my fault. If he and Manny had never found me …' Guilt sweeps through me. I promised Manny I would look out for his brother.

Elgee grips my shoulders. 'You da the best thing he ever found.'

'I told him that he doesn't matter,' I whisper.

'He's a stubborn fella, if you ain't already noticed. He knows you'll realise he does matter. When you're ready, he'll be there, waitin."

'What if they kill him just to make a point?'

Elgee wipes a lone tear off my cheek. 'We ain't gonna let that happen.'

I nod, desperate to cling to some kind of hope.

There is a knock at the front door. 'We haven't got time for the code,' Ryen yells through the wood.

I run across the room and let him in. 'Where's Saxon?'

'The Governess has him.'

'Is he okay?'

'He's alive and he'll stay that way until she gets what she wants.'

'Me.'

Ryen nods.

I stand tall. 'Then let's give her what she wants.'

I won't let Saxon die. He saved me. He never gave up on me. Now it's my turn to fight for him.

Chapter 95

Saxon

The night passed slowly once they brought me here. Sleep was impossible. Now, with the daylight, I concentrate on the crack in the ceiling. I imagine sealing it up and making it disappear. Anything to keep my mind occupied. The four walls crowd me, yet the room is spacious and bare. I walk around and around in circles, trying to guess the Governess's next move. She must have been behind my arrest. The Agent who stopped me might have been the Primo Dictor's personal Agent, but obviously his allegiance doesn't lie with the Governor.

The Governor knew Kerina was hiding, but is he on her side? Or did his wife coerce him into her way of thinking? If they went after me, then Kerina must have left undetected. The thought gives me some comfort.

'Damn it!' I slam my hand on the ground.

Frustration runs through my body, pent up and ready to explode for not having more answers. I stand and walk the length of the room. Fifteen steps long and seven steps wide. A noise comes from the doorway. The small camera in the corner angles toward me. I move backward, away from the door. It swings open and I find myself face to face with evil.

The Governess enters the room, flanked by two Agents. One moves toward me, his stunner poised on my chest. The other remains at her side, like her own personal bodyguard.

'I shouldn't expect any trouble from you, should I, Saxon?'

My eye twitches as she addresses me by name. She smiles, and in that moment I have never hated somebody so much. My fists clench and I breathe deeply to control the urge to attack her right there and then. I need to stay calm and be smart about this. I wouldn't make it two steps before her bodyguards stunned me into a coma for the next three hours.

'I don't want you to be here any longer than you have to, Saxon. But it seems my *daughter* is rather illusive and inventive when it comes to being pursued. I should know. I've been trying to find her for years.'

She walks closer to me, goading him. 'I had to get creative after trying for these past few months to find her. It took so long to locate her initially. I've been so close, so many times, but alas she has slipped through my fingers each time. Until now.'

'You'll never catch her,' I say.

The Governess takes the last step and inclines her head toward me. The Agent nearest kicks the back of my knees, making me buckle under the force. I groan and collapse to a kneeling position. She curls her finger beneath my chin, forcing me to look up at her.

'You inspired my creativity. When I saw you last night, I knew I had the answer to my problem. You are my bargaining token. Why should I do all the work when I can make Kerina do it for me?'

'She won't meet you to trade.'

The Governess grips my jawline. 'Yes. She. Will.'

'If she meets you, she'll kill you.'

'Not if I kill her first.' The Governess smirks, then retreats from the room. At the doorway, she stops and calls over her shoulder.

'It's nothing personal against you, Saxon.' She turns to face me. 'Just like it was nothing personal against your parents.'

She watches my reaction, waiting for it. A guttural mix of pain and rage roars out my mouth. I lunge toward her. I don't even get close before an electric current zips through my body and I collapse on the hard ground.

Chapter 96

Kerina

People move about their daily business in the centre of town, oblivious to the drama unfolding around them. Pots of warbles are scattered on windowsills just like in Nevertyre, creating a familiarity. Vera pulls her hood down further, but swivels her head about, searching the area around them.

'Try to be inconspicuous,' I say, sitting on the same bench seat as the day we met Lace.

'There's too many people around. I can't contain the situation if something happens.'

'Remember that you're not alone, so calm down.'

There should be at least twenty people aligned with Raider and Lace planted around us. Their job is to have eyes on me at all times and stay alert for any suspicious individuals. Vera slumps on the bench seat, her legs jiggling as if trying to heat them up. The weather is already warm, though.

'I don't know Lace's crew and I don't trust nobody I don't know.'

'You don't trust anybody you do know,' I say.

'That's not true. I trust you and Ryen. You trust Saxon and he trusts Elgee—so that's four people.'

I grin. 'Four is a good start.'

Vera jumps up. 'Here comes Ryen.'

'It's done,' he says. 'The message has been sent. Now we wait to hear your mother's response.'

'She's not my mother,' I say.

'How long?' asks Vera.

'I doubt it will be long.'

The words have barely left his mouth when a young girl approaches us. Vera stands guarded. The girl stretches out her arm. Her hand is clasped around something. Vera stands in front of me protectively.

'The Agent told me to give this to the pretty girl with the long hair.'

I gesture for the girl to walk closer. The girl smiles and dimples form on her cheeks. She hands the offering to me.

'A gift for you,' she says, then scampers away.

I squeeze my eyes shut when I see what it is. I rub my fingers around the metal ball that holds the ashes of Saxon's parents.

If you want the rest of him returned, dear daughter, I suggest you meet me tonight when the moon is at its highest. The abandoned warehouse where your friend betrayed you. I look forward to being reunited with you again.

Mother

'Let's go,' says Vera. 'There is so much to plan and the sun is already starting to set.'

'We have to get Saxon back,' I say.

'She won't harm him,' says Ryen.

'This is the first piece.' I shove the proof of life in Ryen's face. 'How many other pieces do you think she is willing to supply?'

Ryen grits his teeth. 'Okay, let's go.'

I follow behind Vera. A plan for the meeting forms in my mind. I can't let anything happen to Saxon. The last thing I want is more gifts from my *mother*.

Chapter 97

Saxon

A bag covers my head. The material is scratchy and dust gets up my nose. I remember a night long ago when Manny and I camped with Rudolph. We were fast asleep when the wind picked up suddenly. I was blown awake. The dust made me squint and I could barely see Manny and Rudolph, let alone make my way inside. The dust got up my nostrils and didn't leave for days. The smell reminds me of that night.

The bag is thick and blocks out much of the light, but I know it's nighttime again. The air has dropped. If I squint downward, I can see my feet and make out the ground, but that's it. The road we travel along is bumpy. It makes me dizzy. My head flops about and I reach toward the door for a handle to grip. The car halts to a stop, skidding with the sudden brake. The door is wrenched from my fingers. Somebody drags me roughly from the car. My hands are secured in front of me so it's hard to keep balanced as they jostle me about.

'Walk,' they order.

Something pokes me between the shoulder blades. Probably a stunner like the one used on me previously. I do as I'm told, hoping there are no obstacles in my path. My ears strain for any distinguishable noises, but the only sound is the crunch of my boots on the ground. We walk silently with the Agent twisting and turning me. After a while I notice there is some light every now and then. It makes me think we must be on the streets of Middtown.

'Stop,' says a voice I wish I didn't know.

The bag is ripped from my head.

'Good eve, Saxon.' The Governess smiles.

I can't help but notice the physical resemblance to Kerina. If I didn't hate the Governess so much, I could see where Kerina gets some of her features from. But that is where the similarities end. Kerina is nothing like this woman before me. Kerina has a pure heart and caring soul. She'd never hurt somebody on purpose like this woman.

'What do you plan to do to me?'

'I told you she would come.'

'No! What are you going to do with her?'

I look around the deserted area and recognise the location. It's where Lariel set us up to hand Kerina over. The Governess probably arranged that as well.

'Once this is over, Saxon, you can go back to your old life. I'm sure you would like to meet your nephew.'

I can't hide the shock on my face. I picture Manny holding a small, newborn boy. I am overcome with a longing to meet him and protect him.

'Such a sweet, innocent thing. It would be awful if something were to happen to his parents.'

I step toward the Governess. 'You will pay for all you've done.'

The Agent steps in front of me to intervene, but the Governess waves him off.

I move closer. 'If something were to happen to my nephew, I'd come for you. And I'd kill you. That I promise.'

The Governess shrugs. 'You speak like a man, but I think deep down, you're still a boy.'

'Perhaps, but I never make a promise I can't keep.'

We stare at one another, neither willing to turn away first.

The Agent intervenes. 'We need to move him.'

'See you soon, Saxon. Try to remember what I said.' She smiles. 'Manny is quite taken with his son. Shayne is his name, I believe. Wasn't that your father's name?'

I lunge for her, but the Agent grips me and tugs me away. I struggle as hatred runs through my blood. The Agent pushes me through the doorway of a nearby building. I choke as a gag is stuffed in my mouth and I'm locked in the small room. Thoughts of my family and new nephew are the only things to keep me company this time. There is no window for light and no way to escape my captivity.

Chapter 98

Kerina

The secret knock echoes off the door at Raider's house. He stands quickly to open it.

'Lariel!' I run toward my friend and hug her fiercely. 'Are you okay?'

'Ryen made sure I was safe, just like he said he would.'

Ryen stands in the doorway. 'Thought we better get her out. My cover will be blown after tonight anyway.'

'Then you better get in here so we can make plans,' Lace yells from the table.

Ryen and Lariel squeeze into the room along with the others.

'Any whispers about the Governess?' asks Raider.

Ryen shakes his head. 'She must be using only those she trusts.'

'That's good,' says Lace. 'Means she won't have big numbers on her side.'

'No, but she'll have the force of weapons and the advantage of a surprise attack.'

Elgee pushes his chair back. 'I'll kill her myself if anything happens to Saxon.'

'Nobody's killing anyone. We'll do the swap and then Lace's people will be ready with their roadblocks,' says Ryen. 'We can highjack the cars and get her back.'

'Yep. We got people set up on every road out of that area. They're ready and prepared. Nothing will get through our roadblocks.'

'This is stupid! Kerina could get hurt, killed even,' says Vera.

'It's my life and that's a risk I'm willing to take,' I say.

'Well, I'm not. There has to be a better way. We need you in one piece.'

'Vera! This is the best plan. There's too little time to come up with anything else. We have to get Saxon back and this is the only way,' I say.

'How can I help?' asks Lariel.

'Our original group will go with Kerina,' says Ryen. 'We'll keep her safe and surrounded until the handover.'

'What if it's another ambush?' says Elgee.

Lariel flinches at his words.

'If my mother wanted me dead, it would have been done by now. She wants me dead, I'm sure, but she wants something else first.'

'What?' asks Lace.

'I don't know. But whatever it is, it's been enough to help keep me alive so far.'

'What about the Primo Dictor? Did he get the message?' asks Vera.

Ryen shrugs. 'I don't know. It was dispatched, but time is limited.'

I survey the room. A couple of months ago, the only person I knew in the group was Lariel. Now these strangers are all willing to put their lives on the line to help and protect me.

'Before we leave, I just want to thank you all,' I say. 'For everything you've done and everything you're willing to do. I promise if this works, I will do everything in my power to govern well.'

'You better be worth all this fuss,' Vera says, rolling her eyes.

When Rudolph first told me that I was the Okodee leader, I thought the old man was a fool. I couldn't believe that my destiny was so great. Now I relish the opportunity to prove myself and make things right.

'It's time, people,' says Lace, clapping her hands. 'Let's go.'

Ryen places a hand on my shoulder. 'Are you ready?'

His sacrifice has been just as great as anyone's. His father devoted his life to the Okodee cause. Rudolph might have lived a double life, but he was an honourable man. I don't want his death to be in vain.

All eyes are on me and I realise they are waiting for me to lead them. 'Let's go. I don't want to be late to my family reunion.'

Chapter 99

Saxon

It's been quiet for a long time. If anybody were nearby, I would have heard them. I'm sure they transported me here and dumped me, ready for the exchange between Kerina and me. The Governess will be making arrangements to ensure it goes smoothly. She won't want any mistakes tonight. This is probably her last chance to get what she wants: Kerina.

I pick up the dirt from the ground. The coarse feeling washes over my hand and I let it slip between my fingers. It reminds me of my garden and the vegetables I've planted. The solace I find working in it is something I crave. It gives me a sense of peace and fulfilment, plus the extra money helps support us. Hopefully Manny has tended to the garden, although he might be busy now Constance has had the baby. My nephew. The thought makes my heart ache. Did they really name him after his grandfather? I can't let anything happen to that baby or his parents. No child should grow up without their parents around. I know that better than anyone. But to protect my family, I might have to let Kerina go. Am I willing to do that?

The door swings open and an Agent appears. His gun is pointed at me.

'Get up.'

I struggle to my feet.

The Agent shoves me in the back. 'Let's go.'

I step out of the room with darkness all around. There's not even any moonlight tonight. I turn my head in all directions, trying to get my bearings. I know it's the same place Lariel set us up.

So, I also know it's a dead end. When Kerina arrives, there's only one way in and one way out. The Governess has planned her trap well. She will not let Kerina escape this time.

'Move it.' The Agent pushes me again, urging me to walk faster.

I stumble but manage to stay upright. I'm hungry and thirsty and weak from the stunner used on me. It knocked me out cold and I still feel the aftershocks in my muscles as I try to walk.

A group of Agents stand in a circle. One Agent, taller than the others, points in different directions. The others move about, following his orders. He turns to face me. It's the same Agent who arrested me—the Primo Dictor's personal Agent. However, it's clear that it's the Governess's orders he follows. She must be paying him well.

The Agent makes no effort to move, just watches me as I'm marched toward him. When I'm close enough, he gets so close, our noses almost touch. His sour breath assaults my nostrils.

He speaks softly. 'You're a disgrace to your own kind, Saxon. Sympathisers like you should be shot. If I had my way, I'd do it myself, right here, right now.'

I want to reply, but the gag is still on. Instead, I push forward with my chest, forcing the Agent to step backward. He punches me in the stomach.

'Oomph.' I double over in pain.

Another thud to the back and I sprawl on the ground. The Agent wrenches my head back by the hair.

He leans down and sneers. 'Lucky for you, I follow orders, or else you'd be dead.'

He shoves my head to the ground and kicks me in the ribs. I groan and he leaves me there, curled up in the middle of the road. My body aches. I try to push myself from the ground, but I have no strength left. That's when I notice a car parked alongside the building. The interior light turns on. The Governess sits in the front seat, watching me. She's been watching all along. She's waiting for her daughter to arrive and I'm the trap, laid out to ensnare her.

Chapter 100

Kerina

Darkness surrounds us like a blanket. The streets are deserted, as if people know something is happening but want no part of it. There is no point trying to hide our arrival. The Governess will have her people in place already. Besides, there is only one way into the area. That's why the ruse worked so well for Lariel last time. The only thing to do is to walk straight in.

'I've got your back,' whispers Vera, squeezing my shoulder.

I am comforted by the words. Vera, who cares about nobody, has been fiercely protective of me. She is one ally I'm glad to have found.

'We're not going to let anything happen to you,' says Ryen.

Vera and Ryen flank either side of me while Elgee and Lariel bring up the rear. There was no sign of Lace or Raider's crew on the way here. I'm confident they are in position, though. I have to put my trust in them and hope they can stop the Governess. I cringe when I think of this woman. How can a mother hate her own child so much?

The rendezvous point is close. Ryen stops the group to address everyone.

'We're nearly there. Now is your last chance to back out.'

Nobody moves.

'Good. Let's do this.'

We turn into the street. It's dark and deserted. Silence surrounds us. Suddenly a bright light illuminates the centre. A shape lies motionless on the ground.

There is a sharp intake of breath from Elgee behind me.

'Saxon,' I say.

Ryen grabs my arm. 'She wants to rattle you. Don't let her.'

My heart pounds against my chest. We walk slowly, each step closer making us more vulnerable. With two hundred metres to go, I stop.

'Show yourself,' I yell.

A car door slams shut from the same direction the light came from. We were right about the escape vehicle. They came prepared for a quick getaway. An Agent appears in the light.

'Dat's the guy who arrested Saxon,' hisses Elgee.

The Agent walks toward the shape on the ground. He drags the body upward and forces him to kneel. I can see Saxon is gagged.

'Let him speak,' I call out.

The Agent looks toward the car before removing the gag.

'Saxon? Are you okay?'

He doesn't respond. His head lolls forward. His eyes open and close as he seems to fight for consciousness.

'Saxon?' I yell louder.

'I'm sorry, Kerina,' he says.

The relief to hear him speak overwhelms me.

'Leave me here,' he says. 'Don't do this.' The pain in his voice is unbearable.

A figure emerges from the car and passes through the headlights to stand beside Saxon. The Governess faces us, her hands clasped in front of her. She stares at me. Even from this distance, I see the hate in her eyes.

'Let him go,' I yell. I step forward, moving away from my companions. 'You've got what you want, I'm here. Now release him.'

The Governess takes one step toward me, her arms open wide. 'If you want him, my dearest daughter … come and get him.'

Chapter 101

Saxon

The light hurts my eyes, but I see Kerina in the distance. I grit my teeth to make sure I stay upright. I try not to sway from the pain in my ribs. The Agent raises his weapon and points it at me. Ryen leans into Kerina and says something. Vera raises her weapon and points it in my direction.

'Release him first,' Kerina calls out.

'Come closer,' says the Governess.

Kerina approaches. As she gets closer, I see she has her eyes fixed on me. She stops halfway.

'That's close enough, now let him go.'

The Agent hauls me to my feet.

'You can both walk at the same time,' says the Governess. 'Don't do anything stupid or my Agent will put a bullet in the back of your precious Saxon's head.'

The Agent shoves me toward Kerina. It's then I understand that she does care for me. Maybe even as much as I care for her. I stumble until we meet in the middle.

'I'm so sorry this happened to you, Saxon.' She grips my restrained hands.

'Kerina, you can't let them take you. There's still time to leave me. You're too important.'

'And you matter too much to me. *You matter*, Saxon.'

She removes the necklace around her neck and places it around mine. My parents' ashes are back where they belong. She caresses my cheek once, then steps around me. She walks fearlessly to the woman who has pursued her. The woman who should have protected her above all others.

I stumble toward the exit point of the laneway where the rest of the group waits.

'You okay, mah friend?' Elgee grabs me.

'We can't let her go,' I say. 'We can't just abandon her.'

'It's under control.' Vera cuts the restraints.

'There is a plan in place,' says Ryen.

Kerina faces her mother. The light casts a shadow across their faces. They seem to be speaking to one another. Suddenly shots echo through the night and the lights on the car are smashed. Darkness falls across the rendezvous point.

'Is this part of your plan?' I ask.

'Not exactly. Who fired?' yells Ryen.

'It came from their direction,' says Vera.

'Why would they shoot out their own lights?' says Lariel.

'Don't shoot back!' yells Ryen. 'We might hit Kerina.'

More shots sound and we all scamper for cover. Ryen goes down, hit.

'Ryen!' I yell, reaching for him.

His breathing is fast and he groans in pain. Elgee helps me hoist Ryen's arms over our shoulders as we drag him from the road.

Blood seeps from his chest. It gushes from the wound even as I apply pressure. Continuous gunfire bounces around us.

'Stay with me, Ryen.'

Ryen's eyes roll around before focusing on me. 'Protect Kerina, no matter what.'

'Ryen no! You're not doing this.' I apply more pressure to the gunshot. 'Ryen! Don't you die on me.'

Ryen's throat gurgles. Bubbles of blood foam at his mouth. Then he stills.

Chapter 102

Kerina

Gunshots ring out around me and I try not to panic. I stay low and crawl through the chaos.

'Grab her,' yells the Governess. 'She can't get away.'

Shots continue to fire. I have no weapon and no idea who's shooting. Ryen wouldn't have planned this attack. He would have had something else arranged. My mother can't have known about it either. She was just as surprised as I when the lights were smashed out. What the hell is going on? Did Lace and Raider double-cross us?

I scramble my way along the edge of the building in the darkness. This might be my only chance of escape.

'Kerina!' yells the Governess. 'Don't you leave me!'

I ignore my mother's voice and continue in the opposite direction.

'*Kerina!*'

A thud hits me and I slam into a building. Broken glass slices my skin. I kick out at the Governess but miss my target. Something metallic glints in the light. I try to move, but I'm too slow. My mother lunges for me and smashes my head with the weapon. My vision blurs and I fight to keep conscious. Warm, sticky blood oozes from the gash on my forehead. The Governess straddles me and glares down. I feel her contempt wash over me.

'For years I searched for you. For years I watched Gerrard wither under the guilt of giving you away. Never confiding in me, never taking much notice of me at all, really. As the years passed, he barely governed at all. I was competing with your ghost! I had to make the decisions. The communities were stupid enough to think it was him.'

'Why didn't you just have me killed?'

'Because I wanted to watch you suffer,' she snarls. 'Just like I've suffered all these years. But none of that matters now, because I will get to watch you suffer at the very end. You should know I have big plans in store for your friends.'

The gunshots have ceased and an eerie calm descends on us. Headlights turn into the street, illuminating the tops of our heads. I use the momentary blindness to lash out, knocking the gun from my mother's hands. I punch upward, just like Saxon taught me. The Governess doubles over. Her screams of pain ripple across the space. I scramble for the weapon, but my mother grabs my hair, pulling me backward. The car door opens and a figure climbs out.

Through the blood I see the Primo Dictor, my father. He walks toward us, a slow but steady gait.

'Gerrard, help me,' yells the Governess. 'We were attacked.'

She staggers for the gun and bends down to grab it, just as I lunge for it. We both wrestle for control. *Bang!* The shot rings out and the Governess sinks to the ground. She clasps her hands to her stomach. I push myself off the woman who wished me harm for so long.

The Governess reaches for me and pulls me close. 'You ... will never ... govern.'

'Yes, I will. And you can no longer stop me.'

I look down on the woman who has hunted everywhere to find me. A woman who has killed good people to get to me and now can do no more to hurt me. She gasps one final breath before releasing her grip on me.

I close the dead, unforgiving eyes of my mother. I don't want them haunting my dreams.

'Kerina? Come out now and feel safe,' the Primo Dictor calls out. 'I promise you won't be harmed.'

I stand tall from the shadows and walk toward my new future. My destiny.

Epilogue I

Saxon

Shayne bowls the ball to me and I hit it back softly.

'Good catch! You've been practising like I taught you,' I say.

I visit Manny and Constance whenever I can. Manny says it's not often enough, but Constance defends me. She understands my job in Middtown is important.

'Uncle Saxon, how long are you staying for this time?'

'I'm here for the whole week.'

'Can we visit Elgee at the market?'

'Sure, he'd love to see you. Mumma Bear might even have a surprise for you.'

Constance waddles out the back door. Her stomach is swollen and ready to burst.

'If this baby doesn't arrive soon, I might just pull her out myself,' she says, wiping the sweat from her forehead.

'Uncle Saxon, is Kerina tryin' to make Nevertyre better?'

'She is. Where did you hear that?'

'My best friend Brayden told me. He said she's makin' Nevertyre a better place for people like him.'

'What do you mean like him?' I ask.

'He's Okodee, but I don't care. I still bowl better at cricket.' Shayne skirts past his mother and goes inside.

'So, tell me, Saxon, how is the Governess?' says Constance.

'You can ask her yourself when she gets here.'

I move past Constance before she can question me further. I work alongside Kerina in Middtown, but she doesn't always approve of my methods. That will probably never change. We're both too stubborn to back down on anything.

Kerina

I let Lariel tend to her father's memorial alone. It holds no remains because they never located a body. We discovered he was dead all along, just like my adoptive parents. Everyone risked so much to ensure my survival. Now I am doing everything in my power to make the communities thrive.

The Agents nearby give me enough space that I'm almost fooled into thinking they're not handpicked to protect me at all costs. It took some getting used to, having such security around me. But my father insisted on it once my existence became public knowledge..

'Let's go already,' says Vera, destroying the solitude that surrounded us.

'Haven't you learnt any patience yet, Vera?' I tease.

Vera has become one of my closest confidants. Although, she still takes little notice of orders and does whatever she likes. It drives Ryen crazy. He commands the security teams within the communities. It was a long recovery for him after the standoff four years ago. He nearly died more than once.

We walk toward Manny and Constance's house. The light in the front window shows a silhouetted head waiting for us.

'I could gobble that kid up,' says Vera, breaking into a jog.

Shayne is the only thing in this world that can make her turn to mush. He runs out the front to greet us. Saxon joins him. His eyes scan the perimeter first, checking his Agents are where they should be. Then he watches my approach, waiting for me. I get a shiver every time I visit Saxon's brother and his wife. If it weren't for them, I would not be where I am now. They took me in, gave me strength and made me part of their family. My family. I know we are creating a world worth fighting for.

Acknowledgments

Earl Nightingale once said, 'Never give up on a dream because of the time it will take to accomplish it. The time will pass anyway.' How true he was! The path to this publication has been long and uncertain. There were many times when I thought The Ruby Locket would not make it into the published book it is now. I admit to almost giving up. Almost.

My sincere gratitude to Michelle Lovi and Odyssey Books for helping to bring my hopes and dreams of the publication of Kerina and Saxon's story to fruition.

Thank you to the Maurice Saxby Creative Development Program, which offered me a once in a lifetime immersion opportunity into the world of writing. During the two weeks of the program I was inspired, motivated, challenged, and supported to grow as an author. A special mention to Helen Chamberlin for chaperoning me throughout the program, and Rosalind Price, who was the first person to read the whole manuscript of The Ruby Locket. Rosalind gave me such supportive feedback, advice, and ideas that the seed of determination was planted to make it the best novel I could write.

To my family Jamie, Toby, and Molly, I thank you for your patience and support, and the indulgence of time that you give to me, which allows me to write.

And to you, the reader, thank you for your support. I hope you have enjoyed this story as much as I loved writing it. Remember to always Dream Big … Read Often.

About the Author

Melissa lives on the Bellarine Peninsula with her husband and two children. She has always loved reading and grew up near her local library, where she spent most of her time browsing and borrowing books. Melissa is passionate about education, in particular literacy, and believes the ability to read and write gives power to change.

Her debut young adult novel Destiny Road was released in 2012 and she was selected for The Maurice Saxby Writers Mentorship Program in 2015. Her work has won honourable mentions and features in several anthologies. She completed a Master of Education in 2017 while researching Picture Story Book use in the classroom.

'Things work out the best for those who make the best of the way things work out.' This is the motto Melissa has lived by most of her life. She loves to travel and has been to many places including Egypt, Italy, Spain, and Africa. She has also travelled closer to home and been to every Australian state and territory. Her bucket list is still long, both at home and abroad!

Melissa believes everyone should Dream Big … Read Often

www.melissawray.blogspot.com